Ranger McIntyre: Down Fall River Dead

The Ranger McIntyre Mysteries
by James C. Work:

Unmentionable Murders

Small Delightful Murders

The Dunraven Hoard Murders

The Stones of Peril

The Mystery of the Missing Bierstadt

The Big Elk Murders

The Lawn Lake Murders

Down Fall River Dead

Ranger McIntyre: Down Fall River Dead

A Ranger McIntyre Mystery • Book 8

James C. Work

Encircle Publications
Farmington, Maine, U.S.A.

DOWN FALL RIVER DEAD Copyright © 2024 James C. Work

Hardback ISBN 13: 978-1-64599-536-4
Paperback ISBN 13: 978-1-64599-535-7
E-book ISBN 13: 978-1-64599-537-1

Library of Congress Control Number: 2024941687

ALL RIGHTS RESERVED. In accordance with the U.S. Copyright Act of 1976, no part of this publication may be reproduced, distributed, or transmitted in any form or by any means, or stored in a database or retrieval system, without prior written permission of the publisher, Encircle Publications, Farmington, ME.

This book is a work of fiction. All names, characters, places, and events are either products of the author's imagination or are used fictitiously.

Encircle editor: Cynthia Brackett-Vincent

Cover design by Deirdre Wait
Cover images: illustration of Ranger McIntyre by Robert Work; all others © Getty Images

Published by:

Encircle Publications
PO Box 187
Farmington, ME 04938

info@encirclepub.com
http://encirclepub.com

*To Sharon,
who listened lovingly to
the ideas for this story
but could not remain
to read the finished copy.*

Chapter One
What Is Eleanor Up To?

Wearing no shirt, hair uncombed, chin and jowls in need of a razor, he leaned nearer the shaving mirror and grinned into his own refection. The mirror image grinned back at him.

And why not? It was a fresh mountain morning. In early summer. At the deeply shaded log cabin of RMNP District Ranger Tim McIntyre, up the hill behind the Fall River entrance station, the chill of the air felt like a breath of new life. Why settle for a bit of a grin? Why not smile broadly? Thus far, at least, everything around him was in its proper place and satisfactory. Life "all proper and accounted for, sir!" as the squadron sergeant used to bark. Although McIntyre had stopped to look at himself in the shaving mirror, he wasn't about to shave—shaving would come later. Dressed only in his uniform trousers (held up with black galluses over his bare shoulders) the ranger stood washing the dish and pan from a satisfactory breakfast—fresh trout, fried hash, thick toast with plum jelly. And coffee.

Dish and pan dried and stowed away, McIntyre refilled the tin basin with hot water from the cook stove's reservoir, placed the basin in the sink beneath the window, dropped a fresh blade into his safety razor, and set his shaving mug on the drain board.

He slid the window further open so he could inhale new summer air as he shaved. Like in the old Christmas carol, in the Fall River valley all was calm, all was bright. Chilled air calm, sunshine bright.

Earlier, it was a very, very small thing that triggered McIntyre's pleasant mood: he realized he had not torn the previous month from his wall calendar. The oversight amused McIntyre. It even made him feel smug, because it reminded him of his indifference to numbers on a sheet of paper. He could tell you how far the winter snowpack had receded above timberline in Rocky Mountain National Park, whether the pasque flowers were in bloom, and whether the hummingbirds and mountain chickadees were back for the summer. When he went fishing the color of the river water told him how much the spring thaw had advanced. Often he could tell you the day of the week, usually in terms of how many days it would be until he got a day off. But he couldn't say for certain whether it was the sixth or the sixteenth. If he couldn't remember when his next day off would be, he wasn't troubled by it: his boss, Supervisor Nick Nicholson, would probably mention it. Or Jamie Ogg, McIntyre's assistant ranger would. Or Nick's secretary, Dottie.

McIntyre usually knew what month it was. However, when asked for his birth date he needed to stop and think. The only calendar number actually entrenched in his memory was November 11 of 1918, the day the officers and men at his squadron's airdrome learned about the signing of the final armistice. The Great War was over at last, the great muddy, brutal, chaotic, inhumane war. It was as if the world had been holding its breath until November 11, when it finally exhaled.

McIntyre had lathered his face and was making the first razor stroke down his cheek when he heard a car coming up the road.

No. Not a car. Heavier engine. A truck, maybe. It emerged from the trees in the distance as a yellow speck.

Razor poised mid-air he leaned to see out of the window. His heart thumped. His eyes narrowed, trying to identify that loud yellow vehicle. The glamorous lady detective? The fashionable fascinating flapper with the concealed .38 automatic, Vi Coteau of the sexy ear-stroking voice? She drove a lemon yellow Marmon convertible coupe. If ever he were to fall in love again, or admit to the possibility of love, it would be Vi…

McIntyre listened. His head was cocked like a spaniel scenting a sausage.

Nope.

Not Coteau.

For one thing, the engine of her Marmon Six gave off a feline purr, a kind of throbbing growl. The engine coming along the road sounded like a delivery truck. It was doing no more than twenty miles per hour, another reason to think it couldn't be her. Vi Coteau drove slowly only in driveways or church parking lots. McIntyre was a calm breed of man, one who avoided gratuitous excitement, which led him to experience feelings of tense apprehension whenever Vi gave him a ride in her convertible. Her way of accelerating from zero to fifty miles per hour made him feel like he was back in his Nieuport biplane approaching takeoff speed.

The road's curve brought it into view, a yellow tour bus from the New Mountain Stage Company, one of the four buses the company bought from the White Motor Company to replace Stanley Steamer mountain wagons. Fancy open side vehicles, wide pneumatic tires, powerful engines, seats enough for a dozen passengers.

It was too early for anyone to be on duty at the park's entrance station, but McIntyre lifted his field glasses from the nail anyway and focused on the entry kiosk about fifty yards down the hill. The door was closed, no one at the window.

No problem. Locals referred to the national park entrance as "the gate" but there was no actual gate. The park was open twenty-four hours a day, like Kitty's Café down in the village. Administrators of the new national park were still debating whether to charge an entry fee for each vehicle, or for each person. He turned the field glasses back toward the bus. How many riders would it be carrying so early in the morning?

One? The driver and one rider. McIntyre blinked, adjusted the focus, looked again. The driver was wearing the New Mountain uniform coat and hat, but it was a woman. More than a woman. It was Eleanor Pedersen.

And now the ranger's smile vanished. A furrow formed between his eyebrows. The guy on the seat behind Eleanor was smallish and angular and wore an oversize cloth cap. Looked like the greasy little weasel they call Ladro. Ladro Topo. One of New Mountain's "managers" imported from the Chicago underground. He was leaning forward and waving an arm, apparently giving instructions.

McIntyre hung up the field glasses and dipped his razor into the hot water. What the heck was Eleanor Pedersen doing driving a twelve-passenger tour bus up the Fall River road into the Rocky Mountain National Park?

While he went on shaving he also kept watching until the tour bus passed through the gate and went out of sight around the bend. It was not only odd: it was downright bizarre to see Eleanor at the wheel with Topo leaning over her shoulder. Topo was a city boy, one of four or five from back east hired by the New Mountain Stage Company. New Mountain did hire one local driver, ice merchant Zig Whortle, but the villagers, especially the gaggle of coffee shop consultants, thought the company should only use local men. Locals would be better for showing tourists around the national park.

Although it was undeniably an addition to the village economy, New Mountain was not popular. The two Jones brothers, Joseph and Lou, arrived one day, driving a fancy eight-passenger touring car, and in two weeks the newspaper announced their purchase of the spacious livery shed and National Park Tours business, located in the center of the main street. Not only bought the tour company lock, stock, and fuel barrels, but immediately divested it of the classy Stanley Steamer mountain wagons, replacing the steamers with White gasoline buses. More than one local man, including Zig Whortle, resented not being given a chance to bid on the steamers. A man could make good summer money with such a vehicle, hauling tourists up from the railroad station and chauffeuring them around the park. There were people willing to pay to ride in a Stanley Steamer no matter where it went.

Scrapping the steam wagons was only the beginning. New Mountain's next scheme was to apply to the Department of the Interior, in Washington, for a "sole and proprietary" license to offer "all hired and chauffeured" transportation within the park. Exclusively. In other words, a monopoly. Or as the honorary chairman of the Coffee Shop Opinion Committee eloquently put it, "now nobody 'cept them damn Jones and their Chicago thugs can drive anybody into the National Park 'less it's for free, damn their eyes."

It was a declaration of war.

Thus far, at least as far as McIntyre knew, the "war" consisted primarily of talk and blustering and vague threats. On one side was New Mountain Stage Company with its fleet of shiny open buses and Dodge touring cars. On the other was a disorganized, disgruntled bunch of local men who owned an assortment of vehicles and dubbed themselves the "Jitneys." Each summer gave them three or four months in which to make sufficient money to last through the winter. They waited at train stations in Berthoud, Longmont, and Loveland for a chance to drive fares to the village, or else they parked at village hotels and offered tours of the national park. Thanks to the completion of the Fall River Road, Jitney drivers could even take fares all the way to Grand Lake on the other side of the mountain. It made for a full day's excursion up the steep mountain road and over Milner Pass to Grand Lake. Lunch not included, twenty-five bucks a person.

Thanks to political shenanigans, the government granted "sole and exclusive" permission to New Mountain Company to "engage in the carrying of passengers for payment" not only in the park but along the roads leading to the park. Outraged, the Jitney men found ways to defy the law by various covert and overt means. The freelance drivers, it seemed, had innumerable cousins and other relatives who needed a ride from the train station to the park. When independent drivers came through the village with passengers the New Mountain tough boys stood with arms folded and glared menacingly.

Eager to accommodate their shady constituents, the Denver politicians unwittingly created a problem for the park rangers: enforcement. Technically speaking, the new road over Fall River Pass was a state highway, Highway 34, but there would be no agency tasked with policing state highways until 1935 when the first Colorado State Courtesy Patrol was formed. Of course, Rocky Mountain National Park was federal territory, however, could rangers legally regulate traffic on a state-owned highway? The State of Colorado ducked the issue by delegating "legal priority" to the county sheriff. Rangers, who weren't even certain whether picking flowers was legal, were asked—or told—

to arrest any private citizen they observed driving a vehicle containing tourists. The Jitney drivers swore they would not go quietly. The New Mountain boys vowed to regard Jitneys as scabs and administer the same baseball bat treatment they used in the city to correct the behavior of disloyal factory workers.

No wonder it puzzled Ranger McIntyre to see Ladro Topo coaching Eleanor Pedersen as a new driver. Eleanor came to the valley a few seasons ago as one of the very first female park rangers. And she was a good one. In the green uniform and wearing a badge, she made a formidable figure, one who could be kind and helpful and at times even diplomatic while urging visitors to keep their vehicles on the established roadways and their children on a leash.

"For you see," she would say politely, "when our bears come out of hibernation they are hungry and of course they look for the weak and slow-moving meat first."

During the affair of the purloined oil painting Eleanor and Vi Coteau became acquainted, became co-conspirators, and eventually saved Ranger McIntyre from an imminent demise. The two women eventually agreed it would be fun for Eleanor to quit the park service, become Vi's partner, and launch their own detective agency, catering especially to women who either lost track of their husbands or wanted to. McIntyre knew Eleanor and Vi were operating the Pedersen Investigation Agency in Denver and were doing well with it, well enough to afford hiring a jazz musician, Eddy Hazzard, as their assistant. Eddy served with McIntyre in France.

McIntyre finished his shave and put away the razor and brush. He sat on the bed to pull on his socks and boots. Halfway through buttoning his uniform shirt he paused beside the card table to put a piece of the jigsaw puzzle into place. Jigsaw puzzles, like fly fishing, helped him think. On his desk in the other corner of the cabin he kept a framed photo of Vi Coteau with her challenging eyes and smile. It did not help him think. In fact, looking at her photo usually muddled his mind.

Why was Eleanor back? Maybe she and Vi got into an argument and Eleanor returned to the village. Well acquainted with the national park, driving a tour bus would be a natural job for her. Or maybe she knew someone who worked for the company and she was filling in for them because they were ill. Or… and most likely for the pair of women in question… she and Vi were investigating either the company or one of the employees.

He smoothed the knot in his necktie, buttoned his tunic, fastened his belt and was ready to put on his flat hat and go to work. As for the Sam Brown belt and revolver, they could remain in the closet. Ranger McIntyre was seldom seen packing a pistol. Ninety-nine percent of the time it was simply a nuisance, an encumbrance when a man was using a fly rod. And it would snag the arms of his chair when he sat down to a Pioneer Inn breakfast. At any rate, whatever happened today probably wouldn't require a weapon. There would be only routine jobs to take care of. If he happened to run into Eleanor Pedersen he would pretend to be surprised. He'd let her lead him into a casual conversation.

A less casual conversation took place some days earlier. It was about Eleanor Pedersen, but it did not take place in the national park. Not even in the village. It happened at the lunch counter of the small railway station at Longmont, thirty miles down the canyon from the national park.

"Yeah, and I still don't like how she's a woman and a ex-ranger," Ladro said. "Rangers are too much like cops. Plus bein' a private snoop. Don't like it."

"Nobody's asking you to like anything," replied the senator's aide. "Hell, I don't like havin' to come all the way up here from Denver to explain things. Wanted to call, but if any nosy telephone operator was listening in and got wind of it, well…"

"Okay, fill me in," Ladro said. "How come you want this dame drivin' a bus?"

"We think—Senator Speckle and me—there's some kind of investigation goin' on. Pedersen's partner, the broad named Coteau, she used to work for the feds. She's gotten real curious about the senator's finances, right? All of a sudden she's doing private eye work? With this Pedersen woman? They set up a detective office a couple blocks from the state capitol. One day the Pedersen dame comes to the village and says the sleuth business is in a slump etcetera and she applies for a driver job 'cause she knows the park better'n most. We're darn sure they're suspecting how the senator's got invested in the tour company. But his reasons don't matter. He's your boss and if he says 'hire her' you do it."

"Yeah, fine, okay. But I'd sure like t' find out why."

"Okay, dummy, lemme spell it out. Somebody's out to get the goods on Senator Speckle, probably Senator Blume. Nosy do-gooder bastard. Whoever it is, they hired the female detective agency to do the spying, got it? Being women they can wangle information outta secretaries, hostesses, companions, hell, maybe even wives. Okay. The Pedersen dame thinks she's pulling a fast one, telling you all she's after is a summer job, sayin' she wants to be back in the mountains again, lets you know she was a ranger and still is a detective. See? She's all up front with you. The senator and me, we say let her snoop but keep a close eye on her. Let her be a driver, talk to other drivers. It'll even maybe mean good publicity for the company because she's female. All the time you'll watch every move she makes. If she looks like trouble, maybe finds out somethin' to screw up the monopoly plan... maybe she'll be in a kind of accident. Or she vanishes. People disappear into those mountains all the time, don't they. Her car could go off the road or she could be standing on the edge of the road, showing sightseers the view from Currant's Curve, and accidentally trips and falls over."

"I see," Ladro said. "Yeah, okay."

"Good. You're our boy in the operation. You keep manipulatin' Pedersen, keep her thinkin' she's really about to learn something. With her busy it'll leave nobody but the Coteau dame to bother the senator, snoopin' around in his financial affairs. But we're on to her, too. We'll deal with Coteau in Denver. You handle Pedersen up at the national park."

"Got it."

"Good thing you do. Train your drivers, make sure the road's safe and everything's on the up-and-up and looks legit. Oh, one more thing. The senator was readin' in the village newspaper about how locals are upset because we got rid of the Stanley steamers. Locals thought those Stanley's were picturesque. Quaint, y'know? See what you can do. Maybe hand out some free tickets for rides in the Whites, anything to soothe their feathers. Oh, and make friends with the rangers while you're at it. Maybe pretend to ask their advice, see? It makes 'em feel important."

"What about these maverick drivers, the ones hijacking our payin' passengers?"

"Jitneys. We got a hired gun who's gonna take care of 'em. You and the boys keep your noses clean, don't ask questions. Pass the word to your drivers. No trouble."

With that, Frank Elmerton paid the lunch counter tab and climbed aboard the Denver-bound train. Ladro fired up his Model T and drove off in search of gasoline. It was cheaper here than it was in the village; he filled the tank, filled a spare gas can, and went chugging back up the canyon. He didn't like being told what to do, didn't like the senator's aide, didn't want to order the drivers not to start trouble, and he didn't like the idea of a woman driving a tour bus.

* * * * * *

At the New Mountain Stage Company the other drivers shared Ladro's bias, all except for one. Three of them impressed Eleanor as Chicago tough guys, probably ex-truckers, recruited by the Jones brothers. Each morning they clustered in a corner of the dark, chilly old livery barn, drinking coffee and waiting for their day's orders. John Smith, who told Eleanor he was thinking of buying a small house in the village, was the only one to socialize with Eleanor. To Eleanor he seemed like a quiet, unassuming sort of gent. When he did speak it was usually to ask Eleanor questions about the village life. Church functions, schools for kids, the best place to buy groceries and so forth. He seemed to take his job very seriously, asking her about the national park, its roads and trails, sightseeing spots, private summer homes and shelter cabins, how the law enforcement worked and where the park work crews lived. Part of his interest in socializing seemed genuine to Eleanor; at times, however, she suspected him of overdoing it.

Eleanor leaned back against the bus fender, cradling a mug of tea to warm her hands. John Smith sat on the running board with his coffee. She raised her mug and took a sip.

"Tell me something, John," she said. "Every morning I see you guys drinking coffee while the boss figures out the daily schedule. But what do you do when the coffee catches up with you? On the road, I mean."

"I don't see your point," John said.

"If you're driving a load of tourists, for instance. Up the Fall River Road. And the coffee kicks in and you need to pee."

John Smith gave an embarrassed laugh and studied the dirt floor.

"Oh," he said. "Emergency telephones."

"What about them?" she said.

"One of the first things I learned. The park service, they've strung emergency phone lines along the river. Up Bear Lake road, too. There's wide places on the road to pull over. Not all of 'em where there's a phone, either. If I gotta 'go' I park the bus and tell the passengers I need to check in with the company. Like a night watchman? How he turns a key in a station box when he's on his rounds? I tell people there's a phone back in the trees and they need to stay in the bus while I go use it."

"The riders, they don't catch on?"

"Nah. For one thing they're new to the area. For another, most of them only take the tour once. I can stop anywhere and they don't know if there's a phone there or not. As for the riders, when we get up the road a ways further I'll show you where we pull over to let 'em 'stretch their legs.' There, the rule is 'ladies into the trees to the right, gents to the left.'"

"Cute," Eleanor said. "Tell me one more thing. If there's any tips from passengers, do we keep the money or turn it in?"

John snorted and tossed down the remainder of his coffee.

"These boys," he said, jerking his thumb at the knot of drivers sitting on the oil drums, "they've got what they call the 'Chicago system.' They figure out an average amount a driver ought to earn in tips on each trip. You keep your tips, but you have to report them after every trip. At the end of the week Ladro deducts the average amount from your pay and puts it in a separate ledger. Once a month he divvies it up. Everybody has the same share. I got a sneakin' hunch he keeps part of it for his trouble."

"We're paid every week?"

"Every two weeks."

"By check? I'll need to open an account at the local bank, maybe. I had one when I was a ranger, but I closed it."

"Nope, no checks. Cash only. And lemme tell you, between us two, some of those bills are brand new. Fresh from the mint. I mean, what does Ladro do, drive to the Denver mint for cash?"

At that very moment the selfsame Ladro appeared, popping up in the dusky livery shed like a weasel sniffing cheese. A self-important weasel.

"Let's hop to it, drivers," he announced. "Diego, you got a half-dozen backpackers to haul to Bear Lake. They want to be dropped off at a trailhead. Take Number Three bus. And arrange with 'em when they want picked up again. Oliver, you load ten passengers at the Stanley and give 'em the all day excursion over to Grand Lake. Number Two bus. Antonio, Number One needs oil changed and lube. Better do it quick in case we need it. John, take a Dodge touring car, go to the Baldpate Inn, see the desk clerk. He's got four or five guests wanting a tour of Longs Peak and Wild Basin."

"What about me?" Eleanor asked. She already knew the answer. No more customers. And the only bus left was the one most likely to break down, Number Four.

"Well, Honey Cake, I think you need t' smooth out how you shift down through the gears," Ladro whined, studying his clipboard. "So's your brakes don't overheat. Find yourself a long downgrade and practice downshifting. Take Number Four. In fact, why don't you deliver a carton of our brochures up to Fall River Lodge. Go on up the road, go ahead and drive past Chasm Falls, practice your four-point turnaround. Shift down to a dead stop a half dozen times until you think you can do it smooth, see. Afterward come on back here. You can clean the office and sweep the waiting room. I'll find other stuff for you to do."

Chapter Two
Wreckage and Women

Finally, Ranger McIntyre's day off came around again. After the sun came up and after breakfast, he was going to go fishing. Worm drowners rose in the dark and hiked through chilly dew-damp grass until their pants and boots were soaked. They baited their hooks in the cold, shivering until the sun came up; but because the trout didn't begin to hit insects until mid-morning, a fly fisherman could sleep late, indulge in a large breakfast, and wait for the sun to warm the riverbank.

He was crossing his porch, fishing rod in hand, when the telephone shattered all peace and quiet with its rattling, jangling racket.

Fifty years since Mr. Bell invented the darn thing, McIntyre thought. He carefully set the fly rod in a corner of the porch where it wouldn't fall over, slipped off his creel's shoulder strap, and hung the creel on a peg. Fifty years and nobody's found a way to make a telephone buzzer less irritating. He was tempted to take a screwdriver and disconnect the wire, except somebody might need him in an emergency.

He sat down at his desk and put the earpiece against his head.

"Fall River station," he said.

"Tim," said the voice. "Nick."

His boss, Rocky Mountain National Park supervisor Nick Nicholson.

"It's my day off," McIntyre said.

"Yeah, sorry. But this is bad. In fact it's awful. A hiker who'd been coming down Fall River road reported it. Six passenger Dodge touring car. Went off the steep stretch above Aspenglade. There was only one person in it, the driver, thank God. But, dead. Well…"

* * * * *

After hanging up the phone McIntyre went back out to the porch. There was a grim set to his jaw. He stared into the dark distance of the Fall River canyon while absently disassembling his fly rod. The telephone jangled for a second time. Sections of rod in hand, he returned to his desk.

"McIntyre," he answered.

"Tim?"

"Yeah?"

"Are you all right?"

"Hi, Vi," he said.

He strained to sound like his usual lighthearted self.

"How's things in Denver?" he said. "Matter of fact, I was thinking about calling you."

"What's going on?" she demanded. "Are you clenching your teeth? Aren't you glad I called? Were you busy and I interrupted?"

"No. I mean yes. I mean… Nick phoned a minute ago—you remember Nick—bad news. I need to hurry up Fall River road. Accident."

"What accident? What's happened?"

"A car wreck. Not far from Fall River Lodge, up the first steep section of road where it drops off a long ways toward the river. According to Nick a hiker saw it happen and told one of the drivers from New Mountain Stage Company. They reported it by emergency phone... driver went off the road. Killed."

"Not Eleanor!" Vi cried out. "Oh, God, I've been so afraid she'd be hurt! Not dead, tell me she's not dead!"

"No," McIntyre said. "No. As far as I know, she's okay. Eleanor's not involved. The New Mountain driver was coming down the road, apparently, and the hiker stopped him. The hiker said he'd seen a Dodge touring car go off the road and roll all the way down the mountain. Nobody in it except the driver, and he's dead. Soon as I hang up I'm on my way to the site."

"You're scaring me," she said. "You're very upset. I can hear it in your voice."

"It's Arthur. Arthur Ogg. Jamie's dad. He's been driving tourists in his four-door Dodge."

"No! Hauling people? Oh, poor Jamie."

"Arthur's wife told Nick he drove a hiking group to the Mummy Range trailhead this morning. Four of them. No, five. Said he started out with four, but she was watching him go and saw a fifth person flag him down. They got into the car. Anyway, Arthur was the only one in the car when it went over the edge."

"Has Jamie been told?"

"Yeah," McIntyre said. "He's already up there. Wanted to help carry the body to the ambulance. I got to go, but what's with Eleanor? And why's she driving a bus? What the heck made you think she was in the crash?"

"Let me catch my breath," Vi said. "Tim, Eleanor decided to step up our investigation of the senator. Thought it might stir things up if she applied for a job with New Mountain, because we heard a rumor he was financially involved with them. But

New Mountain hired her too quickly, see? Right away. It looked really suspicious. And since everybody's aware that the senator's a member of Denver's KKK. I'm afraid for her, I really am. It's why I called. I'm coming up there for a few days."

"Okay," he said. "Listen I need to go. I'll see you at the Pioneer Inn later."

"I'm not staying at the Pioneer this time," she said. "I'll be in touch. Tell Jamie for me… well, you know."

He hung up the phone and hurried out the door. He knew? That was the problem. He didn't know. He didn't know what to say to Jamie. He didn't know what happened. He didn't know anything.

Yet.

* * * * *

A summer temp in park service coveralls unchained the barricade and swung it aside to let McIntyre drive through. The ranger was glad Supervisor Nicholson sent a man to close the road. Several pickups and a ranger coupe were parked nearby, at the bottom of the grade; McIntyre left his own pickup there and hiked up the road. Near the top of the steep grade he found Ranger Russ Frame looking down into the Fall River gorge.

"Russ," he said.

"Tim," Russ replied.

"Jamie?" McIntyre asked.

"He and the guys got his dad wrapped in a blanket. Instead of hauling him up here they moved the ambulance down around the switchback. Carried Art down the trail along the river. Gonna drive him into town. Jamie was upset as all hell. Said he was going to make Doctor Lipp—the coroner?—examine the body, go over it until he's sure what killed him. I couldn't tell, what with the head being all bloody."

Down the slope, mostly loose rubble from road construction, McIntyre could see Art's black Dodge touring car jammed against the trees.

"Looks like it bounced over a log there and went into the ponderosa head-on," he observed.

"Yeah," Russ said. "I've been keeping everybody from messing up the tire tracks. Come look at them. Over here. You can see where he left the road. See how a tire dug into the gravel? It's like Arthur jerked the steering wheel to the right. If you look at this track… no, this other one… I'd say he hit the brakes too late. The front wheel was already over. See how the tire track looks like a skid mark?"

"Good job. We'd ought to take photos."

"Already done," Russ said.

"Who's down there at the wreck?"

"Dan Post. And a fisherman who heard the car hit the trees and came to see if he could help. And Marley the blacksmith's down there, too. I called him to see if he knew anybody with a winch or tow truck. Nearest one lives in Lyons. But Marley thinks he can rig up his chain hoist and drag Arthur's car back up here to the road. Leave it up to him, he'll figure a way to tow it to town. You give Marley a pry bar and a pulley and he can move anything."

McIntyre was still studying the tire tracks. He walked slowly up the road, keeping his eyes on the track left by the right hand wheels. He turned and came slowly back again.

"Russ, you were down at the wreck. How were the tires?"

"Nearly new. The tread pattern's the chain design, same as I've got on my Ford. Dunbartons."

"Okay. Take a look at these marks in the dirt. Dunbarton chain tread. Nice and clear. This track runs all the way down there to where it went off the road. He was coming downhill, so this track's from his right-hand wheels. C'mon. Let's take a look up the road a ways."

Both rangers studied the ground as they walked.

"There," McIntyre said, pointing. "Another skid mark in the dirt. What does it look like to you?"

"Well," Russ replied, "it looks like the wheel jerked sideways a little. See how the tire imprint's blurred? Dirt plowed up to the side? It'd be the front wheel because the back wheels don't turn sideways. Like it hit a rock in the road, except there isn't a rock. Smooth all the way."

"I'm thinking the same," McIntyre agreed. "Let's backtrack a few yards. I noticed something else."

McIntyre pointed again.

"Look right there. Another skid?"

"Okay, yeah, I see it. Same wheel. Say, that tire mark in the dirt, it's wider. Twice as wide, almost. Kinda blurry, too."

"I think it was a blowout," McIntyre said. "On the right front tire. A blowout jerked the steering wheel. The flat tire made him veer off the road."

"Why didn't he correct for it?" Russ asked. "He would've heard the tire blow, or at least felt it. He should have steered away from the edge."

"We'll probably never find out. Maybe he got distracted. Remember your first year with the park? We went hunting deer? You took a bead on a nice buck—with your .303 Savage—and a rabbit jumped out next to you. You seriously wounded a boulder instead. We didn't see another buck the whole day."

"You're saying maybe there was an animal in the road," Russ said. "I'll look around and see if I find any tracks."

If there were any animal tracks, Russ Frame would have found them. On days when it didn't rain, cars moving along the dirt and gravel road always kicked up a haze of dust; in Colorado's dry air it settled back as a layer of fine silt. Man, beast, or automobile, nothing could move on the roadway without leaving tracks.

McIntyre studied the ground like it was one of his jigsaw puzzles.

"Easy to see," he told Russ. "These wide tire tracks? See the crisscross tread pattern? They run closer to the uphill side of the road. They're from the White bus that came down. They drove over Arthur's uphill tracks, mostly. But coming back down Arthur stayed near the dropoff edge. Maybe looking down the gorge for something. What did you find?"

"Come up here and look," Russ said, "further up the shoulder."

Footprints.

The soft dirt of the road's shoulder added an entirely new chapter to the story. Fifty or sixty feet uphill from where the tire went flat, the chain design tire tracks showed how all four wheels skidded, throwing little ridges of loose dirt to either side. The two rangers read the tracks and agreed what had happened. Arthur's touring car stopped here. Somebody wearing size ten or eleven smooth sole shoes stepped down from the car to stand on the shoulder. He stood there facing the car. Apparently the car began to drive away while the person stood on the road's edge and watched it go.

"Here's where he went next," Russ said from the other side of the road.

"Sure enough," McIntyre said, coming to look at the shoe prints. "I think he got out of the Dodge, watched Arthur drive off. Apparently he went across—see the foot print in the middle of the road?—and walked along the opposite shoulder. Let's see where he went next."

They worked their way down the road, following traces of heel prints and a few full, clear footprints. And…

"Here. Here's where our man stopped and turned. About halfway from where he got out to where Arthur went off the edge."

"And no more footprints," Ranger McIntyre observed. "This must be the spot where the New Mountain driver stopped. If I've got the story right, this hiker got out of Arthur's Dodge. He stood on the shoulder of the road, maybe looking down at the river, and Arthur drove away. The hiker turned around, crossed over to the other side of the road. He probably saw Arthur's Dodge go over the edge. I think he was still standing there when a New Mountain bus came down the road. Seems natural he'd wave it down and tell the driver what he'd seen. It looks like he got into the bus and the bus continued down to where Arthur went over. I guess we might've found their footprints there, since they would've gotten out to look. Maybe one of them climbed down to see if Arthur was injured or dead. Too bad people've walked all over the place. But it's natural that the hiker and the driver went down to the wreck. Looked it over and drove to the nearest emergency phone to report it."

"Makes sense to me," Russ Frame agreed. "Only who's the hiker? Who got out of Arthur's car and into the New Mountain bus?"

"We need to find out," McIntyre said grimly.

"Simple," said the young ranger. "All we do is find out who the New Mountain driver was who came down the road and he'll tell us who the other man was."

"Maybe," McIntyre answered. "But not too likely. They're a tough bunch. Don't like to answer questions. Or, there's the four customers Arthur took to the trailhead, they might have exchanged names with the fifth passenger."

The rangers returned to the wreck site and stood on the

shoulder of the road watching Marley and Dan Post clearing the slope of large rocks and weathered logs. Marley sent for his chain hoist and ropes, and as soon as they arrived he would set about winching the Dodge up the embankment. Russ Frame lit a cigarette.

"I hate this canyon," McIntyre said. "I don't like anything about it. To me it's like Longs Peak, makes me nervous. When I'm up there it feels like the mountain's waiting to get me."

"Get you?" Russ said.

"You've never noticed it? Like it has an evil spirit? I almost always have a feeling like the mountain's waiting for a human to make a mistake. Same with Fall River. Other places—well, take Hidden Valley, for instance—feel real welcoming, like you can relax there. Catch a few trout, take a nap under a tree. But this canyon, whenever I'm in it I want to be out of it."

"I've heard people died here. I mean, besides your… friend. Sorry."

"It's okay. You heard right. My first season as a ranger there was a guy drowned at Chasm Falls. Later there was a woman who disappeared hiking up the road. It hadn't been finished beyond Willow Park. She told people she meant to climb Mount Chapin, but she vanished. Never did find her. Last fall a kid got into the river and got stuck between two logs, drowned. And there's the old miner, of course. The one with the strange cabin. Round, or maybe octagon. With high pointed cone roof. He locks himself in whenever there's fog coming down the canyon. He even puts a heavy flat rock over his chimney. Claims there's a demon hidden in the forest, comes prowling when there's a thick mist."

"Since you mention it," Frame said, "whenever I drive up this road I always feel relieved to come to timberline where everything opens up."

"Same here! Jamie told me much the same. He doesn't come up

Fall River unless he absolutely has to. He said there's something antagonistic about the place. And it's killed his dad, dammit."

"I bet Jamie didn't use a word like 'antagonistic' but I know what you mean. Well, what next?"

"I'd better go down and open the road. There's a temp on the barricade. I'll send him up here to help you keep traffic moving. Don't need a bunch of tourists stopping to gawk. When Marley's hoist shows up you might need to block traffic for him."

"Got it," Frame said. "See you later."

* * * * *

Arthur was liked and respected by everyone, and his death caused a somber mood throughout the community. The night felt longer than usual, and colder, and when morning daylight returned, it was to a brooding, silent village. The little shops and houses sat dejected and lifeless between the mountains like prisoners with hands folded and heads bowed, awaiting a judge's sentence. The sun climbed the cloudless crystal blue sky but seemed to lack any power to penetrate the deep-forested canyon of Fall River. People on the street who happened to glance westward into that unforgiving valley sometimes averted their eyes and went on about their business. Whether walking on the street or going about their business inside the buildings, everyone moved as if in a slow-motion cinema scene. Even the usually cheery dining room of the Pioneer Inn was wrapped in an atmosphere of quiet pain. McIntyre sat at his customary place, the table by the front window overlooking the village. He poked his fork into the scrambled eggs as always, but had no interest in carrying on his usual banter with the owner and chief waitress Charlene "Charlie" Underhill.

He wanted to be with Jamie at the doctor's clinic, but Jamie said he would only be in the way. Jamie persuaded the county coroner to drive up to the village and assist the local doctor in preparing his father's body. Jamie needed to learn if it was a heart attack, or stroke, or what. Jamie deeply appreciated McIntyre's sympathy and support, but his mind craved silence. The young ranger paced the tiny waiting room, or went outside to smoke a cigarette and stare down at the sidewalk. He wrapped himself in a shroud of contained rage. No matter what the doctor and coroner discovered, Jamie was already blaming his dad's death on the war between the tour drivers. Maybe they didn't physically push his car off the road, but they sure did start the damn stupid feud. Everyone including his dad felt the tension. It could've been what gave his dad a stroke, maybe. But whatever killed him, it was New Mountain's fault.

At the blacksmith shop Marley took a note pad and stubby pencil and grimly began an inventory of Arthur Ogg's Dodge touring car. He, too, was angry. Arthur was one of those guys who liked everyone, a man who didn't see why people couldn't simply be nice to each other.

As Marley already told McIntyre, the car's frame was bent. The radiator was mashed and the engine block was cracked, but he could salvage and sell other parts. The widow would be needing the money. Besides, keeping busy making a list of parts was the burly blacksmith's way of grieving. He needed to be doing something with his hands.

The rear wheels and tires looked okay. However, a sharp rock had torn the front left tire beyond repair. The tire on the right front was part way off the rim and the rim itself showed scratches from being dragged through the dirt. It was already flat when the car rolled off the side of the road and down the slope. However, he couldn't see any sign of a blowout. No jagged hole. Marley jacked up the front of the Dodge, reached for a wrench, and removed the wheel entirely. What he found was curious and odd. There was a round hole in the tire. Maybe the Dodge ran run over a spike lying in the road, except it would have been a good size one. The hole was at least a quarter inch across. He inserted his pencil into it.

Marley tugged the inner tube out of the tire and found a corresponding hole, a larger and more ragged one. He held the tube up and rotated it until a small object fell out. A deformed pellet of lead.

He went to his telephone and tapped the cradle a few times to signal the operator.

"Jane? Marley. Any idea where to find McIntyre?"

The telephone exchange building overlooked the village's main intersection. Through her tall corner windows the operator could see up and down both streets without leaving her switchboard. And since her job was to connect all incoming and outgoing phone calls, she usually knew who was at home and who was at work.

"At the Pioneer, Marley."

"Thanks."

Near the other end of the village, in the rented room of a small house on a narrow side street, two women sat on two beds opposite one another. Both were young. The woman in the chauffer uniform had a defiant set to her jaw and sturdy shoulders. Her cool, unwavering way of looking into a person's eyes showed her to be strong and self-willed but interested in them and very pleasant once they got to know her. The other woman, more slender and more apt to be whistled at by rough men, wore fashionable driving attire including tailored jacket and nicely fitted long skirt. The shade of the silk stock around her neck complemented but did not mimic the hue of her lipstick.

"Okay," Eleanor said, "fill me in real fast. I need to report for work."

"Right, partner," Vi began. "First, everyone in town recognizes who we are. There's no point using phony names or pretending we've just met. Let's stick to the real fact: I was concerned about you and came up from Denver. But let's do pretend how our detective agency enterprise isn't doing too well and that's why you took this summer job and why we're staying here in Mrs. Spinney's house. It's cheap."

"Good. What are you going to be doing, though, while I'm working?"

"Two things, both very logical. Our friends, Charlie, Dottie and the other ladies, they're aware of my interest in Ranger McIntyre. Since business is slow right now, in Denver, I'll say I was bored and drove up here to see him. Secondly, I accidentally dropped my gun and damaged it. And it's true, I actually did drop it."

"Also true is the part about you setting your cap for tree cop McIntyre," Eleanor commented.

Vi ignored it.

"I'm going to visit the local gunsmith, Doctor Hayward," Vi went on. "About fixing it. I think he would make a good local contact, should we need one. A handy source of information. Like Kate Warne says in her handbook, men tend to do their loitering and gossiping in gun shops, tobacco shops, and magazine stands. "

"Tim McIntyre isn't going to like you hanging around with Hayward. He's good-looking, a bachelor, intelligent, well-spoken..."

"McIntyre is?"

"No, the gunsmith. But speaking of the war between genders,

what's actually going on with you and McIntyre, anyway?"

"That's partly what I came up here hoping to find out. I'm worried about my good ol' business partner, of course, but Eleanor, there's something vaguely out of joint with Tim and me. At times we can be very chummy, even passionate, but he pulls back. He stayed the night in my guest room. I mean, he actually stayed in the guest room. All night. During our camping trip, looking for the white rocks? We slept in his tent and cuddled most of the night away, but..."

"Maybe I might put a bug in his ear for you," Eleanor said. "Drop hints to him. Maybe he doesn't think he ought to... you know. There actually are men who take the risk of pregnancy seriously. Or... and it's none of my beeswax... how can I put this delicately... he was in France during the war. Maybe he caught the clap. Or maybe he was wounded to where he can't, well, perform."

"I'm glad you put things delicately," Vi replied. "But no, it's deeper. When I'm with him and things begin to turn tender and romantic I can sense a wall. Or a gap. It's like when a person's talking to you but staring away into the distance."

"The other woman," Eleanor suggested.

"Other woman? Who?"

"The one who died. Mind you, I only heard about it as second hand gossip while I worked for the park. But when he first came here either he already knew or he met a woman he fell hat over boots in love with. One day she was apparently hurrying back down the Fall River road—locals said she and McIntyre were up there 'dallying' at the old patrol cabin the night before. The patrol shelter at timberline? And she was going to be late to work—her car went off the embankment and down into the gorge. Killed her. Listen, my time is almost up. Gotta dash. See you this evening, okay?"

"Sure," Vi said. It was her turn to stare absently past her friend. "Sure."

Seeing Eleanor leave, Mrs. Spinney came to see if Miss Coteau needed anything. When Eleanor first told Vi about the little house with a rental room, Vi expected the landlady to be a dowdy widow who eked out a living renting her spare bedroom to working girls, a gentle elderly lady dressed in outdated clothing. Mrs. Spinney, however, was quite up to date. Her silver hair was permed into coy waves. Her housedress and sweater ensemble, Vi realized, were pictured in *Vogue*'s 1922 overview of styles for modish householders.

"Anything you need, dear?" Mrs. Spinney asked. "Find the towels and bath soap? I do have an extra bathrobe if you require it."

"Thus far, so good," Vi replied. "I do like your house! It feels so comfortable. Eleanor tells me you were active in the WCTU?"

"Yes," Spinney said, her eyes brightening behind her tortoise shell spectacles. "Our local bachelor park ranger, your friend McIntyre, says that the initials WCTU stand for the four scariest things he can imagine. Women's. Christian. Temperance. And Unionized."

Vi Coteau laughed gaily. It did sound like McIntyre.

"I carried a placard in many a parade, let me tell you!" the older woman continued. "Carried a concealed gun as well, but you don't need to repeat that information. And I wrote pamphlets, screamed at politicians, did it all. Well, you can see the good we did. Take this village, for instance, there isn't a single saloon or whiskey mill anywhere. No late night drunks staggering along the streets or vomiting into people's flower beds. I realize prohibition has been very hard on folks, sure. But until we got the Eighteenth Amendment in place everything connected with booze was simply out of control, out of hand. Not in places like this, of course, but in the big cities… well, I could go on and on."

"I'd love to hear more," Vi said. "Perhaps at supper? At the moment, though, speaking of guns, I'd like to go see if the gunsmith shop is open."

"You mean Doctor Hayward," Spinney stated. "He doesn't keep regular hours. Of course, why should he? He's single and retired, he told me, and gunsmithing is only a hobby. He does a great deal of walking and bicycling. When he has the urge to go out, I believe he simply hangs up his 'Closed' sign."

"Perhaps I'll catch him. I'd like to ask him about this pistol."

Vi put her hand to her clothing and drew out a streamlined silver automatic, a pocket size Remington in .380 caliber.

Mrs. Spinney smiled in admiration.

"Well!" she said. "What a cozy way to carry a concealed gun!"

"Our secret, okay?" Vi replied. "Not knowing where I keep it drives Ranger McIntyre nutty."

"What fun," Spinney agreed.

Vi put the Remington automatic into her handbag. From her suitcase she took another gun, a small, compact revolver. As with the automatic, the silver plating and mother-of-pearl grips made the revolver almost dainty.

"My old gun," Vi said. "A Colt .38 Police Positive. Two inch barrel."

"I like you," Mrs. Spinney said. "Most girls hang on to a few old pairs of shoes, or an old purse. You keep your old guns."

Sliding the Colt revolver into the same cozy concealment her Remington had enjoyed, Vi donned her light jacket and cloche.

"See you later!" she said.

Chapter Three
Much Ado About Guns

Marley pushed through the door of the Pioneer Inn and advanced apologetically toward McIntyre's table. Charlie silently brought him a mug of coffee and a menu and returned to her cash register.

"Kinda late for you to be here," Marley suggested.

"Didn't have the heart to go back to work," Ranger McIntyre replied. "Besides, you could say I'm working because I'm sitting here thinking what to do about this feud between the drivers. What's up with you?"

Marley put the piece of lead on the table.

"Been going over Arthur's car," the blacksmith said. "Found this thing inside the front right tire. Dunno what it is nor how it got there. Looks like a bullet, but it ain't. Is it? Figured you might know."

"It's awful mashed," McIntyre said. "Sit down."

The ranger may not have been in the habit of carrying a pistol, but rarely did he leave his cabin without a large handkerchief, a multi-blade pocket knife, and a small magnifying lens. He slipped the lens out of its leather case and examined the chunk of lead.

"Might have been a bullet," he agreed. "I've never seen one like it, though."

"My money says it's what made the hole in the tire," Marley said. "Same size, about the diameter of a pencil. Maybe a little thicker. By the time it hit the inner tube I guess like you said it was mashed outta shape. Left a good-size rip in the tube."

"Small, for a bullet," McIntyre said. "But not as small as a .22 bullet. And look here… use the lens… it's bent, but you can see how the base is concave. It reminds me… when I was a kid I used to hang around with Old Man. It's the only name we ever knew him by, Old Man. He owned a Civil War rifle. It fired what he called 'Minnie ball' bullets. They weren't round, like most muzzle loaders use. They were pointed. Their base was concave like this. But heck, Marley, those were sixty caliber or more. Lethal things."

"Whatever it is," Marley said, "bet you a dime to a dollar either Arthur ran over it or somebody shot it into the tire. Maybe a hunter in the park illegally, up on Fall River. Maybe an accidental shot."

"Maybe," McIntyre mused. "Let me keep this. I think I'll wander over to our gentleman gunsmith's cottage and see if he can identify it."

After finishing his meal and paying the bill, McIntyre walked out of the Pioneer. Standing a moment on the porch, adjusting his flat hat, breathing the mountain air, looking all around at the buildings and roads and the towering granite peaks, he knew in his heart why he was deliberately stalling. He hoped to see the yellow Marmon convertible coming up the street.

"Silly ranger," he muttered. It was one of Vi Coteau's affectionate terms for him.

There was no yellow Marmon car, but the ranger did see Jamie Ogg running toward him. McIntyre hurried down the steps to meet him.

"Didn't anybody ever tell you not to run at this altitude?" he said. "What's going on?"

Jamie stopped and braced himself on the fender of the nearest car to catch his breath. He opened his clenched fist and held out his hand. The small leaden object in his palm was almost identical to the one in McIntyre's pocket.

"Doc found it in Dad's shoulder," Jamie told him. "Close to his spine, high up almost at his collarbone. A kind of bullet. Tim, it's those damn New Mountain boys. I'm sure of it! One of them must've been waitin' up there where the road drops off steep and he shot at my dad to make him go off the edge. They want all the tour business. Kill the competition like how they do in Chicago."

"Jamie," McIntyre said, "Jamie, let's not go off half-cocked. We'll look into it. Quietly. Calmly."

"Then if you're with me we're gonna calmly go over to their bus shed and take it apart 'til we find the gun and whoever owns it, dammit. I don't suppose you've got your service revolver. C'mon, I'll need you behind me. Gun or no gun. Let's go."

McIntyre took the young man by the arm and led him to the park service pickup truck.

"Climb in," McIntyre ordered. "Sit there. Breathe. Calm down a minute. You know better than to go dashing off in all directions without studying the situation. In these mountains, it's how greenhorns end up dead. Settle yourself down, Ranger Ogg."

McIntyre climbed in behind the wheel and proceeded to tell Jamie about the other lead slug, the one Marley found inside the Dodge's front tire. He held both of them in his hand.

"I was on my way to the gunsmith," McIntyre said. "Maybe he can tell what kind of gun would fire these things. Maybe he knows where a man might buy them. Maybe he made them for a client. But you need to calm down."

"Okay," Jamie said. "Okay, Tim. Okay. You're right. You're right. It's only I'm damn mad, see. Alright, no use t' charge in there and maybe get myself beat up. You're right, gotta do it your way. Take it slow. Look everything over real careful. Like you're always tellin' us. Say! I reckon the gunsmith guy sees probably every gun in this village. Okay, let's go see him. Maybe while we're at it we could ask if he has a service revolver he'd lend you."

"Good idea, kid. But you still need to come off the boil and cool down. Rushing into things won't help your dad any. In fact, thinking about it, I believe we'd better start by driving up the Fall River road instead. The gunsmith can wait. We need to go back to where your dad went off the road, have a good look around before traffic or maybe a rain storm wipes away any tracks. Okay? You okay with it?"

"Yeah, okay." In his frustration Jamie stomped his boot on the floorboard and released a stream of locker room language directed at the blankety-blanks who killed his dad. Having vented, he felt a little better.

"Okay, you're right," Jamie admitted. "Let's go find evidence. Let the damn killer steam a while longer. I gotta agree, we need t' get back up there, search the whole place right away before it's messed up. We can talk to the gunsmith later."

* * * * *

Ranger McIntyre didn't realize it, of course, but his decision not to interview the gunsmith, to drive up Fall River road instead, saved him from walking into an awkward situation. The car he hoped to see, Vi Coteau's yellow coupe, was parked in front of a tidy painted picket fence two streets away from the Pioneer Inn. A small meticulously lettered sign on the cottage's front wall included an arrow directing visitors' attention to a neat little sidewalk leading to the back yard. The sign said, simply, "Dr. T. Hayward, Gunsmith."

Hayward's handsome face brightened considerably—without losing any of its dignified reserve—when he answered the knock on his door and discovered Vi standing there. He remembered her, of course, from an earlier incident when he helped her examine extractor scratches and primer dents on various .22 shell casings. With his hand on the small of her back he ushered her into his meticulously clean, brightly lit workshop. He invited her to sit on one of the stools beside his bench and offered her tea. She politely declined. He courteously inquired as to her health, the weather in Denver, the state of affairs regarding the women's detective agency, and the condition of the roads. Vi replied with equally polite but discretely general answers.

"I'm pleased to see you again," Hayward said at last. "How may I be of assistance?"

Vi removed a square of velvet from her bag and unfolded it to show Hayward a chromed automatic with pearl grips.

"It's this," she said, "my .38 Remington. You see, in the course of our investigations, I carry it concealed in... well, concealed. The other day I was about to return it to the holster when I dropped it. On a stone step. Luckily I was already planning to come to the village, to stay with my business partner a few days, and I hoped you might take a look at it. There's something wrong with the sight. And as you can see, I scratched the slide and possibly put a dent in it."

He took the gun and held it gently, almost as if he wanted to fondle it. Instead, he reached for his magnifier.

"I'm sure we can put things right," he said. "If the sight isn't misaligned, the lack of accuracy might be due to a pitted or worn out bore. It would take weeks to send away for a replacement barrel."

"Oh!" Vi exclaimed. It was time to begin being an investigator. "Oh, I don't want to be without it. Not for weeks! Frankly, Dr. Hayward…"

"Please. Thomas."

"Thomas. We have heard there's a new element in the village, tough men from out of town trying to take over the transportation business. Possibly gangsters! I hope they're not like some men in Denver who make rude comments when I pass them on the street…"

"I can well imagine," Hayward said.

"…and having my gun, well, it gives me a sense of safety, you see."

"Of course," he said. "Let's look at the bore and rifling, After I give it a thorough cleaning I'd like to shoot it a few times to check the sight. The rear sight on this model gun is notoriously delicate. The way it's mounted in a groove makes it susceptible to lateral misplacement. This scratch and dent, though, might be another matter. But first things first. If you can reach the drawer behind you you'll find a bore scope. Perhaps you'd hand it to me."

Hayward could have retrieved the bore scope himself but as he expected, when Vi twisted around on the stool he was afforded a pleasing glimpse of her shapely calf and black stocking.

While disassembling the Remington, carefully cleaning each screw and spring, even removing the grips to clean the inner surfaces, Dr. Hayward described the "war" between the transportation monopoly and the "Jitneys." Not bad for business, he admitted, with the new gentlemen from Chicago coming to him for gun cleaning and repair.

"When the drivers feel bored or restless, or both," he said, "they take their guns out of town and shoot at cans and bottles. I do a brisk business cleaning and adjusting their weapons."

Seems odd, Vi thought. Why not clean their own guns? Unless they simply like to hang around a gunsmith shop.

"There's a jitney driver who carries an unusual German rifle," Hayward went on. "He practices shooting with it, but it requires custom-loaded ammunition."

As he spoke, Vi couldn't help but notice how the gunsmith seemed almost deferential to the invading bus drivers, saying that he hoped the village would "become used to them" in time, and how he met several who were "good lads" and "anxious to fit in."

"And there we are," he said after twenty minutes. "All cleaned up. I see nothing wrong with the sight, although in shooting such a pistol one isn't apt to use the sights. I did find dried oily residue under the grip safety, possibly affecting the way it handles. There was also residue around the safety, causing it to stick."

"Thank you," she said. "And about the scratch and dent?"

"Ah. It could be a serious problem. If you'll leave it with me a few days I'll see what I can do. I'm afraid, however, I may need to send it to an expert, an acquaintance of mine. At any rate, it's all clean and will operate more smoothly. Why don't we go downstairs and fire a few rounds?"

"Downstairs?" Vi asked, looking around at the one-story cottage.

"Basement," Dr. Hayward smiled. "A basement target range. I never show it to people, but after buying the place I paid to have a narrow tunnel constructed for shooting. It leads from the basement out under the back lot. Scarcely three feet wide and four feet high. But it extends a good twenty-five yards. The basement itself is soundproofed so no one will hear me firing a gun. I keep my most unusual firearms and other items down there. Come, have a look."

The room at the bottom of the steps was as tidy as the upstairs workshop. And, once Hayward turned on the lights and secured the thick door, it was silent as the proverbial tomb. He unlocked a steel drawer set into one wall and brought out a box of .38 auto cartridges.

"I keep my ammunition here," he said. "As you can see, I have my metal lathe and a boring machine down here. Although the forge and anvil have to be kept in the garage. A little inconvenient. The desk is where I do my custom reloading."

"Do you build guns yourself?" Vi asked.

Hayward deflected the question by taking a cartridge from the drawer and holding it up.

"Being a gunsmith allows me to collect very unusual firearms. Because I can make ammunition for them, you see. People sell me their antique weapons because they can't find ammunition. For instance, I recently acquired an old shotgun, a very short barreled .410 designed to shoot this unusual brass cartridge. But I don't wish to spend an hour talking about guns! Let's load this little beauty of yours and you can tell me whether my cleaning has helped her performance. I tightened the trigger pull a tiny bit. A quarter turn of the adjustment screw. You may not even notice."

Hayward turned a switch and the far end of the shooting tunnel was illuminated. Although a person could crawl down the tunnel in order to change targets, the ingenious Dr. Hayward instead created a simple rope and pulley arrangement. He clipped a cardboard target to the rope and ran it downrange.

"Your honor," he said, courteously waving Vi toward the narrow padded bench rest at the mouth of the tunnel.

She took her stance behind the bench, cocked the Remington, and slammed three shots very close to the bullseye.

"Excellent!" Hayward exclaimed. "Your posture is nearly perfect. One would think you learned to shoot in the military. Or the Secret Service. But, if you'll allow me, I would suggest a slight modification of your position. May I?"

He stepped in close behind her. She could smell his hair oil. With the toe of his shoe he nudged her foot a couple of inches to point directly at the target; taking her shoulders in his hands he turned her body slightly.

"There," he said. And he remained uncomfortably near to her.

Vi took aim and with three more shots shredded the target's center.

"Gracious!" Hayward said. "Very deadly shooting, Miss Coteau. Very deadly indeed. I wonder… in your line of work… have you needed to turn your weapon on anyone?"

Vi twisted away from him. She cleared her pistol's breach, handed Hayward the clip to refill, and replied to his question.

"As my mother always said, a lady must never shoot and tell."

* * * * *

Being at the accident scene again seemed to help Jamie "get his head back in one piece," as Old Man often said in reference to young McIntyre. The two rangers stood side by side where Arthur's Dodge had left the road. McIntyre recognized the distant, distracted look in Jamie's face, for he, too, once gazed down at scarred trees and displaced boulders as if staring at it would make it all go away, would bring everything back the way it was before the accident. It helped Jamie to have McIntyre beside him, another human who once felt the same numbing pain.

In the way of humanoid males sharing grief they opened up to one another. McIntyre put his hand on Jamie's shoulder.

"Goddamnit, Jamie," he said.

"Yeah," Jamie replied.

Having thus eloquently broken the icy awkwardness, McIntyre began to re-enact the accident, performing an odd pantomime of a man driving a car down the narrow road along the long, steep drop-off into the river valley. He went up to where the flat tire had smeared the silty dust. Returning toward Jamie he held his hands up as if he gripping a steering wheel. He walked in the center of the road, since Arthur would have been on the left side of the car, driving. He pretended to be twisting the steering wheel for control after blowout.

He threw his hands up and veered to the lip of the roadway.

"I think I've got it," he said. "The top was folded down, right? The Dodge was open. That's important. If the brakes were working okay your dad should have been able to stop as soon as he felt the front tire blow. Any good driver could steer away from the edge and come to a stop. But I think, Jamie, I think a few seconds after the tire blew, he got hit with the piece of lead the doc found. Got hit in the back. His hands jerked up—like this—and the car went over."

"One of those New Mountain thugs," Jamie growled. "Waited for him, shot him. Bastards."

"We can't tell who it was," McIntyre said, "not yet. But I don't think it was planned. Remember the foot tracks, further up the road? I think another man was in the Dodge, one your dad maybe picked up along the way. What if the same man was on the prowl, watching for a way to sabotage an independent driver, waiting for any chance that might come along—didn't matter who or what—and he asks your dad for a ride. As they're coming to this steep part with the long drop, he says maybe 'why don't you stop and let me out, I'd like to walk from here,' something along those lines. The guy dismounts but just as your dad starts to drive away he pulls out a gun and shoots the tire. See, to do it he'd need to stand on the very edge. What I mean is, he wouldn't be already hiding and waiting up there in the rocks. Maybe he works for New Mountain, saw a chance to sabotage a jitney, thought he'd give it a flat tire and leave your dad to fix it while he strolled on down the road."

"Yeah," Jamie said. "I guess it makes more sense. If he shot out the tire on the right side he'd have to be there on the shoulder of the road, the shoulder nearest the river… like maybe he said to stop the car and he got out and stood looking down at the creek. Maybe he said he was goin' to hike down there and take the fishing trail back to the lodge. Something like that."

"Okay," McIntyre continued, "let's say your dad starts to drive off. The mystery hitchhiker shoots the tire. But your dad, he's keeping the car under control. No harm done, see? It would be like any other flat tire. Happens all the time. You stop, you fix it, you drive on. But maybe on an impulse, the guy with the gun fires again, maybe hopes to hit the windshield or the gas tank, maybe even your dad. The slug goes in your dad's shoulder, he jerks, the car goes over the edge."

Jamie stared off into the deep, hostile shadows of the river canyon, mentally replaying his father's final moments.

"Shots," he said.

"What?"

"Shots," Jamie repeated. "Maybe a fisherman down there or your anonymous hiker, or even the New Mountain driver, the one who 'happened' to be comin' down the road about the same time and picked up the hiker, one of them woulda heard two shots. I mean, in the canyon like this? Hell, you'd hear a shot a mile away. We need to find those guys. Remember when I was new to the service? Suspected a poacher? Remember how you told me to make sure it was a poached deer and not a natural death? Told me we gotta put a shooter in the scene. Do it first and it can tell you who the shooter was. It's like that."

"Good," McIntyre said. "Speaking of shots, let's look and see if we can find any cartridge cases. If there was a sniper, and if he stood on the very edge, and if he took two quick shots, he must have ejected at least one shell. It probably went down over the slope."

Their search was difficult and diligent. Using a rope from the truck, Jamie looped a bowline under his arms and with McIntyre belaying him from above, he descended the loose rubble and methodically examined every square foot.

"Nothin'," he said, when McIntyre finally hauled him back up to the road.

"Nothing up here, either," McIntyre said. "What kind of gun... unless it was a revolver... but really small caliber. It'd take a really good shot to hit both the tire and your dad from here."

"I'm betting it's a rifle," Jamie said. "The shooter picked up his brass."

They were coiling the rope and preparing to leave when one of the New Mountain buses came chugging up the road. The driver was Diego, short but muscular, swarthy and inclined to be insolent. He wore the New Mountain chauffers' uniform and cap, and a pair of smoked glasses with round lenses. Seven passengers of assorted sizes, wearing assorted 'outdoor' costumes, sat on the four rows of seats.

Diego stopped beside McIntyre's pickup, shut off the bus engine, set the brake, and climbed down from the driver's seat. He was one of those men who display toughness by standing closer than other people find comfortable. When he positioned himself in confrontation with McIntyre, however, the ranger thought he merely looked like a self-inflated little bantam rooster.

"Howdy there," Diego said. "Mister Ranger McIntyre. We boys been lookin' to find you. Got a complaint, see? I see you finally decided to open the gate and let the taxpayers use their own road again. I missed out on three full loads 'cause of you. Oughta sue the park for damages."

"The way I heard it, suing people is a major pastime in Chicago," McIntyre answered.

Being short and broad in the shoulders, and arrogant, Diego customarily stood with his fists on his hips and his chin up; the unbuttoned front of his uniform gaped open, giving McIntyre a glimpse of an automatic pistol carried in a waistband holster.

McIntyre leaned nearer to whisper.

"Everything okay?"

"What you talkin' about?"

"Trouble? You bein' kidnapped? Need help?"

"What?"

"Your hat," McIntyre whispered. "The badge on your hat. It's upside down. Like a signal for help."

Diego reached up with both hands for his hat—as McIntyre knew he would—and quick as a cat the ranger snatched the gun from Diego's waistband.

"A Colt .380, huh?" McIntyre said. "Let's see if it's loaded."

"Gimme it back, dammit."

"Nah," McIntyre said. "Guns not allowed in the park. I'm afraid you're breaking the law."

McIntyre stepped around the sputtering bus driver and faced the four rows of passengers.

"How about you folks? Any guns among you? Let's have them.

I'll leave them at the entrance station for you to pick up as you leave. If I need to search you people and find one, I'll put the owner under arrest."

One fat man sheepishly produced a pocket pistol, a Browning .25, and handed it down to McIntyre.

"A .25," McIntyre said, unloading the little gun. "For bear, maybe? What's your plan, wait until a grizzly swallows you and shoot your way out?"

"As long as you're harassing tourists," Diego snapped, "you'd oughta find a damn jitney driver, the one drivin' a Franklin car. Hell, he's always carryin' a little German carbine under his front seat."

"Thanks, I will. I'll tell him you squealed on him, too. But I hear another car coming up the grade," McIntyre said. "You either move this heap or pull it off the road. When you're done with your tour you can stop at the entrance and pick up the pistols."

* * * * *

The pasteboard "Back At" sign with movable clock hands told visitors Dr. Hayward would return from his walk at three p.m. McIntyre decided to wait. And sure enough, prompt at three, here came the man himself hiking vigorously up the lane. He wore a shoulder bag and carried a thick walking staff.

He greeted the ranger and invited him to step into his shop.

"Welcome," he said when they were seated at his workbench, "what can I do for you?"

McIntyre produced the two chunks of lead and put them on the bench.

"This one," the ranger said, "apparently penetrated a car tire. The other one wounded the driver. If they came from a gun I need to identify the owner. If not from a gun, I still need to find out where they came from. I figure you've probably seen more of this village's guns than anyone else."

"Undoubtedly," Hayward said. "However, let me say one thing at the outset. I do not wish to acquire a reputation as a snitch. When I repair a firearm, or manufacture ammunition, I keep their name in the strictest confidence. To do otherwise would be to lose both their confidence and their business. But let's see what we have here."

He opened the glass door of a small cabinet and brought out a jeweler's scale of the type once used to weigh gold dust. After determining the weight of the two bits of lead he reached into a cloth-lined drawer for a pair of calipers and a magnifying loupe.

"You were in the war, I believe," he said as he peered at the bits.

"More above it than in it," McIntyre replied. "Mostly I flew over the battlefield and took photographs."

"Perhaps from the air you couldn't see our doughboys picking up combat souvenirs. Bayonets, pistols, rifles, helmets. These are badly distorted, but I believe them to be homemade bullets for a Model 177188 German carbine. The primary clue is the weight, of course, but also the diameter. The base of one of them measures exactly 7.9 millimeters."

McIntyre frowned. Millimeters meant very little to him.

"In other words, almost but not exactly a quarter of an inch."

"Oh. Twenty-five caliber," McIntyre suggested. "I showed my assistant ranger the concave base, like a Minnie ball. Except a Minnie ball would be fifty or sixty caliber."

"Correct," Hayward said. "As I remarked, these appear homemade. The lead is likely salvaged. You can see tiny flecks of contamination in it. Dug out of a tree stump, probably. The concave base is common to what's termed a "Nessler ball."

When fired, it expands like a skirt in the barrel, forming a more perfect seal and resulting in more power and accuracy. Your shooter, whoever it is, probably owns a handheld bullet mold of very small caliber and scrounges used lead from old logs or tree trunks. As for the concave base, a simple tool rounded on the end could be pressed into the lead while still molten."

"What about the brass?"

"Cartridge cases for such bullets? They could be re-used a half dozen times or more. You'd need new primers, of course. But they'd be a standard metric size. One could order them by mail. I suppose the local outfitter's store could order primers for you. You might ask Mister Schuel, the store owner."

Ranger McIntyre left Hayward's cottage. Two gunshots killed Arthur. Russ Frame—and Jamie—were talking with everyone they could think of to see who might have heard the shots. The mysterious "hiker" was a missing piece in the whole puzzle picture. The New Mountain drivers were acting smug; one of them likely saw and talked to the unnamed hiker and probably gave him a ride into town. But they weren't about to share any information unless they scored a boon in return. That, apparently, was how it was done in Chicago.

Dr. Hayward's theory presented another problem. How could a hiker be carrying a rifle without anyone noticing, even a short one like a carbine? It was a clear infraction of park rules. Even a smug bus driver like Diego would feel it was in his own interest to report it.

At Fall River Lodge McIntyre learned more about Arthur's final group of riders, the party of hikers he had dropped at a trailhead. They were due back from their long camping hike in two days. They would have seen the additional passenger Arthur picked up at the edge of town. Probably spoke to him as they drove up the road to the trailhead. They darn sure would notice if he was carrying a carbine. Besides, Arthur would have told the hiker he couldn't bring a gun into the park. Even a New Mountain driver would protest anyone carrying a rifle on a tour. Although… if McIntyre was figuring this particular part of the puzzle correctly… a man with a gun hitched a ride with Arthur Ogg. He probably either got out along the way, or he stayed in the touring car after the other passengers were dropped off at the trailhead. Back down the road where there's a long, steep drop-off he got out of the car and the car drove off again. He stood on the lip of the road, shot a tire, shot Arthur, picked up his spent cartridge case or cases, flagged down a New Mountain tour bus to report the "accident," ended up riding the bus into town and vanishing. And no one saw the gun. Even the New Mountain driver would have reported it, if only to keep from being a suspect himself.

As McIntyre directed his steps toward the nearest mug of coffee, a sneaky little notion crept into his brain and caused his lip to turn up into what a romance novelist might call a "wry" little grin. *No one saw the gun?* Maybe the shooter was Vi Coteau. She kept her gun hidden and never would she allow him to find out where.

Chapter Four
Amour, Arson, and an Admirer

Once again she was at the Pioneer Inn, back at the familiar table by the front window, looking out across the porch and down over the village. Houses, cottages, little stores and small cabins, even the streets and walkways were awash with morning sunshine. Vi enjoyed a warm and peaceful moment of realization, sitting there: the inn, the people, the valley and the mountains themselves were becoming special to her. Often while at her desk in Denver it was here she wanted to be instead, and when she was here there was nowhere she'd rather be. On this particular morning she felt a deeper, more inexpressible understanding of McIntyre's affection for it all. There was the inn with aromas of coffee and bacon and new-baked rolls, a room of people lingering over breakfast, exchanging murmured words in casual, unhurried conversations. This morning even the fierce granite wall of mountains looming behind the valley and village seemed more kind than cold, more protective than daunting.

She sipped her tea, took a dainty nibble of her sticky bun. Her eyes lingered on the ranger sitting opposite her.

"I don't see how you do it," she said.

"Oh?" McIntyre replied.

He pushed aside the empty plate, recently harboring a flotilla of sausages and over-easy eggs, and addressed his fork to the steaming pancakes on the second plate. He smiled a "thank you" to Charlie when she reached over his shoulder to refresh his coffee.

"Well," McIntyre continued, "it's like this. Some people think they need to build the border first. They'll spend an hour searching the pile to find all the straight edge pieces and the corners. But I can't do it that way. If I put the whole border in place it kind of hobbles my thinking process. Even with the border done there's still all the pieces in the middle. No, I like to find the pieces of one feature, like a house or maybe a bunch of flowers, another and another piece in place until…"

"I don't mean your jigsaw puzzles, you silly ranger. I'm talking about your breakfasts."

"Oh! Hey, I'm a working man. Why, at any moment they might call me out to climb a mountain and rescue someone, or dash up a canyon to put out a forest fire, and I'd need my energy. Might have to wrestle an injured deer or bear."

"Or do a fly rod census of Fall River rainbow trout?"

"That, too."

"Tim, how can you afford huge breakfasts?"

"Uh, oh!" he said, forking a chunk of pancake into a pool of syrup. "When a lovely woman asks an eligible bachelor about his finances, look out! Things are getting serious! Anyway, I told you before. I budget. I calculate how much I save by living in a government cabin, I put that much away from the paycheck, and once in a blue moon I treat myself to a full breakfast cooked by somebody else."

"Okay," she replied. "I remember. It's like me saving my

pennies to buy a new hat."

"Yup," he said. "The one you're wearing is really swell."

Really swell? Her new cloche with patent leather swirl strips and the merest hint of a brim, with one leather strip the color of her eyes and the other one a suggestion of deep red wine, cost her over ten dollars. And all he could come up with was "swell"?

"Fill me in about Eleanor," he said. "What's she found out thus far?"

Maybe we should discuss my hat first, Vi thought.

"Okay," she said. "First of all, everybody over there at the bus shed, the boss, the foreman, all the drivers and two mechanics, they're all very tight-lipped. They've been given instructions not to socialize with locals and not to start trouble with the jitney men."

"They're ordered to stay out of trouble, huh?" McIntyre said. "Might account for what happened when I had a run-in with the one who wears dark glasses. I took his gun away from him but he didn't try to stop me. Didn't even protest. Maybe his boss warned him to keep a lid on his temper. And stay out of trouble."

"There's more," Vi continued. "The little rat-faced foreman warned drivers not to ever tell anyone how many passengers they carried, or who the passengers were. Or if they were picked up or dropped off at a certain lodge or hotel. Oh, and Eleanor thinks the owners tamper with the payroll. She's only received one paycheck and can't be certain. But she thinks they're skimming the tips, probably manipulating the records, too. And she's heard hints about some drivers getting sizable bonuses under the table."

"For special jobs, probably," McIntyre mused. "Or maybe to keep quiet. Like about the name of the driver who picked up a hiker the day Arthur was killed, and who the hiker was."

"Maybe."

"Speaking of hikers, the group Arthur dropped at the Mummy Range trailhead finally got back. Ranger Frame interviewed them at the lodge. But he says their heads were all full of scenery and peaks and lakes and vistas and such. After a week of camping none of them could remember anything but a general impression of the hitchhiker Arthur picked up at the edge of town. Floppy hat shading his eyes, plain short jacket, ordinary hiking shoes, a walking stick. One of them managed to recall the man's hiking stick was very 'sturdy'. Frame thinks he meant 'thick'. Not much of a description. And none of the New Mountain boys are going to tell who picked the hiker up. What about your senator?"

"Speckle? Same thing. No word. Although… Eleanor did have a charter group from Denver. Drove them to Grand Lake and back. From conversation she overheard, she's certain they not only knew the senator but were KKK people themselves. Know how you can tell people are bigots, from words they use? She heard one saying how the park made a real cozy deal for the tour monopoly, how the taxpayers were dumb to fork over their tax money to pay for a national park and allow one outfit make all the money from it. Another guy made a crack, right to Eleanor's face, about how it was smart to hire women because they're cheaper and how a clever foreman ought to 'train some Blacks' to drive and save even more on wages."

"And Eleanor didn't push them off into a canyon?" McIntyre suggested.

"Drivers aren't supposed to engage in fights, remember?" Vi said.

Charlie came up and reached for McIntyre's two plates and the side dish, all three of looking as though they'd been licked clean.

"Honestly!" she said, addressing Vi. "One of these days our

ranger's liable to eat the painted flowers right off the plates!"

Vi laughed. Under the table her foot pressed affectionately into his shin, a gesture to tell him they weren't laughing at him. Except they were.

"Now," Charlie continued, "what about dessert?"

"What have you got?" the ranger asked.

Vi pulled back her foot and kicked him.

"Just pay the bill," she said. "I'll wait for you outside on the porch."

Leaning on the porch railing, looking down over the village and up at the granite cliffs and spires of the Rockies, Coteau and McIntyre could have been mistaken for honeymooners. The tall ranger in his off-duty riding jodhpurs, high boots, plain shirt and Stetson was the very picture of contentment, largely owing to having eaten a large breakfast. The slender young woman in walking skirt of tweed and jacket of chamois-thin leather appeared to be satisfied with the peaceful mountain scenery while at the same time poised for an adventure, virtually any adventure at all.

There exist numerous phrases in the human female lexicon, phrases certain to arouse fear, or nervousness, or grim-jawed resentment in the male. Phrases such as "do you like to dance?" or "we need to talk" or "guess who's coming" are only a few examples. In the present case, a man who has not been fishing in a week or more is taking notice of a bright, warm, absolutely still day. He is thinking of a calm, remote bit of river where lunker trout swim in the deep shadows of the bank. He can almost see the instant splash of a fish taking the dry fly, almost feel the line tugging through his fingers and the bamboo fly rod bending toward the water.

And in the midst of his daydream an attractive, bright-eyed, free range female next to him innocently utters one of those female questions.

"What would you like to do today?"

At times, when a woman asks a man this particular question she is simply being polite. She already knows what the two of them are going to do.

"How about a nice drive up toward Bear Lake?" Vi went on to suggest. "You once pointed out an abandoned tunnel up there, remember? Along the Bear Lake road? I'd love to see it. Will you show it to me? We could take a picnic."

Two automotive mechanics operated repair shops in the village. According to local coffee bar comedians, the rough road to Bear Lake had put the repairmens' children through college. Another joke claimed there were two kinds of sections to the Bear Lake road, those under construction and those needing to be. It was more than merely rough; it was bumpy, impassible in bad weather, and usually blocked by various steam shovels and tractors. Drivers frequently had to share the road with jackhammer hoses from the huge air compressors.

"We'd better use my truck," McIntyre replied. (In male talk this suggestion translates as "why don't we go somewhere else and try fishing.") His private truck did have narrower tires and higher road clearance than her heavy Marmon convertible coupe and was less likely to leave its muffler hanging on a boulder. McIntyre acquired the little Ford pickup when the Small Delights lodge went out of business; therefore, any female riding with him felt as if she were the object of raised eyebrows—actual or imagined—when people saw the legend "Small Delights" lettered on the door.

"When are you going to have those doors of yours painted?" she asked, and not for the first time.

"When are you going to tell me where you hide your .38 Remington?"

"Touché," she said.

"Doesn't 'touché' in French mean 'touch me'?"

"No, it means put your hands on the steering wheel and keep them there."

It was one of the private pleasantries of their friendship, the lady detective pretending to be annoyed by the truck's door signs and the ranger feigning curiosity as to how—and where—she could conceal her sidearm. He secretly liked it when she kidded him about his three-plate breakfasts; she was glad when he mentioned her weakness for egg salad sandwiches. And nonpareils candies.

The journey to the Bear Lake road felt like old times, calling up McIntyre's memory of the first time he and Miss Coteau escaped the village and shared their first private picnic in the woods.

Small Delights chugged happily. The air was warm and rich with the scent of pines; the sky was clear. Those picnic memories surged again when they arrived at "Tiny" Brown's roadside grocery, delicatessen, bait shop and camping supply store at Beaver Point. As they did on their very first picnic date, they chatted with the three hundred pound Tiny while he created sandwiches—roast beef this time—packed potato salad into cardboard containers, selected bottles of pop, cut wedges of fresh apple pie to wrap in waxed paper, and finally arranged everything carefully in a little basket. For the ranger, no deposit needed for the bottles and basket. Tiny knew McIntyre would bring them back. He also apologized for not having egg salad sandwiches, a particular favorite of the lady.

On the wall behind Tiny's cash register there hung a framed photograph of an "Under Construction" sign from the Bear

Lake road. A caption claimed it to be a venerable sign, an ancient sign, possibly the oldest such sign in the United States. Next to it a hand-lettered notice said "Yes, We Stay Here All Winter, No, We Don't Get Lonely." Beneath these two bits of wit a third sign proclaimed "In God We Trust, All Others Pay Cash."

On this particular sun-washed day the road to Bear Lake certainly lived down to its reputation. Small Delights crept cautiously from pothole to washboard, tilted alarmingly while detouring around a recent rockslide, and held its mechanical breath as it ventured across a rain puddle that might be an inch deep or might be bottomless.

The mine tunnel Vi Coteau wanted to investigate turned out to be no more than a shallow hole in a cliff beside the rushing creek. But it could be a "drop," she said, a place for an illegal drug wholesaler to leave goods to be picked up by a local dealer. However, the hole turned out to contain no prohibition liquor, no drugs, no contraband military weaponry, no counterfeiting plates, nothing except a rusty blade from a broken shovel. Finding it to be merely an old hole in the rock and in no way sinister, the ranger and Vi hiked a few minutes downstream to a sunny patch of grass where the creek flowed with less splashing racket. Vi spread the car robe and unpacked their lunch. McIntyre unpacked his fly rod and assembled it.

"Going to murder the poor little trout?" Vi asked sweetly.

"I might," he said with a smile. "After all, it's part of my job. The brookie population needs to be kept under control. Besides, what else is there to do on a picnic, after you've eaten the food?"

In reply she rose from the car robe, took hold of his fly rod, tossed it aside, and used both hands to pull his head down for a sizzling kiss on the lips.

"Oh," he remarked.

He thought he might quip "well, sure, there's that." Luckily for him her mouth was in his way.

Later, leaning on his elbow looking at her, contented as a man might be with a lovely woman and a fine roast beef sandwich, McIntyre popped a question.

"What are we doing here?"

"What?"

"I mean, your story about wanting to investigate the old mine tunnel. Seems to me like pure malarkey. How come we came here, really?"

"Really?" she answered. She sipped her soda pop and thought about it.

"Wanted a little time alone? Because you were missing me?" he asked.

"No," Vi said. "Because I was missing us."

* * * * *

Back in the village, on their way to Mrs. Spinney's house, they came upon a scene of much commotion at the New Mountain Stage Company's bus barn. They could see a little smoke drifting up from the roof and the volunteer fire department's hose cart and hand pumper standing in the street. Half the population of the village and valley seemed to be crowded around trying to see into the dusky shadows of the barn.

Volunteer Fire Chief Andy Schuel came out as McIntyre was dismounting from his pickup.

"What's up?" McIntyre called out to him.

"Ranger! Say, I'm glad to see you! I need you to take a look at where the fire was."

"Not really my jurisdiction," McIntyre said, looking over his shoulder at Vi, who was still seated in the truck. Behind the "Small Delights" lettering on the door. Their plan was to clean up and go share an evening supper.

"C'mon," Andy said.

Reluctantly, with a resigned shrug of his shoulders and another apologetic look at Vi, McIntyre followed the fire chief into the barn. Despite the wide open doorways at either end, the place reeked of smoldering rubber.

"Small fire," Andy told him as they made their way toward the grease pit at the back of the barn. "One of the drivers, Oliver, he was soldering a radiator when a fire broke out all around him. They took him to the Longmont hospital, poor guy. He's burned awful bad."

McIntyre looked at the scorched bus and scratched his head.

"Looks like they'll need to repaint the fenders. Need new tires on the front, naturally. You say the radiator was busted?"

"Just a small hole is all," Andy said. "But look, Tim, you're the guy who can read signs. The minute I got here and we put the fire out, I thought to myself, 'McIntyre ought to be here, he could figure out what happened quick as lightning.' Take a look around, would you? I wouldn't ask, except the so-called accident with Arthur Ogg has me spooked. Oliver, he might die and I'm going to be asked a lot of questions."

"Got your fire axe?" McIntyre said.

"Right here."

"Okay, smash a hole in the wall where those scorched boards are. We need sunlight in here."

The front tires of the bus were still smoking. The concrete floor was wet.

"You do that?" McIntyre asked.

"You mean the water? Yeah, we hit it with buckets of water first, but it was gasoline. We finally smothered it with a couple of asbestos fire blankets."

"Where'd the gasoline come from?"

"See the gas can over there next to the back wall? We knocked it out of place, smothering the fire, but it looks like it was standing there and sprung a leak, the gas dribbled out across the floor, pooled all around the driver, and his blowtorch ignited it."

"There's the blowtorch, probably where he dropped it. And look, there's a stick of solder lying next to it. Anyone around who might have seen the fire start?"

"A dozen people. But they were up at the other end of the barn waiting to go on a tour. I think Zig Whortle was the one who first saw the flames shoot up. He was about halfway down the barn, coming toward the office. He'd been talking with Hayward."

"Hayward?"

"Hayward. Starting out on one of his walks. Often comes here to the car barn. See, if a bus is going out with an empty seat they let him on for half fare. Rides the bus into the park, dismounts somewhere along the way, walks back to town."

"Let me look around. You might go outside and tell Miss Coteau what I'm doing. I'll be with her in a few minutes."

Miss Coteau, however, was not a woman who could be told she needed to wait for a man. Andy delivered McIntyre's message: She shot the messenger with an icy, pitying smile before turning on her heel to walk into the gloomy barn. She joined Ranger McIntyre and asked what he was doing.

"Looking for anything suspicious," he replied.

The word "suspicious," added to his curtly official tone of voice, prompted her to adjust her own tone, and her cloche, to become Violet Coteau of the Pedersen Investigation Agency.

"Is it supposed to be suspicious?" she asked. "Why are we suspicious?"

"I don't know yet. Fire Chief Schuel asked me to look around."

The tires no longer smoldered. McIntyre squatted in front of the White bus as he imagined the victim did. The fire brigade left Oliver's blowtorch where it was, probably near the man's right hand. He probably held the bar of solder in the other. McIntyre felt around under the radiator and found the soldering iron. The gas can was off to his left, near the wall, far enough away not to catch fire. The floor sloped: leaking gasoline would flow down directly in front of the bus. McIntyre was hunkered down there, going through the motions of soldering the radiator, when he overheard a smooth, cultivated voice talking to Vi.

"Terrible thing," said the voice. "Awfully fortunate, though, since the building might have ignited as well. Entire village might have gone up. Gone up in smoke, as the saying goes."

McIntyre rose to his feet to see Dr. Hayward. The gunsmith was standing a few inches too close to Vi. And he looked, McIntyre thought, a little too impeccable. He was dressed for walking, from his rich-looking Stetson down to his tweed knickerbockers and sturdy brogues. He pointed his thick walking staff at the splintered outer wall.

"Explosion?" he said. "I heard no explosion."

"Dark corner," McIntyre said. "We broke out part of the wall because we needed the daylight. Oliver was working with a miner's lamp because it was dark back here. I heard you were in the barn when the fire started?"

"Indeed," Hayward said, continuing to look at Vi rather than at McIntyre. "I was, in fact, weighing my options. Oliver told me he intended to take a test drive once the radiator was repaired—and I said I might go with him. I believe he was thinking of driving up the Moraine Park road. But the other driver, Antonio, also had space on his bus. He was scheduled to leave for Deer Ridge junction."

"But you didn't see the fire start."

"Matter of fact," he replied, continuing to smile at Vi, "I did. I believe—I cannot be certain—people were talking and engines were running, echoes bouncing all over the place—I believe I heard something hit the back wall. I distinctly heard the gasoline can fall over onto the concrete. You know, the thunking sound a half-empty can would make if it fell over? Well, I stepped away from the others who were waiting for Antonio's bus. I intended to investigate and also see how the radiator repair was coming along. I was half way to Oliver's bus when a flash of fire lit up the whole barn. Everyone retreated onto the street except for Ladro and two other drivers who seized the fire buckets and attempted to rescue unfortunate Oliver."

"He didn't try to save himself?"

"I've no idea. Never saw him until the volunteer firemen arrived with blankets. Perhaps he slipped, fell down in the flames. Might have saved his life, being near the floor."

McIntyre turned away to go look around outside on the off chance of discovering how the gas can got knocked over. A thrown rock, for instance? Rock might still be there, somewhere, or left a scar on the wall. Or a scuff mark from somebody kicking the wall with their foot. Or a crack wide enough to shove a stick through and push the can over.

"Miss Coteau," he heard Hayward say, "terribly bad timing of course, but I was wondering… I must ask… the fact is, I have a reservation at the Stanley this evening and wondered if you'd care to join me."

"Reservation?" she asked.

"Supper and film. They do it every two weeks. The supper's

a set menu, I'm afraid, but usually quite good. Tonight's film is called 'The Goat' with Buster Keaton. It turns out I won't be going hiking this afternoon. Perhaps I could pick you up? Say around six o'clock?"

Miss Coteau informed him, politely, of her previous dinner engagement, Hayward wished her well, and he, his hiking stick, and his male pride made a dignified exit.

Did everything but kiss her hand, McIntyre thought.

She was standing in front of the scorched bus, wondering why the driver hadn't simply jumped away when he saw and heard the flames, as the ranger returned through the hole in the wall.

"Anything?" she asked.

"Nope. Chief Schuel said the gas can sprung a leak. Didn't fall over like Hayward thought. Let's see… from the way the concrete is stained, I would say the flow of gasoline started right over there. The stain spreads out from there, see. I'll get the can and put it back where it probably was."

When he picked up the can he saw the quarter inch hole near the base. When he shook it to see if any gas remained inside, he heard the rattle. And when he unscrewed the cap and turned the can upside down, he saw what fell out.

A lead pellet. With a concave base.

"If you should wish to discover a most suspicious clue," McIntyre said, mimicking Hayward's diction, "I suggest we need look no further. For here, my dear, is how the petrol was permitted to flow out. The container has been targeted by a shooter."

"I'd rather not have a forest ranger call me his 'dear'," she countered. "He might be confusing me with his four-legged ones. The kind with antlers?"

"Question is," McIntyre continued, ignoring her little joke, "why didn't Oliver simply move away from the spilled gas and the flames?"

"Are you ignoring my little joke?" she asked.

"Yes," he answered. "Now, are you free for supper, or not?"

"Do you have reservations?" she said.

"Several," he quipped, "but I'm willing to risk eating with you anyway."

"Old joke, ranger. If I wanted humor I would've opted for the Buster Keaton film."

Unlike Vi Coteau's bit of wit, Ranger McIntyre's attempt at levity obviously sounded forced. He knew it, and he knew why: having snapped a few pieces into place, his mind had shifted into its serious mode, preoccupied with finding the next piece. But so far he didn't like the emerging picture. Perhaps Oliver had been shot, like Arthur Ogg. Maybe he'd been shot and fell to the floor where he was not able to move away from the burning gasoline. Searching for connections, it popped into McIntyre's brain that Jamie Ogg's favorite small game rifle was a .25-35 Winchester, firing a bullet less than seven millimeters in diameter.

In Mrs. Spinney's tidy little parlor, McIntyre gingerly situated himself on the fragile-looking settee to wait for Vi Coteau. Vi was in her room doing what females have been doing ever since Eve needed forty-five minutes to decide which fig leaf to wear. The ladies refer to it as "freshening up." Like most males of the species, McIntyre had no clue what "freshening up" might entail. To himself it meant running a pocket comb through his hair, using his hand to brush lint and dandruff from his shoulders and possibly checking to see if his fly was zipped all the way. The ritual might make him feel less nervous, but hardly "freshened."

"I truly appreciate your sharing with me," Mrs. Spinney said to McIntyre. "But who do you think is behind all these apparent shootings? Somebody trying to start a shooting war between the New Mountain stage drivers and the jitney fellows? Doesn't it look that way to you? I'm reminded of a time when our WCTU group was infiltrated. The liquor interests hired tough women to mingle with us and start fist fights during our peaceful protests."

"Not sure what it means," McIntyre replied. "All we have are a few little lead slugs. Might be another one made the hole in the radiator. You're probably right. Seems obvious to assume it's someone trying to start trouble between the monopoly and the independents. Not sure who it would be or why they'd start a shooting war. But the pieces seem to fit."

"Say!" Mrs. Spinney said. "I've got a theory for you. Let's say he wanted this Oliver person out of the picture for whatever reason. Revenge, jealousy, fear? He's really good when it comes to fixing a radiator. Good at soldering. The attacker punches a hole in the radiator and arranges the gasoline can, figuring Oliver would move the bus to the far corner, out of the way of customers, to work on it. Then all the shooter needed to do was wait in the shadows and shoot the gasoline can."

"And also make it so Oliver can't move away from the fire? No, I can't buy it," McIntyre said. "Too complicated. Timing for one thing. He might not get around to fixing the radiator for several days. Or, he might have it fixed in a matter of minutes. No, I think they saw the opportunity and took it. I'm starting to think the same about whoever killed Arthur Ogg. It wasn't planned. I think our shooter—if there is one—is an opportunist. But do me a favor? Keep all this under your hat for now."

"Hats?" Vi Coteau said, coming into the parlor. "You two are discussing hats? Tell, me, sir, what do you think of this one?"

She did a pirouette to show off her latest new hat, a design incorporating the lines of a man's Homberg with those of an old-fashioned lady's bonnet.

"What do I think?" McIntyre said. "For one thing, I think I know better than to answer the question."

"Go ahead," she urged. "Be a brave ranger."

"Well, okay. It looks real spiffy. On you."

Vi responded with an icy look that made Mrs. Spinney wince, then simply said, "Let's go."

Chapter Five
What the Ranger Missed

"Anything to report?"

Vi, Eleanor, and Mrs. Spinney were sitting down to an early morning breakfast in Mrs. Spinney's kitchen.

"Not much," Eleanor replied, pouring tea. "I'm on full pay now. And Ladro's put me in the driving queue like a regular driver."

"The what?" Mrs. Spinney asked.

"Queue? It's what they do with taxis in the city. At hotels and train stations, mostly. Basically it means when I'm assigned to a vehicle I wait my turn to take the next load of passengers, whatever it might be. And wherever they want to go, except of course we've got a set menu of certain routes and destinations for customers to choose from."

"Nothing queer going on, though?" Vi asked.

"Nothing you wouldn't expect," Eleanor said. "I'm almost certain the Deer Ridge tea room, and the gift shop, Arts Place, out on the Longs Peak road, both give Ladro a kickback when we stop to let passengers buy stuff. Plus, when we pick up passengers at the railroad station we're under orders to take them to certain specific hotels and not to other lodges or dude ranches. Oh, and there's the business with your admiring swain. Doctor Hayward."

"Hayward? What about him?"

"He's in the habit of hitching rides into the park. He either hikes back to town or catches a return bus. Does the same with jitney drivers, I found out."

"Seems innocent enough to me," Mrs. Spinney said. "Maybe he has a *quid pro quo* arrangement. Maybe he loads ammunition for them, repairs guns, sells them ammunition, in return for rides."

"Maybe," Eleanor said. "But here's what looks like funny business: he wanted to ride my rig one morning, heading for Moraine Park, and Ladro bumped a man and woman and their kid to let Hayward have a seat. Ladro told them he'd give them a reduced fare on the next bus. Plus, other drivers tell me Hayward always asks people to move so he can sit on the back seat. They've seen passengers bumped for him too."

"I have to admit, I've only chatted with him briefly," Mrs. Spinney said. "At the church social. And a few times at the grocery, mostly. He seems like the breed of smooth gentleman my mother used to caution me about."

"Exactly," Vi said. "I've noticed him watching me... you ladies have seen the sort of look I mean... the other day he said he needed to deliver a repaired gun to a summer cabin in Tahosa Valley and asked if I'd like to make the drive with him."

"A conveniently remote place to run out of gas," Eleanor said. "We should keep an eye on him. He's awful chummy with the New Mountain gang, for instance."

"Agreed," Vi said. "I've left my Remington automatic with him as an excuse to make a surprise visit to his shop, should the situation call for it. I got the idea from Kate Warnes' handbook for lady detectives. Too bad she didn't offer any advice about how to deal with smitten males."

"My mother's advice was to steer clear of them," Mrs. Spinney said. "More tea?"

At Dr. Hayward's gunsmith shop Ranger McIntyre was also being offered a morning cup of tea. But he turned it down. For one thing, he would be expected to return to duty. For another, he couldn't warm up to Dr. Hayward enough to sit around passing the time of day with him.

"Wondered if you could tell me anything about this slug," McIntyre said, putting the lead pellet on Hayward's pristine workbench.

Hayward examined it with his jeweler's loupe, weighed it with his dainty balance scale, measured the base with a micrometer, and returned it to McIntyre.

"Same as the other two, I'm afraid," he said. "Same weight, approximately, same very faint rifling marks, same diameter. I'd say you're looking at homemade ammunition for a rifle of twenty-five caliber or between seven and eight millimeters. Probably a single shot, but not necessarily."

"Single shot?" McIntyre asked.

"The shape of the head. The point is nearly blunt. In a lever action or bolt action rifle it could hang up when you tried to push it into the chamber. I'm no detective, but I would suspect the owner to be an indigent, such as a hermit, who scrimps on both lead and gunpowder and who uses a single shot rifle to hunt rabbits and squirrels for the pot. His bullet mold and the pot he uses to melt his lead are probably very old and quite primitive."

"Interesting," McIntyre said. "If you were a detective, would you have a theory as to how this slug could end up inside a gasoline can? What I mean is, how did it go in one side and not come out the opposite side?"

"Well…" Dr. Hayward said, "one explanation would be that the shooter scrimped on gunpowder, creating a round capable only of knocking over a rabbit at close range. Such a round would probably penetrate one side of the can, but not both. The liquid inside, the petrol, would stop the bullet. Or… exactly where did the projectile strike the can? Near the base?"

"Yes. An inch or two up from the base."

"Well, there's your answer. The liquid in the can stopped the bullet. The gasoline leaked out, you see, leaving the projectile in the can."

"Right," McIntyre said, rising from the stool. "Thanks very much."

"I've thought of one thing more," Hayward said. "And I have a question for you, too."

"Oh?"

"While you are looking for a suitable weapon, it might turn out to be a light deer rifle, such as a Winchester .25-35, but the owner could be saving money by reducing the powder charge, in order to hunt small game more economically. And as I said, he probably needs to chamber his cartridges one at a time. As you would a single shot rifle, you see."

"Thanks. What's your question?"

"Rather hard to put into words. Let me say I've heard local rumors, rumors linking a certain park ranger with a smashingly glamorous lady who happens to be a detective. Being a bachelor chap myself, and quite, quite fascinated by the selfsame lady, I wonder…"

McIntyre interrupted him.

"You'll have to go on wondering," the ranger said, trying to sound pleasant about it. "Out here in the wild west we don't discuss ladies."

But to Doctor Hayward, seeing how quickly Ranger McIntyre snatched up the lead bullet and hurried for the door was a picture worth a dozen details. There would be competition for Miss Coteau's attention, and the competition would be wearing a dark green uniform.

McIntyre made one more stop on his way back to the Fall River ranger station: Moraine Park Outfitters, Andy Schuel, proprietor. The same Andy Schuel who served as the village volunteer fire chief.

"No," Andy said, "haven't sold any primers, or any reloading supplies in months. Leon Counter came in for a pound of black gunpowder a few weeks ago. But I suspect he puts it in his moonshine for added kick."

"Or he might be blasting a bigger cave to hide his hooch in. Making more room. He thinks I don't know about his liquor cache."

Leon Counter was one of Ranger McIntyre's unsung assets. The ranger never made any move to have the grubby hermit evicted from his "house," a pile of brush and rock concealing a lean-to and cave where Counter manufactured white lightning. From the vantage point of his "house" on an otherwise uninteresting barren ridge Counter could make a short walk in one direction to look down on the Fall River valley, while a walk the other way took him to a spot overlooking the Moraine Park country. Equipped with binoculars, and in return for being left alone, he acted as an unofficial warden for the park service, alerting rangers to poachers, illegal campers, troublesome animals and fires.

"Hey!" Andy said. "Speaking of black powder and reloading,

the new shooter's catalog arrived yesterday!"

Andy brought out the heavy catalog of guns and camping equipment and placed it on the counter with all the reverence of a priest presenting a bible. In the weeks to follow nearly every man and boy in the valley would come to the outfitters and linger over all the hundreds of pictures of guns and equipment.

"Would you look at this," Andy said respectfully, turning pages of the gun catalog like a man handling the Old Testament. "Every gun, foreign and domestic. Every kind of ammunition. And neat articles on stuff you never heard of. Look, look here. This page is all about a company in England still making flintlocks! And up to… can you guess? Up to a damn four gauge. Four gauge! A lead ball nearly an inch wide? It'd weigh a quarter of a pound. And look back here in the knife section…"

The telephone rang. Andy went to the back room to answer it, leaving McIntyre browsing through the catalog's section on small caliber Winchesters.

"It was the doc on the phone," Andy said when he returned. "He said to tell you why the bus driver didn't stand up and move away when the gasoline spilled all over the floor. Because he'd been shot. And ranger, Doc's description of the slug they dug out of him sounds like the ones you showed me."

"Dead?"

"Nearly. Got him in the neck."

"Damn. Well, let me know if you hear anything else, okay? I'll come back and look through the catalog in a day or two when I have more time."

"Okay," Andy replied. "But before you go, I thought of one thing you might look into."

"What?"

"Your little nine year old? Or ten? Anyway, your pal, the little girl who's president of the McIntyre fan club. Gala Book. The one who's always finding ways to make money. She asked me if I'd buy used cartridge cases. Brass. She's been scrounging brass all over the valley, anywhere people do target practicing. I told her I got no use for old brass. She's saving it up anyway. Plans to sell it to the metal scrap man down in Longmont. If I know Gala, she'll con a local citizen into taking it down there for her. Anyway, if anybody's been fooling around reloading or modifying their own bullets, Gala might've picked up their discarded brass. Cartridge cases they couldn't reload, like they were bent or split open. You said you didn't find any shells when Arthur was shot, huh?"

"Nope," McIntyre said.

Andy's remark sent McIntyre's mind flicking back to the day he and Jamie were at the death scene. Something, some little thing, was troubling McIntyre about it. It was like doing a jigsaw puzzle and not being able to find a piece even though it seemed like it ought to be easy to spot. There'd be no point in returning up the Fall River road, though, not with the recent rains and the traffic. Maybe the photographs would show him what he'd been missing.

"I know what it was," Andy said, breaking into McIntyre's brief reverie.

"You what?"

"I remembered," Andy said. "Back at the bus barn. You were asking who was there and what they saw. When I got there to help put out the fire I asked the little Italian guy, Ladro, if everyone was okay. It's what we're supposed to do in case of fire, make certain there's nobody injured or trapped. Check for any humans involved before we attack the flames. Well anyway, Ladro looks all around, see? He says 'all the passengers are out here on the sidewalk. Antonio's bringing a bus around to the curb. Secretary was in the office but she's come out. Nobody else was inside,' he told me, 'except a jitney driver who'd been askin' about a job.' Ladro said the jitney man was halfway along the barn. He'd been hangin' around, hopin' to talk to the boss about jobs. He might have seen what happened, see? But when I got there he must have gone."

"Who was he?"

"Ladro didn't recognize him. All he said was the guy wore a green plaid cap. The kind that's supposed t' look like a Scotch tartan."

* * * * *

In keeping with the local way of doing things, McIntyre's visitor rapped twice on the log cabin's door, opened it, and entered without waiting.

"Why don't you come on in," said the ranger. He knew it was Vi Coteau. There was no mistaking the growl of her yellow Marmon coupe's engine.

"Thanks," she said. "I will. Do you have anything for lunch?"

"And hello and how are you, too. I'm fine, thanks. What were you expecting for lunch? Hoping I'd brought egg salad sandwiches from Tiny's, maybe?"

"No, silly ranger. I was coming down from Fall River and thought I'd drop in for a bite to eat. I was ready to raid your ice box, since I expected you to be out in the forest being a ranger. Rangering? Or is it called ranging? Anyway, you're here. It looks as though you're sitting there playing with your jigsaw puzzle."

"Nick told me to stop hanging around the village and to finish my late reports and overdue forms."

"I don't see any paperwork," she said.

"On the desk. Over there. But look at this piece of puzzle. Could this be part of a ship's mast, or is it a fence post, do you think?"

"It's a shadow," Vi answered, opening his ice box. "What do we have in here for lunch? I see you've been helping yourself to taxpayers' trout."

McIntyre stood up, stretched a kink from his back, and, looking back at the puzzle with a sigh, went to put kindling in the stove. Before too long he and Vi were sitting down to trout, fried potato slices, homemade applesauce (courtesy of Odette Book), and hard boiled eggs.

"Sorry the milk went sour," he said. "But ol' Rocky Mountain spring water is plenty good enough. Do you want to get married?"

"Not particularly," she replied. "Why do you ask?"

"Gala Book suggested it. Again. I gave her an assignment to very secretly see if she could find any brass cartridge cases to fit a bullet about a quarter inch in diameter. She skipped off to begin investigating. Loves to play detective. She still wants to be you, of course."

"And this means you and I should get married?" Vi said.

"You know how Gala's little pigtailed brain works. She finds a worm on a lawn, finds a tin can in the trash, and presto! She's going up and down the river selling cans of fishworms at ten cents a dozen."

"Or two dozen for a quarter," Vi laughed. "And no charge for the can."

"Right. She wants to be a detective like you, but she can't see herself leaving mom and dad and her little brother. Therefore, you'll need to move the Denver detective agency up here to the village. She's got a building spotted for you, one next to her dad's barbershop. It used to be a fabric and sewing store. Gala says she can get it for you at twenty bucks a month or less, furniture not included. She intends to work for you until she learns the detective business, she'll live in the back of the shop, and you'll move in with me, and you and I will have both my government truck to use, and my Small Delights pickup."

"What?"

"Gala wants your Marmon, too. As soon as her legs are long enough to reach the pedals. On time payments. She's got it all planned. But you and I need to get married to make it work for her."

"I see," Vi said. "Well, speaking of marrying a mental case, and speaking of cartridge cases, how are the murder cases coming along?"

"Let's say they're challenging. And I feel like I'm looking for dynamite with a lit fuse and it's about to blow up. Jamie's on edge, looking at every tourist suspiciously, brooding around the barracks when he's off duty, and he's roped Russ Frame into helping him harass the New Mountain bus drivers until one tells who shot his dad. Even Marley's been acting edgy. Everybody wants answers."

"Right," Vi said, pushing her empty plate to one side and taking out a pocket notebook and pencil. "Let's go over it. What are the questions?"

"First, who shot Arthur and who shot the driver, Oliver. Who dismounted from Arthur's car up there on Fall River, and who picked him up? Was he the shooter, and if not the shooter, what did he see? Why didn't the fisherman hear any shots? Who was the jitney driver hanging around in the bus barn when the fire started, and what did he see? And why didn't anybody hear those shots? I don't know. I can't even figure out what's bothering me about the foot tracks Jamie and I saw up where Arthur's Dodge went over the edge."

"Maybe we should begin there," Vi suggested. "We could drive up to the same place and maybe it would jog your memory. We can take my car, or your truck. Either way."

"I've got a better idea," McIntyre said.

He went to his desk and picked up the telephone.

"Jane?" he said to the operator. "Would you please see if you can get me Tom, the hostler at Fall River Lodge? Thanks."

He covered the mouthpiece with his hand and looked at Vi, who was still sitting at the table.

"Are you wearing pants?" he asked.

"I do beg your pardon," she replied.

"I mean, is that one of your split skirt things? Can you ride a horse in it?"

"My friend," she said, "I can ride a horse wearing nothing but your hat."

"Good," the ranger said. "Tom? Hi. McIntyre here. Got a Kodak camera I could borrow? No, I'm kidding. Only kidding. Could you saddle up a horse, for a lady? In half hour to an hour? Yes, you know the lady I mean. No, I've got no idea what she's doing up here. Okay. Well, we'll be there soon. I need to clean up the lunch dishes and find her one of my hats."

Vi Coteau took her Marmon coupe to Fall River Lodge. Ranger McIntyre rode Brownie along the river trail shortcut. Brownie trotted proud as a ranger horse can be, head high, ears straight up, watching to left and to right for fish poachers, injured animals, lost children, or tourists wanting directions. Her ranger sat well in the saddle, boots polished, dark green tunic brushed, flat hat set squarely on his head. Nick the supervisor would have admired how impressive one of his rangers looked, especially if he hadn't seen all the unfinished paperwork gathering dust on the ranger's desk. And if he wasn't aware that the ranger's riding partner was not one of his assistants, but an extremely attractive woman.

Vi was in the saddle and waiting for him when he got there. Side by side they trotted up the road, crossing over the noisy little cascade called Roaring Fork, passing through the white-pillared aspen groves and finally breaking out of the forest at the point where the first steep upgrade began. There McIntyre paused, considering whether to continue up the roadway or veer off onto the fishing path along the river.

"I don't think our mystery hitchhiker went near the river," he said. "Let's stay on the road."

Seeing how intently the ranger was studying the ground left and right, Vi dropped back half a horse length, not wanting to be in his way. There was a look to the man, a noticeable tension in his posture, an unusually grim set of his chin. He was into one of his very serious moods. The further up Fall River they rode, the more morose he seemed to become.

She said nothing.

The canyon narrowed in the far distance, taking on a foreboding, hostile appearance. It's only the shadows, she told herself. And it's how the trees up ahead crowd the road in a solid wall. The high cliffs and the thick forest block off most of the sunlight in the upper canyon. Even on a warm day the chilly gloom makes a person shiver.

Vi looked over the edge of the road. At the gorge's rocky bottom the river flowed in and out of sight, foamed around boulders, settled into long mirrored pools, sent the faint, constant murmur of its voice up the rubble slope. This, she learned, was where Tim McIntyre's first love met her death. Not much further away, Jamie Ogg's father died in another car crash. McIntyre had not confided in her his own sadness about either tragedy. God only knew what thoughts were behind the steel-hard clench of his jaw.

As expected, recent rain and motor traffic had erased the tire marks and footprints. McIntyre looked sadly down the rubbled slope at where Arthur Ogg's car came to rest. He slowly made his way along the shoulder of the road, leaning down to study the ground. He halted at the place where Arthur stopped the car and where Arthur's passenger alighted. Vi saw McIntyre cross his hands on the saddle horn and saw his shoulders slump as he stared down into the valley.

Whatever McIntyre's thoughts were, they were broken into when Brownie began pawing a hoof into the dirt. Ranger horses don't simply stand around looking at scenery, especially with a civilian livery horse looking on. The mare's impatient gesture drew McIntyre's attention to the road's shoulder again, looking to see what she was pawing at, and Vi saw him straighten up, smile a tiny smile, and gaze back off into empty space.

"Eureka," he said flatly. "Got it."

Vi urged her horse alongside his.

"Good!" she said. "What have you got?"

"A tiny detail, that's all. But it's like with a jigsaw puzzle. You know, when you look at a piece and think there's part of a flower petal on it, but it turns out to be somebody's ear? It gives me one of my 'aha!' moments."

"Like your 'aha' moment in Denver when you first met me. And your jaw dropped open?"

"My jaw did not drop open. When I met you for the first time it was a 'hoo, boy!' moment As in 'hoo, boy, trouble ahead! Run away!'"

"But you didn't run away," she said.

"My mistake. Anyhow, when Russ Frame interviewed those hikers, the ones Arthur hauled to the Mummy Range trailhead, they told him they picked up a hitchhiker outside of town or at the edge of town. Anyway, he was carrying a sturdy walking stick. The way they described it, it was thick and was about waist-high. Like the one Hayward usually carries."

"Okay, a walking stick? And?"

"Looking at the tracks, Russ and I figured that Arthur stopped right about here, on the side of the road where it begins to drop off into the canyon, and a man got out. Arthur had let the four hikers off at the trailhead, that's for certain. The only passenger left in the car was the unknown hiker. Probably he said, to Arthur, something like 'it's only a few miles to the lodge, I'll get out here, thanks, and walk the rest of the way.'"

"Sure. Plausible," Vi said. "Common thing to do, especially if you're not in a hurry."

"But no sign of the walking stick. The two of us tracked him from here to over across the road there, down the road about ten yards, saw clear footprints where he got into a New Mountain bus, saw where the New Mountain bus stopped at the wreck site and he and the bus driver got out and stood on the edge of the road. What I didn't realize at the time is that we didn't see a single mark of a stick. I would have seen at least one small round hole in the ground next to his footprints, but I didn't. Why not?"

The pair turned their horses homeward and rode side by side back down the road.

"Did he leave it in the car?" McIntyre mused. "Or if he used a takedown rifle to shoot Arthur, and used the stick to steady the rifle, maybe he cached both gun and walking staff before the New Mountain bus showed up. Darn, I wish we'd searched the other side of the road. The uphill side. The day it happened, I mean. Maybe he hid the gun up there and came back later to retrieve it."

"But you said it yourself," Vi pointed out. "A mark left by a walking stick is a very tiny detail."

"Yeah," Ranger McIntyre replied. "Maybe I'm going at it all wrong. Maybe where I'm making my mistake is wasting time thinking about how it was done, of who made those homemade bullets, how he could shoot without being heard, what kind of gun it was, how it was concealed from the hikers in Arthur's car, how to fire a shot inside the bus barn without it being noticed. Important details, maybe, but they're still nothing but tracks. Like when you follow an animal's tracks backward and find out where it's been. No, I need to figure out where our shooter was going. What he was intending to accomplish, see? Been studying the wrong details."

"Let me suggest a little strategy," Vi said, reaching over to put a hand on his arm. "The gunsmith, Doctor Hayward, has shown an interest in me."

"What man wouldn't? Unless he was a hundred year old monk? And blind."

"Hush. Why don't I flatter him up a bit? I'll turn on the charm and persuade him to show off what a gun expert he is. Maybe he'll say something, remember a customer with an odd gun. He claims to know most of the guns in the village. Maybe there's a murder clue he's seen but doesn't think it important. What I'm saying is, let me keep on nosing around, looking for the 'how', and you see if you can dope out the 'why' of these two shootings."

McIntyre didn't like the picture of Vi hanging around with the smooth Hayward, especially considering Hayward's apparent connection with the New Mountain thugs and possibly with the bent senator. Like the missing impressions in the dirt, there was something not quite right about the gunsmith. Early in their relationship, however, the ranger learned that once she had made plans to do something, Miss Violet Coteau could not be dissuaded. In a miscellany of previous encounters she ignored all his protestations as she arranged for him to look like an amusement park sex pervert, a dinner dandy in a tuxedo, and a slow-moving target for a sharpshooter on snowshoes. And now he thought he could tell her not to flirt with another man?

After a few moments he uttered a carefully considered response.

"Be careful?" he ventured.

Chapter Six
McIntyre Gets Serious

Fall River entrance, midmorning. The day was warm, the sky was columbine blue, the Rocky Mountains were a postcard photograph, and visitor traffic was light. On the four miles of road between the village and the Fall River entrance Vi Coteau overtook only two other cars. She never regarded her speed as excessive or risky, but when she arrived between the entrance's two log buildings and skidded to a stop the Marmon's tires did leave ruts in the loose gravel.

A tall (dark and handsome) ranger in full uniform stepped out and approached her car. He put one polished riding boot on her running board, like a cop about to write a ticket.

"Welcome to Rocky Mountain National Park, miss," he said. "And exactly how many cars did you overtake illegally this grand morning?"

"Only two, officer," Vi replied.

She noticed him looking down at her knees. The airstream in the convertible often disarranged the hem of her skirt.

"And anyway, one of the cars I passed was already slowing down to pull off of the road."

"Probably terrified when he looked in his rear view mirror and saw you coming."

"As long as we're asking each other questions," she went on, "what are you doing guarding the park?" she asked. "Or are you only intercepting innocent women? I didn't expect to see you this morning."

"The temp came to work without his flat hat. I sent him back to the barracks for it. I took over the gate until he's back. Why don't you drive on through? You can park your car beside the building. If you want to stay and talk."

He's awfully official lately, she thought.

A Chevy four-door with a family in it stopped at the entrance to ask the way to Chasm Falls. As McIntyre gave directions, the driver and the wife kept throwing satisfied smirks at the sporty convertible. They were obviously glad to see the ranger detain the snooty flapper who sped past them earlier.

After the Chevy family drove on, McIntyre strolled to the Marmon and lounged against the front fender. Vi opened her door and swiveled on the seat to set her feet on the running board.

"What do you call this color?" McIntyre asked, running his finger over the smooth enamel. "Lemon? Or banana? I've been thinking I might have my pickup painted. With this color I could hide it in the autumn aspen grove when I sneak out to go fishing. Anyway, what brings you to our beautiful national park, lady?"

"The color is called 'Arizona Sunrise', smarty-pants, and I doubt if you'd ever paint Small Delights. If you did, women might actually not mind riding in your truck. You probably feel like a real ladies' man when one of them objects to sitting behind a 'small delight' sign but does it anyway. Speaking of the man-woman thing, though, it's the reason I'm escaping from the village."

"Man trouble?" he asked.

"I might ask you to go locate your service revolver and shoot our chivalrous Doctor Hayward," Vi said. She stretched out a leg to admire how nice her shoes looked with the tartan skirt.

"I'm afraid I haven't time to shoot any of your admirers this morning," he said with a straight face—while watching the lower edge of her skirt—"busy schedule. Maybe tomorrow. As soon as the temp comes back I need to make my rounds. Nick is a little upset how I've been spending time in town when I ought to be in the park where I belong. But what's the problem with Hayward?"

"For one thing, whenever I walk in the village he seems to be watching me. Always coming from the other direction, touching his hat brim, stopping to chat. It's as if he's either waiting for me, or sees me and runs around the block in order to accidentally bump into me. And when he does, he always stands a little too close. But here's the corker, Tim. Yesterday I was coming out of Murphy's with a few groceries? He accosted me. Wanted to carry my groceries for me. And 'have a chat' about a proposition of his. The house adjoining his cottage is for sale. He has the idea of buying it and then renting it to me! Like Gala, he thinks the village needs a detective agency and wouldn't it be a wonderful advantage if a lady detective could find a combination office and living accommodation at a very low monthly rent. Oh, and I would be welcome to use his underground target range. 'Any time,' he said. He was practically drooling at the idea of having me for a neighbor. He even hinted that his 'connections' might eventually make a nice sideline for me. I don't whether he means drugs, or influence peddling, or what. Honest to Pete, Tim, the next killing you need to investigate might be him, and I'm your murderer. You might as well arrest me now."

"Does it mean I can search you for a weapon?" McIntyre leered. "I've always wondered where you carry your little pistol."

"Don't you start," she snapped. "I'm leaving. I'm going to drive—slowly—over to Moraine Park now. I want to relax, enjoy the scenery, spend time alone. Okay? Now, you can recognize Hayward's car, the plain brown Franklin coupe? If he comes along after me, do me a favor and shoot out his tires."

"I don't have a gun," McIntyre said.

"You're wearing a Sam Brown belt and holster," she pointed out, swinging her legs back into the convertible.

He shut the car door for her.

"Of course I am," he said. "Part of the uniform. But there's no revolver in it. Maybe I'm trying to be like you and hide my .45 inside my unmentionables. Or maybe I left it at the cabin because the holster is much lighter without it. But you take it easy. After I've done my checkpoints, maybe about two o'clock or a little later, I'll stop at Tiny's Beaver Point store for a roast beef sandwich. Maybe catch up with you there. We can sit in my truck and eat."

"How romantic," she remarked, pressing her foot against the starter switch.

Fifty to a hundred yards outside the Fall River entrance the road builders provided a wide place where motorists might turn around if they decided not to enter the park. There, screened by pine trees, a man with binoculars sat in a brown coupe. The entrance station was too distant for him to see faces, but he knew the yellow convertible. And he knew the tall, straight figure walking back to the information building. It was Ranger McIntyre, Vi Coteau's oh-so-chummy pal with nothing to offer a woman except a horse, a pickup truck, and a fly rod.

What to do about McIntyre, the watcher wondered. Maybe Senator Speckle's aide might arrange with the park service to have McIntyre transferred. Or maybe McIntyre might meet with an accident on one of his trips into the woods. Among the villagers he was famous for risking his life in pursuit of criminals; perhaps if another murder happened, and there happened to be evidence of the perpetrator having fled to the wilderness, to the high cliffs and deep canyons, maybe Miss Coteau's friend might investigate. And not come back.

The watcher knew it would be awkward to drive through the gate as long as McIntyre was there. Instead, he might go back to town and place a telephone call. He knew a person who could become the beginning of McIntyre's final investigation.

* * * * *

The moonshiner emerged from his "house" and blinked at the bright sunshine. His "house," as Leon Counter described it, was "half brush pile, half shack, half mine tunnel and half rock outcropping." His lawn furniture consisted of two flat stumps and a section of pine log. McIntyre chose a stump. The ridge where Leon built his whiskey still was largely bare of trees, a mundane piece of scenery. With so many spectacular trails and vistas in the park, no one ever hiked up Leon's hill.

After exchanging customary remarks about weather, number of park visitors, the condition of the deer herds, and the possibility of an early winter, McIntyre diplomatically broached the object of his visit, couching it in the most subtle terms possible.

"Leon, have you shot anyone recently?"

"Recently, no."

"See anybody carrying a rifle?"

"You're talking about Arthur Ogg bein' killed, right? Can't

see that part of the road from here. Heard about the crash. Went down there in time to see you and a young ranger, in fact, tryin' to track the shooter. You didn't see me, of course."

"What do you mean, 'young' ranger? I'm young, too," McIntyre protested.

"Well, let's say you won't be gettin' any younger any time soon. No, I thought like you did. Chatted with Marley about it, in fact, 'bout two weeks back, about how the sniper had t' have been on the roadway. Darn strange. You want a drink? I've got fresh popskull. Or I even got a jug I've let age almost a month."

"Thanks, but I'll need my legs to hike back down to my truck."

"Okay. More for the rest of us. Anyhow, I ain't seen anybody carryin' a rifle, not lately. 'Course, it don't mean they might couldn't have one in a car or truck. Or tour bus. You come all the way up here to ask if I shot anybody?"

"Wanted to pick your brain, mostly," McIntyre said. "Thought about you when I heard you bought gunpowder from Schuel's store? I figured you wanted it to blast a new storage area in your cache. I don't have a problem with it, I'm trying to line up as many puzzle pieces as possible."

"Matter of fact, I been thinkin' I might could. Enlarge my warehouse cave, I mean. But it ain't gonna be used for what I bought it for. Turns out I couldn't use it like I was goin' to… ah, hell, Tim, I might as well tell you about it. It'll probably mean you rangers'll be snoopin' around and wreckin' everything, but what the hell."

"Give me a clue," McIntyre said. "You can pour me out a finger or two of your well-aged Who-Hit-John while you're at it."

Leon cheerfully took up the other tin cup and 'barely damped the bottom' with a shot of moonshine liquor from the jug.

"Well," he said, "it's like this. According to a couple of m' customers, th' older jugs of my hooch has really mellowed with age. Tastes like top quality stuff. If I can maybe contact the right speakeasy, or if this prohibition malarkey comes slidin' to a halt, I stand to make a sizable profit. Problem is, too damn many people know about my ol' cache."

Leon took another sip and regarded McIntyre carefully.

"Now..." he resumed, "you remember Miner Bill. He dug prospect holes all over these mountains. You know about the cave on Mount Chapin, up at timberline. Well, there's another'n like it, only let's say it's less accessible. When spring come I figured I'd make a hike and see could I make a new cache in it. Blast out more of the rock. Only guess what?"

"There was a bear hibernating in it?"

"No such luck. I'm partial to bear steak. No, they've built a door outta heavy timber and double padlocked it and stuck 'Danger No Trespassing' signs on it."

"You say it's on the slope overlooking Moraine Park?"

"Didn't say any such. I found me another ol' prospect hole, further up and higher. Hard to get to. Strictly between you and me and this jug, I plan on obtainin' a mule and couple of panniers to haul my products up there. See? I figure this time next summer I could've cached more'n a hundred gallons."

"You still need gunpowder?"

"Once I've cached me enough booze t' pay for my retirement, I plans to blast shut the opening. Like you rangers do when y' figure a tunnel's a dangerous temptation for folks. And whoever closed off the other hole, I wouldn't want 'em to poke around my cache."

"Who was it who built the heavy door? Any ideas?"

"Dammit, Tim," Leon answered. "You gotta swear not t' make it a federal project. People stomping all over the place. One day I was... well, I happened to be over by Moraine Park with my field glasses when this yellow tour bus come up the road. After a while here comes a sedan. They go on up outta sight and by and by the bus come back again, like usual, only a guy in the rearmost seat of the bus drops somethin' onto the road, see? And directly there' the sedan again and they stop and a fella gets out and picks it up. They wait maybe five minutes and drive off again."

"Drugs?"

"What else? I figure they cache their junk in th' old blocked-up tunnel, see. Probably when an order comes in for a couple of pounds of it one of their flunkies sneaks up there, packages the stuff, makes a signal for the customer to follow the tour bus. The dealer takes a ride and drops it off. Probably a different dropoff place each time. Less chance of the law catchin' on. Fewer men meetin' face to face, so fewer witnesses or stool pigeons."

"Would it work?"

"Hell, Tim, sure it would. Slick as hog snot on a marble floor. It's like sellin' moonshine, y' need to take trouble not to have anybody see the exchange. Neither party oughta know who the other one is. A guy rides a bus up to Moraine Park, see, and says he means to hike or fish or take photographs and he lets the bus go back without him. He hightails it to the cache, gets a package of drugs, hides it in his creel or his rucksack, goes back down to the road to wait for the next bus to come along. Meantime there's a car parked along the road, maybe pretendin' to take pictures of be birdwatchin'. They follow the bus, pick up the package the guy drops out the back, and Bob's your uncle."

"Leon," McIntyre said, setting the tin cup on the ground and rising carefully to his feet, "you've got a criminal mind, you have."

"Then how's come I ain't rich?" Leon asked.

* * * * *

That evening Dottie phoned McIntyre. His morning schedule, she informed him, would begin with a visit to Supervisor Nicholson's office. When he arrived, freshly shaved and fully uniformed right down to his holstered service revolver, she looked him up and down with approval.

"Coffee will be ready in a few minutes," she said. "I'll bring it. You're to go right on in."

Nick didn't ask the ranger to sit down.

"Anything to report concerning the Arthur Ogg incident?" he inquired.

"Not anything significant," McIntyre replied. "One key piece of information would be the identity of the extra rider Arthur Ogg picked up. But the New Mountain boys either don't know or don't want to tell me. Right now all we've got are three bullets, apparently from a noiseless gun. Odds are it's got to be a rifle, because of the distance involved. There was a guy fishing on Fall River but all he heard was Arthur's car crashing. Didn't hear the shots."

"Okay. Now tell me what's up with Ranger Jamie Ogg."

"Up?"

"Yes, up. For a few days after the wreck he was hot under the collar. Came in here to resign in order to hunt down whoever killed his father. I mean, the boy was in a rage. I refused his resignation and he said he'd refuse doing his regular duties, he'd go on hunting the killer. His own words. But this week, for the past few days, he and his pal Ranger Russ Frame have been good as gold and thick as thieves. They've both gone about their duties like they're trying to win a Ranger of the Year award. And I don't like the way they hang around outside the New Mountain car barn. After work, almost every day. See what you can find out."

"Yessir," McIntyre said. "Anything else?"

"Yeah. This thing with the New Mountain driver who got

burned… he might not make it, by the way… and the fire at the barn. Not our business. Leave it to the sheriff's office. Stay out of it. Oh, and a party of guests of our beloved senator went camping at Moraine Park last weekend. They caught sight of a strange-looking vagabond up on the ridge. A vagrant, probably. Senator's friends didn't like him spying on them, want us to find him and run him out."

"I don't know if I can do…"

"What you do is tell Leon to lay low awhile. Or we might have to send him packing. While you're talking with him, you might tell him I could use a couple of quarts of his best. I'll leave the money in the usual place under my porch. He'll know."

"Anything else?"

"If you've got time, sit down and have your coffee. You can tell me where the trout are biting. I agree you should keep on investigating wherever the park is involved. And I want you to put a bee in Ranger Ogg's ear, and Leon's too: there's to be no… unauthorized shooting. Got it?"

"Got it. Well, as to the trout question, if I was to go fishing this weekend I think I'd either take a horseback ride up the Thompson River to The Pool, or I'd try the Thompson where it leaves the park boundary. The Hidden Valley beaver ponds have been good for a lot of action, but mostly small brookies."

Dottie brought the coffee pot, cups, and two heavyweight day-old donuts from Kitty's (Always Open) Café. She set the tray down and left again, shaking her head. The two men were having an important government talk? It seemed to be all about number fourteen mosquitos versus a number twelve Rio Grande king versus the virtues of a black gnat.

Honestly.

* * * * *

A national park ranger, especially in the 1920s, lived in a world of men. Men who maintained the roads, men who built the hiking trails, men who patrolled the park. Even when a civilian automobile stopped for information, it was usually the man who got out to ask the questions. A bachelor ranger slept in a barracks full of men, shared a government cabin with two or three others, or, like McIntyre, ate and slept in a cabin where he found not only no female companionship but often no companionship whatever.

One would think, therefore, McIntyre would have greeted the feminine trio of Friday evening visitors with enthusiasm. However, a Scotsman and bachelor appreciates a surprise guest almost as much as he would a door-to-door salesman.

For the potluck supper all three females had donned their "Sunday-go-to-meeting" dresses and hats, attractive but not flashy. With wide eyes and cheekbone-to-cheekbone smiles they seemed ready to overflow with indomitable comradery cheerfulness. To a male, especially one with Scots blood in his veins, they represented a change of plan—or a change of vague intentions, which when interrupted morphed into important plans—and therefore were met with a scowl and refusal.

"I was about to fix supper," he grumbled.

"Oh, c'mon Tim!" Vi Coteau saw his scowl and laughed it off. "You know these community socials! There'll be food galore, plus desserts."

"Yeah," added the little girl Gala, "my mom's bringing the special sugar pie you like. Plus I'm gonna sing. It's a children's talent show. C'mon!"

"And you'll be the only man there with three dates," Eleanor pointed out. "I'll even dance with you. You know you like to show off doing the foxtrot, you devil ranger you."

"I've got a new jigsaw puzzle I was planning to work on,"

McIntyre protested. "And besides, tomorrow's my day off. I wanted to oil my fishing reel and dress my fly line."

"Pooh!" Vi countered.

"Take Brownie for a ride to give her the exercise?"

"Double pooh. We'll wait outside while you put on your suit and tie. In fact, we'll go say hi to Brownie, won't we Gala? I've got apples in the car for her."

As the three females walked toward the stable Eleanor could be heard chuckling out loud.

"Wow," Eleanor said. "What a grouch! Mata Hari herself couldn't talk Ranger McIntyre into a date if he didn't want to go."

"Who's Mata Hari?" asked little Gala.

"Oh," Eleanor answered, "she was a spy. A naughty lady who knew how to make army officers fall in love with her."

"How hard could that be?" Vi Coteau asked.

The festive quartet—or festive trio plus one uncertain participant—arrived at the community hall to find their table already reserved for them. Phylo Book, Gala's father and town barber, stood up to greet the new arrivals. His wife Odette was sitting with a squirmy toddler, little Polis, in her lap.

"Nice of y' to save seats for us," McIntyre remarked.

"Not a bit of trouble, ranger," Phylo said cheerily. "When you're the only Black folks in town there's generally plenty of empty seats near to you. Hope you don't mind Gala coming with the ladies to drag you to this event. She sure does like to hang around with Miss Coteau. And with you too, of course. But when are y' comin' in and let me give you a trim? You're lookin' a little shaggy around the edges."

"Phylo!" Odette protested. "Manners! You don't talk shop at social gatherings! Go get your food. And bring me a plate, too. I don't dare let go of Polis."

The sight of the buffet tables caused McIntyre's mood to improve considerably. It seemed as if all the housewives in town, and several of the husbands, were battling to determine who could do the most creative things with starch. There were potatoes prepared every way imaginable, steaming containers of macaroni, macaroni and cheese, macaroni and chicken, and macaroni with canned tuna. And dinner rolls, light as air, piles of them next to the pans of sliced ham, sliced chicken, sliced pork and sliced beef. Vegetables, too, boiled, broiled, steamed, baked, and raw.

After she and the ranger filled their plates, Gala suggested they grab their dessert before all the good stuff was gone; Vi Coteau, however, reminded the girl not to seem impolite and piggish.

"Or," Vi added, looking at McIntyre's loaded plate and giving him a flirty look, "rangerish."

The entertainment was announced. Gala and McIntyre were finishing the last crumbs of sugar pie. Most of the ladies and a few of the men began clearing away dishes and packing up leftovers while others folded tables and arranged chairs to face the tiny stage. Three husky young men helped Andy Schuel push an upright piano into position. Mrs. Spinney modestly assumed her seat at the keyboard, signaling the children to gather.

"Who are those young men who helped move the piano?" McIntyre asked.

"I don't know much about them," Phylo Book replied. "But I cut their hair a few weeks back. They're summer hires, up at Creagdhur Lodge on the hill. Awful nice fellas."

"Quite good-looking as well. I could investigate them for you," Vi said sweetly.

"I bet," McIntyre returned, "but I couldn't afford your rates."

"You couldn't afford my hat," she said.

There was a motive behind McIntyre's curiosity: the ranger couldn't help but notice how Dr. Hayward kept looking toward the three as if… as if he didn't understand why they were there. Hayward had been watching Vi Coteau all evening, his interest in her not so much noticeable as patently obvious. Why had he become distracted by three young men pushing a piano?

The children's chorus opened the program, standing reverently with hands over where the heart was presumed to be, leading everyone in the Pledge of Allegiance to the Flag. This was followed by a very, very serious rendition of "America, the Beautiful." The solemn tribute to the Union led into a lighter, more energetic version of "Erie Canal" with the children pantomiming hauling a canal boat and petting an invisible mule named Sal.

"Aren't you glad you came?" Vi asked, patting McIntyre's knee.

"You bet. Reminds me of when I was a kid."

"You were cute, of course?" Vi whispered.

"What else? I was born cute. But it wore off."

"No comment," she said.

The music teacher announced a new song, recently written and becoming popular among children's groups, "This Little Light of Mine."

She distributed candles, one per child, and paused to tell the audience that, given the age and unpredictability of certain chorus members, the candles would remain flameless. It made little difference to the children, who enthusiastically waved their unlit kitchen candles and sang—or shouted—"I'm gonna let it shine!"

Eleanor, sitting on the other side of McIntyre, elbowed the ranger in the ribs.

"Good thing the teacher didn't have the idea of turning out the lights and lighting those candles," she whispered. "It would've been too scary, and I don't mean for the kids."

McIntyre silently nodded agreement. And at that moment, if it is possible to coin a cliché, a light began to dawn in the ranger's brain. The light. The corner of the bus barn, where Oliver was soldering the radiator, was dark as a coal cellar. He was using a miner's lantern. The darkness was why McIntyre asked the fire chief to bust a hole in the scorched wall. There was no light. Whoever shot the hole in the gas can, and, as McIntyre suspected, probably shot Oliver as well, needed to be very, very close. Point blank range. He would have to be standing behind the bus Oliver was working on, with the bus hiding him from anyone else in the barn.

"Sure," McIntyre muttered.

"What?" Eleanor asked.

No one saw it and no one heard it because the shooter was in virtual darkness and on the far side of the bus. At such close range the weapon could have been a pistol. As the gasoline caught fire and all the confusion began, the shooter would merely pocket the gun and mingle with the crowd. It wouldn't even need to be planned. Whoever it was, he only needed to wait for any opportunity to do mischief. He found one in the gloomy end of the barn, and took the shot.

"Oh, nothing." McIntyre said to Eleanor. "A puzzle piece clicked into place."

With the entertainment over, volunteers began rearranging the folding chairs. This time the chairs were push back against the walls. The members of a local amateur dance band, The Peak Tones, set up their music stands and chairs on the little stage.

A quartet of mothers rounded up all the smaller children and herded them into the anteroom where they could play and be supervised and, hopefully, be unheard. Other children, the sleepy ones, were bundled off toward their own beds. A few of the "older" kids like Gala were allowed to stay to watch the grownups dance.

The Peak Tones led off with a version of a modern waltz, played with more zeal than proficiency. Eleanor tugged at McIntyre's sleeve.

"Oh, oh, Look." she said, nodding her head toward the doorway.

Vi Coteau was coming back from the ladies' room; Dr. Hayward had intercepted her with his arms open in what was obviously an invitation to dance. McIntyre looked, shrugged, and pretended to be more interested in the other people who stayed for the dancing. Jamie, Russ, and the three piano shifters were in the bachelor line, leaning on the wall with other young men who were encouraging—or daring—one another to go across and talk to the young women.

The waltz tune finally gave its last spasm and expired, and Dr. Hayward gallantly escorted Vi back to where Eleanor and McIntyre were sitting. McIntyre stood up and the two men exchanged polite but cool greetings.

"Tell me," McIntyre said, "it looked like you recognized those guys. The three standing in a clump over there? Know who they are?"

"No," Hayward answered. "Mistaken identity. I thought one resembled a young man I knew. I believe they're from Creagdhur Lodge. Employees. Summer help, you know. But no, never met any of them."

The Peak Tones broke into a bouncy foxtrot. Dr. Hayward sneered at first, but the sneer became a scowl when he saw the ranger wrap an arm around Vi's waist and lead her skipping out onto the dance floor. Hayward's sullen frown was to remain as long as the music lasted, for Miss Coteau obviously enjoyed McIntyre's footwork. Laughing and smiling widely, she matched him step for step, spun away to the end of her arm, twirled back again, did a skipping pattern of steps with him, laughed again when he whirled her away.

Zig Whortle came across the floor to claim Eleanor's partnership for the next dance.

"Let's see what we can do!" Zig said.

The next Tones tune was still a foxtrot, but at a slightly less frisky pace. Vi said she needed a chance to catch her breath, and Gala smiled from pigtail to pigtail when the tall ranger asked her to be his partner instead. It made her feel very grown up, especially since her parents had gone home to put sleepy little Polis in his crib, leaving her on her independent little own.

The foxtrot went well. As the music stopped, however, things took an unfortunate turn for those who wanted to continue dancing. In other words, the band's truant vocalist showed up. The band leader announced that the singer would now treat the assemblage to a sampling of the latest popular songs. Dancers politely lined up against the walls, some people sitting, some standing. Vi, Eleanor, Gala, and McIntyre found seats at a small table in a corner.

"I still wonder who those guys over there are," McIntyre said, nodding his head in the direction of the three young men. "I'd swear our Doctor Hayward recognized at least one of them, except he told me he'd never seen them before."

"If you think it's important to know who they are," Eleanor said, "I guess I could try to find out on one pretext or another. Maybe I'd pretend I have to pick up riders at the lodge."

"A person might ask around town," Vi suggested. "Carefully,

you know. I bet Kitty could tell us. Or Mrs. Murphy at the grocery. But I don't think they're any of the bad guys. Finding out about them doesn't seem worth the trouble."

Gala piped up.

"Hey," said the little girl. "I'm gonna be a lady detective, right? Like Miss Coteau and Miss Eleanor? You just leave it with me, lemme take the job. Let's say... let's say two bucks for the whole operation. Results guaranteed half your money back if not satisfied. I can get their names and ock, ock..."

"Occupations?" Vi suggested.

"Yeah. Ockipashion. Also where they hail from. My dad, he always asks customers he don't know where they hail from. Only charge y' fifty cents more for a hail where from."

"Cash on delivery?" McIntyre smiled. It was not the first time he had bargained with Gala, over her handmade dry flies, her tin can burglar alarm among other things.

"Nope, up front," she replied. "I got expenses, y' know."

Vi contributed one dollar. McIntyre handed her another. Gala tucked both dollars into the small clasp purse hanging from her shoulder and hopped out of her chair. Skipping happily as a little girl who's earned two dollars, she made a beeline for the nearest of the young men.

"Hi!" she said to him. "I'm Gala! What's your name? You come from around here?"

Early during their friendship, while spending an evening at the Trocadero Ballroom in Denver's Elitch Gardens, Vi Coteau was surprised—or shall we say "astonished"—by McIntyre's skill as a dancer. His poise was easy and natural, he was light on his feet, and he controlled his partner with subtlety. Spinning off to his arm's length made her feel free as a sky-curving swallow in flight.

At the village social, therefore, she was not at all surprised when he led her in a waltz smooth and graceful enough to compensate for the local band's occasional lapses in syncopation. What Vi did not anticipate, however, was how boldly the mountain-living women, frontier women, despite being married women, would tap her shoulder and cut in for a few moments in the ranger's arms.

Vi sat at the table, watching him dance with two other women. She politely rebuffed Dr. Hayward when he invited her to waltz with him; she felt rather bad, and a little bit guilty, when she also said "no thank you" to a young man who summoned up sufficient tight-chested courage to cross the dance floor and approach her. The music ended and McIntyre returned to drop into a chair.

Gala was sitting with her elbows on the table and her hands supporting her little face. An impish sparkle in her dark eyes made her resemble an elf usurping the toad's mushroom.

"Well?" McIntyre inquired. "What'd you find out? You look like a cat with cream on its whiskers."

"Next time I'm gonna charge by the piece," Gala chirped. "I'm thinkin' maybe a quarter per fact, three for a dollar. You owe me a half a buck for the where from."

"You've already got my lunch money," the ranger said, trying to look serious with her. "Let's have the lowdown. Smart-aleck."

"Okay," Gala said. "Name, Jon Jules. Says he's born in Holland where people wear wood shoes? Father died in the Great War. I told him our ranger was in it, too. Anyway, his mother sent Jon to the U.S. To Denver. They got family an' stuff in Denver. And a friend in the roads department. But he got the urge to be where's there's mountains, came to our village two years ago, got a room with them other two. They get a free room 'cause they work at Creagdhur Lodge. He works for roads department here, doesn't socialize, never set foot in the Pioneer Inn or Kitty's Café. 'cause he's always out hiking. He even—what'd he say he called it—moonlights? As a guide. Workin' the roads, people sometimes stop and ask where's a good place to take a hike, or go fishin', or take pictures, and for money he agrees to guide 'em. Me, I wouldn't do it. I mean, let's say I got four people, see, and they'd pay maybe two bucks per each and use their own car and gas. Profit, right? But I'm out there all day, couldn't sell no fish worms or tie dry flies or otherwise mind to my business, see. Plus I'd wear out good shoe leather, like my dad's always complaining about anyway and I'd weary myself somethin' awful walkin' all day and so nuts and no thanks to that."

"Okay," McIntyre said. "Now you mention it, I've seen him around the park. But not in a coat and collar and no hat. Tonight he's got his hair slicked back. Sure, I've seen him on the roads in coveralls, or hiking in a hat and with a rucksack. Got it. Thanks, young lady."

Vi enjoyed one last uninterrupted dance with McIntyre, with the tired band extemporizing a waltz with fox trot tempo, and then came the last few minutes when it was time for the evening to end. The band's volunteer vocalist made a full frontal attack on "Good Night Ladies" but having forgotten all but the first three words, tried to shift midstream into "I'll Take You Home Again Kathleen" and ended up simply saying good night for the whole band.

Eleanor, Vi, and McIntyre saw Gala home. What followed was the awkward moment of three persons saying goodnight when two of them want a few moments alone.

"We'd better shake a leg," Eleanor said. "I bet Mrs. Spinney's waiting in the parlor with hot chocolate. Besides, I'm bushed."

"Right," Vi Coteau said. "Give us a minute. I'll be right with you."

Eleanor politely turned her back. Vi put her arms around the ranger's neck and gave him not one but two warm and lingering good night kisses before releasing him and walking away with Eleanor.

They were wonderful kisses, the kind of kisses a man might fantasize, the sort to leave a man wanting more, much more, of the same. Nothing more vulgar, nothing more naughty, simply more moments with her hand warm on the nape of his neck and her lips insistently caressing his. More of that. When she stopped and turned to go it felt to McIntyre like dropping a lit match into the stove and being eager to feel the warmth rising, only to peek in and find the flame was out.

In a hazy, dreamy state of mind McIntyre turned to his truck and reached for the door handle. And as he did, his eyes stopped to read the lettering painted on the metal.

"Small Delights," he muttered. "No kidding."

Chapter Seven

Death's Many Moods

Usually arid due to their distance from the oceans and their two-mile height, Rocky Mountains nevertheless do know days of soft, quiet rain when the great cliffs and spires of broken granite are wrapped in impenetrable fog. On such days one can know a feeling of calm, quiet privacy. There are no noisy hiking groups on the trails, fewer automobiles competing for space on the roadways, and on such days even the outdoor tasks and errands seem wholly unnecessary. On this particular morning, however, the cold, drizzling mist helped Ranger McIntyre's mood not at all. He was at the death site, the long steep embankment halfway up the road, the place where Arthur Ogg's car had plunged over the edge and where Arthur died.

Wrapped in his rubber poncho, water running off the oilcloth cover of his flat hat, he stood in the middle of the Fall River road to direct traffic. Except there was no traffic, nobody attempting to navigate the slippery, fog-bound gravel road. Sodden ribbons of mist hung in tatters from the fir trees. The whole upper valley of Fall River seemed to be glaring down at him from beneath a wet, gray shroud, vaguely hostile, emanating a watchful, foreboding air. He felt as if he might see a ghostly funeral procession coming down.

Not far from where he was standing and dripping, the blacksmith Marley and Marley's teenage assistant Ike Vinter were taking turns cranking a chain hoist to drag Dennis Fife's car out of the ditch and back onto the road. They were being extra careful not to damage it, knowing the Willys four-door was Denny's primary means of income. Late the previous afternoon he was coming down Fall River, with four paying customers, when the brakes failed and he went into the ditch.

Fortunately, no one was hurt. Even more fortunate, in less than ten minutes Assistant Ranger Jamie Ogg came driving down the road. Everyone including Denny managed to squeeze into his pickup. Although the trip back to Fall River Lodge was bumpy and overcrowded, the park visitors actually thought the whole adventure rather a fun lark.

"Okay," Marley announced. "We got 'er back on gravel again. But without good brakes, I dunno. I guess we oughta lash Dennis's front bumper to my back bumper to take 'er down. Any traffic comin'? I'd like to crawl under and check the brake linkage. Might be we could fix 'er right here."

"Go ahead," McIntyre said. "I'll make sure nobody runs over your legs."

Marley slid beneath the Willys, oblivious to the mud, saying he'd like to have some kind of light to see by. As it was, he'd have to feel around to check the cables and brackets. After a minute or two he called for Ike to find a dry rag and hand it to him.

"I'll be damned," he said, squirming from wheel to wheel. "Ike, hand me another rag. Unscrew a gas cap on one of these vehicles and dip the rag in the gas."

Muttering to himself, Marley wriggled from wheel to wheel. Finally he slid out from under the Willys and stood up, holding grease-stained rags out for McIntyre's inspection.

"'Nother mystery for you, Tim," he said. "Grease. Every brake shoe. I'd say Dennis, or a mechanic, went to greasing the springs and joints under there but got a blob of grease on every one of the drums, 'cept I can't fathom how a man could. You'll have to ask Dennis, I guess. Maybe he greased the car this morning before heading out to pick up his riders."

"And he'd not notice he'd smeared grease on his brake drums?"

"Darn odd, that's what. I'm nuthin' but a blacksmith, y' understand," Marley replied, "but my theory'd be if a man was driving on level roads or going uphill, those brakes would only feel a little soft, probably. But on this downhill stretch, and with a load of people, they wouldn't hold."

"Accidental?"

"Don't see how. Not all four wheels. If I didn't know better, I'd say it was done with a grease gun."

"Crawled under with a grease gun? Wouldn't a man be seen doing it?"

"You're thinkin' one of the New Mountain hoodlums maybe did it, huh? Sabotage? They wouldn't need to crawl under. They could stick the nozzle—on the grease gun—right through the spokes and squirt a blob on the drum. But I wiped off the shoes with gas. Ike's gonna have some brakes on the way to town. We're still gonna lash the front bumper to the back of my truck anyhow, just to be safe."

"Damn," McIntyre said, "more deliberate damage. As if I didn't have enough worries already."

"Say, while you're frettin' over stuff, I'll tell you another thing," Marley said. "Your helper, Jamie Ogg? And his buddy,

Ranger Frame? I guess you haven't heard, but they been spendin' a lot of time in town, hangin' around across from the New Mountain's bus barn. A couple of times it looked to me like they was whisperin' about somethin'. I mentioned it to Andy Schuel and he said they'd been in his store askin' about small caliber rifles and ammunition. If I was you I'd give those two boys more chores to do, keep 'em out of trouble. Plus I'd hurry up and find the answer to how Arthur Ogg got killed. People in town got wind of those bullets, see, and rumors are flyin'. People are upset."

"I see what you're saying," McIntyre said. "Maybe you'll do me a favor and keep an eye on things around town. What I mean is, get in touch with me if you see… well, you know. Trouble brewing."

"Yeah," Marley replied. "Sure I will. Say! There's another thing! Dang, I meant to mention it to Dottie to tell you. Day before yesterday. Slipped my mind. Anyhow, one of the other jitney men, Sandy Beech, he brought me his car to see if I could fix the snubbers. I needed to mail order new ones. The straps on the front snubbers was sliced. Almost all the way through. Looks like they done it with a sharp blade, like a cutthroat razor. If a snubber strap broke I don't think it'd cause a wreck, but it'd sure be a bumpy ride home, you bet. Might make for a wreck, though, dependin' on speed an' the road and such."

After Marley and Ike drove away McIntyre stood there listening to the sound of the car engines fading away, letting the mountain silence come flowing back down the mist-shrouded canyon. He scowled at the drizzle dripping off his hat as if scowling would make it stop.

What Marley said about wheel spokes and grease on brake

drums made him recall one of Gala's remarks. It was when she was saying how she didn't much like the Doctor Hayward man. Didn't like what she called "his attitude of looking down his nose." For instance, the little girl explained, one day she happened to see him poking his walking stick at a car's wheels. Looked like he was thinking of buying the car, see? Only he kinda sneered and poked at the wheels and walked away. No, she didn't care for the man much.

The ranger swept his poncho around him and sat down on a wet rock overlooking the canyon. Through the wavering mist he could catch only glimpses of the river below. He felt his mind drifting downward, moving like a wayward river current about to eddy into a whirlpool, and the whirlpool was the first love, the beautiful friend, she who plunged off into the awful canyon. And he knew he needed to grip that awful image, seize it and lock it away and put his mind elsewhere. It was past, it was gone. Not to be forgotten, but not to be lived again every time the mountain fog came roiling down Fall River gorge.

Arthur Ogg. Poor, kind Arthur was what he needed to focus on, force his brain away from memories of her and work on Arthur's death. Match up the pieces and figure out what happened, and do it before Jamie Ogg lost patience. Killing a man he thought killed his dad wouldn't solve anything, and would wreck the rest of his life. McIntyre would definitely need to keep a close eye on Jamie, at least for the time being.

There was another reason to hurry and find out what had happened. McIntyre needed to figure it out because of the women. Eleanor and Vi might find a suspect among the New Mountain men and place themselves in harm's way trying to apprehend him.

What did McIntyre have so far? Cars being tampered with. Bus radiator damaged. A man apparently using bus rides to deliver mysterious packages. It's all about vehicles. The feud between the jitney owners and the New Mountain outfit. Did a jitney driver burn Oliver? Or did Oliver become a risk to the drug smugglers? Maybe he got in the way. Refused to go along with whatever they were up to, or threatened to spill the beans. Setting him on fire was an example to others. But who could plan such a thing? McIntyre still believed it was opportunistic, that the perpetrator happened to be in the bus barn and saw the gas can and Oliver's blowtorch, and nobody was watching, and he said to himself *there's the guy who needs a lesson, what if I knocked over his gas can and threw a fright into him?*

Fall River ran on beneath the drifting shreds of mist. On an outcrop of ancient granite the colors of the moss and lichen were freshened by drizzle. A tall fir tree standing apart from the others looked despondent with sagging branches dripping. Rivulets of water flowed down the gravel road, making ponds here and there. McIntyre rose to his feet and, turning his back on the heartless gloom of the misty upper canyon he slouched back to his truck.

At least there won't be any forest fires any time soon, he thought.

* * * * *

McIntyre awoke the following dawn, looked out the window, and found a gray blanket of cloud spread across the sky. Breakfast was oatmeal and toast for himself, hay and oats for Brownie. After fixing himself a venison and mustard sandwich to take along for lunch, he decided to leave the pickup truck in the shed and go on mounted patrol for a change. Maybe if he rode the Deer Mountain trail, or the virtually unused trail to Potts Puddle he wouldn't meet anybody, wouldn't have to talk to anybody.

The next day was a trifle less depressing, but it was still a taciturn ranger who checked the campgrounds and trailheads. When park visitors asked him questions, and they always did, he answered politely but without much in the way of enthusiasm. He drove over to the ranger barracks to pick up a list of needed supplies—a task any temp could do for him—where he was glad to find the building empty of people. Walking back to the truck he was hit by a realization. He was glad not to find anyone to talk to, and at the same time he needed a human to talk to. Stupid.

He got up as the first light began to streak the eastern sky, made breakfast, then started work early. All day he drove the roads in his district, spoke with park visitors, inspected recent improvements to the Lawn Lake trail, but his brain kept going back to thinking whether Arthur Ogg was deliberately murdered. He worried about Jamie, too. When the hands on his pocket watch finally crawled around to four o'clock he headed back to the cabin. As he drove he tried to sort out his feelings. He was hungry, but not hungry. He wanted to be alone to think, but couldn't think clearly. He didn't feel like seeing anyone, yet didn't like the idea of being alone. He cursed the overcast weather, damned the job, muttered oaths about whoever was causing all the feuding and tension. When he parked the truck and slouched toward his cabin he even swore at the idea of cooking supper. Baked potato and a slice of fried venison. Again.

McIntyre was lighting a fire in the stove when he heard the Marmon Eight coming up the road. *Great,* he thought. *I take off early from work and here she comes. And there goes any chance of taking time to think. I was hoping to spend the evening sorting out what we know about the feud and maybe figure out who could be doing all the trouble.*

He heard the car door slam, heard her high-heeled boots crossing his porch, heard her humming an annoying cheery little ditty. She knocked once on his door and entered without waiting for an answer. She was carrying a pasteboard box loosely wrapped in a car robe.

"Hi, ranger!" Vi chirped. "Guess what I've got!"

"No idea," he replied. "A box of kittens? Whatever it is, it's got you in a happy mood. Egg salad sandwiches and some nonpareils, maybe."

Vi Coteau laughed. She set the box on the table, threw her coat and hat on the bed, turned back toward him, raised her chin, placed one hand across her bosom like a soprano in an opera, and began to sing.

"Oh, I scream, you scream, we all scream for ice cream! Rah! Rah! Boola, boola, you take chocolate, I'll take vanoola!"

"What the…"

"It's a song, silly ranger. Mrs. Spinney has it on a gramophone record. Fred Waring's orchestra? It's fun. It's about cheerleaders at an Eskimo college and they cheer for ice cream. Rah!"

"Okay, the box is full of ice cream."

"Not only ice cream," she laughed. "I was near Beaver Point and remembered I hadn't had lunch. So I stopped at Tiny's store for a late afternoon sandwich, and he had freshly baked apple pies for sale. I bought one, and thought about how nice it would be to have ice cream to put on the pie. Well! As if happened, Tiny had made a batch of ice cream for himself! He was glad to sell me some—and I thought I'd come share it with my moody ol' Scotsman. C'mon! Dig out a couple of your plates and silverware and we'll eat pie for supper."

"Nothing but pie?" he said.

"For supper," she smiled. "Who knows what we might do for dessert?"

The aroma of the pie, warmed in the oven, was enough to take a man's memories all the way back to his mother's kitchen. The ice cream, melting a little on the hot pie crust, made McIntyre go on licking his lips long after the last smear was gone. There was even entertainment to go with the pie and ice cream—Vi Coteau batting her eyelashes like an overly adorable chorus girl attempting to render the words to the song "Ice Cream." Vi's performance brought the baritone chuckle back to the ranger's throat. He smiled broadly and attempted to join her in singing the song, although the impromptu duet collapsed in laughter because she only half-remembered the lyrics and he'd never heard them at all. They abandoned the assault on good music and he lounged back in his chair, looked wistfully at the empty pie plate, and, in short, McIntyre relaxed.

Until he heard a truck coming up the road. And until he heard it turn in at his cabin and stop in front of his truck shed.

The hammering on the door was Jamie.

"There's been another one!" Jamie gasped, bypassing all polite greetings. "You gotta come."

"What are you talking about?" McIntyre said. "Sit down. Relax. Let me pour you a cup of coffee. What other one?"

"Dead. One of those kids from Creagdhur. Drowned and dead in the river. Downriver, down to the beaver meadows this side of the cascades. His buddies found him."

Silently, Vi Coteau picked up the plates and forks and carried them to McIntyre's sink. McIntyre buttoned his shirt collar, tightened his necktie, and put his tunic back on. As he followed Jamie to the door he turned to give Vi a wistful, grim "I'm sorry" smile without words.

"Go," she said. "Go on. I'll take care of the dishes. I'll be at Mrs. Spinney's this evening if you want me."

The park service pickup went up Fall River road toward Beaver Meadows, traveling through the sun-shot mountain afternoon as if the two rangers were merely doing a routine patrol rather than heading for another dead body. Neither Jamie nor McIntyre looked forward to what might be waiting for them.

"Fill me in," McIntyre said

"Yeah, okay," Jamie replied. "The guy's deceased, for sure. When his buddies found him one of them lit a shuck for town and brought back the doc and Nick. Nick sent me to get you 'cause it's your district."

"I did hear a couple of cars go by my cabin," McIntyre said. "Didn't look to see who it was."

"You was busy eatin' pie?" Jamie suggested, trying to grin and failing at it.

"Who's the deceased?"

"Young kid, maybe eighteen. Name of John Jules. I guess early this morning he borrowed his roomate's car to go fishin' and said he needed t' be back before noon for his job, but it got to be midafternoon and they borrowed another car from the lodge and went lookin' for him. Found the car right away, parked on the side of th' road. They drove up and down the road yellin' for him and finally spotted him floatin' face down. About a half mile downstream. Like I said, as soon as they dragged him out of the water one of 'em skedaddled to town for help."

"And the doc came all the way out here?" McIntyre said.

"Yeah! Doc, he says he's gettin' professionally concerned about these so-called accidents. Bad for the village image, see? Doc's on the town council, remember."

"There they are," McIntyre said, pointing at the small group standing on the roadside.

"Yeah," Jamie replied. "I wonder if maybe they're waitin' for an ambulance to come take the body. The younger guy standin' there, the one in the overcoat, he's one of the roommates. The other one went back to the lodge 'cause they're shorthanded."

The men stood in a tight group, their heads bowed and eyes fixed on the ground while they took turns mumbling about dying too young and wondering how the family will take it. McIntyre finally asked Nick if the boy in the overcoat could be dismissed.

"Sure," Nick said. "He's kind of in shock, but standing here isn't going to help him any."

The ranger beckoned for Jamie to follow and walked over to where the college boy was standing.

"McIntyre," he said, extending his hand. "This is Jamie Ogg. We're awful sorry about your friend."

"Thanks. I'm Bernard, by the way. Bernard Cleve."

"Listen, Supervisor Nicholson says it's okay for you to take your car and head on back to the lodge. I'd suggest you try to go back to work, to give yourself something else to think about. Anyway, we'll walk up the road with you. Okay if I ask a couple of questions?"

"Sure."

"First off, Jamie and I will be looking for footprints, any kind of sign to tell us what Jon was doing when he went into the water. Can you recall exactly where you and your other roommate walked, after you saw the car where it was parked?"

"I think I can," Bernard said. "It's parked well off the shoulder. We both walked around it, looked to see if he'd left anything inside, like maybe his fishing gear or jacket. Let's see, finding no gear in the car we assumed he was fishing. We went toward the river—there's a sort of trail there—but we only went until we broke out of the willows, maybe twenty yards? From there you can see up and down stream and we didn't see him. We shouted, but…"

"Yeah," McIntyre said. "Then what?"

"Well, I guess we went back to Dwayne's car. Yeah, we did. Since it was pointed uphill we drove real slow up the road, honking the horn, yelling out the window. Went maybe a half mile? Didn't see him. We turned around and went down the road and right before we got to the cascades I spotted him, face down in the quiet part of the stream. We hurried down there, pulled him out, but he was cold and dead."

"Wow," Jamie said. "That's tough."

"Yeah," Bernard agreed.

"Fishing," McIntyre stated.

"Yeah. He was goin' to take a few days off work and guide a hiking party up the Mummy Range, but they canceled."

"Knew the route, did he?"

"Oh, yeah. Favorite hike of his. Remember the day a tour car went off the road, killed the driver?"

"Yes."

"Well, the driver who died, he was comin' back down the road from droppin' Jon and four or five hikers at the Mummy trailhead. Jon really loved goin' up there."

McIntyre and Jamie watched Bernard drive away before beginning their methodical search of the roadside, the dirt path through the willows, and the river bank.

"Did y' make the connection, Jamie?"

"Meaning our dead guy was prob'ly one of the last to see Dad alive?"

"No. More important. Our dead guy maybe could've identified Art's mystery hitchhiker."

Old Man taught the boy McIntyre his tracking skills, and Ranger McIntyre passed them on to Jamie Ogg. Working as a team, it was said, the two of them could track a horsefly through a field of manure.

"He stood here," Jamie said when they were a few yards from the stream. "Smoked a cigarette."

"Looks natural," McIntyre agreed. "I'd do the same, if I was fishing. Come out of the willows, not go stomping up to the edge of the water and spook the trout, take time to size up the stream. Let's see… if it was me, I'd probably be figuring to make my first cast upstream, there where the riffles run into the calm part."

"Seems right," Jamie said. "He field-stripped his cigarette butt right here. Like you said, he moved toward the river bank. There's a broken willow branch. And part of a heel print."

"It's a start," McIntyre said. "Let's keep looking."

While Jamie studied the ground and bushes, McIntyre re-enacted Jon Jules' probable movements, stepping soft and careful along the edge of the willows to reach the side of the water. There, he pretended to be stripping line from an imaginary reel to make a cast into the riffles.

Startled expressions from the two rangers came simultaneously.

"Another one!" Jamie exclaimed.

"I've got something!" McIntyre shouted.

Jamie, on his knees at the fringe of the willow thicket, was looking at a second track, the clear imprint in a patch of sandy mud. A man's shoe, slick sole, size ten approximately.

"I've got a second man here," Jamie said. "What have you got?"

"His fishing rod! It's out there under the water. I'd say he was making his cast and his hand slipped, the rod went out into the stream. Cut me a long piece of willow, would you? Maybe we can manage to snag it and haul it out of there without having to wade in after it."

* * * * * *

Down in the village, Vi Coteau was intercepted.

She had stepped out of her car onto the sidewalk in front of Mrs. Spinney's house, and was closing the door of the Marmon, when she heard a footstep behind her and felt a familiar hand on her shoulder. A too-familiar hand for her liking. She turned to face Dr. Hayward. His face wore the look of a man with high hopes, and Vi knew what those hopes were.

After back-and-forth banter about what a nice afternoon it was and how peaceful the village seemed and whether she had found the roads in good condition, Hayward came—vaguely—to the point.

"I was wondering, Miss Coteau, if you would have the time to assist me. At my workshop. It wouldn't take long, and I'd be awfully grateful."

"Well," Vi said, considering her options. A cup of tea with Eleanor and Mrs. Spinney, or an opportunity to learn more from the gunsmith who seemed in league with the New Mountain Stage outfit?

"Of course," she said brightly. "Shall we walk?"

As they approached the door to his workshop they were surprised by a man emerging, a man who seemed in a hurry. It was John Smith, a New Mountain driver. With a quick mumbled "gotta hurry" and a "thanks!" to Hayward he half ran, half walked away down the path.

Hayward conducted Vi to the basement shop and shooting range, making certain she appreciated how few people had ever seen it or even knew about it. He made no mention of Smith nor what the bus driver might be doing inside his workshop. After turning on the lights he went to the immaculate workbench and unfolded a cloth to reveal a small, ordinary-looking revolver.

Ordinary except for missing its grips.

"I have noticed your hands," he said. "Glove size, if I'm correct, about size seven?"

"Or seven and a half," Vi said, "depending on the material. In silk gloves, a seven. In kid leather I find seven and a half more comfortable."

"Excellent," he said, picking up the pistol.

From another folded cloth he took a pair of carved pistol grips. "Very nearly the same size as the lady who owns this."

"Ebony," he told her. "Or African blackwood, if you prefer. A lady acquaintance of mine mailed her revolver to me and asked if I would fabricate custom grips for it. It's a light gun, a .32 Iver Johnson, but she doesn't think the factory grips allow her to hold it firmly."

He positioned the unfinished grips on the revolver and tightened the retaining screws.

"What I was wondering," he said, "is if you'd do me the favor of testing these to see if I have the contours correct. As you see, I've contoured the wood to accommodate fingers and thumb. If the grips seem secure to you, I'll go ahead and carve the checkered pattern into them. With a bit of oil and a good polishing they'll be finished. Do you mind holding it and giving me your opinion?"

Vi accepted the gun. It did, indeed, fit her hand nicely. As she aimed it here and there, careful not to aim at Hayward, she noticed three long cardboard tubes leaning in a corner. Noticed them because they seemed out of place in a shop where literally everything was either covered, hidden in a drawer, or secured in a cupboard.

"Fishing rods?" she said. "You've been buying custom fly rods by mail?"

"Uh, yes. Well, no. The tour company, uh, wants to have

fishing equipment available for passengers. People may want to drop off, do a spot of angling, catch the next bus. I'm, uh, installing more durable cork handles you see. But what do you think of the revolver grips? Could I ask you to load up and fire a few rounds to be sure?"

When Hayward switched on the lights of the shooting range tunnel, Vi saw a cardboard target already in place downrange. Was John Smith having some target practice?

"Ah," he said. "There are a few holes in that one, but it's of no matter. Go ahead and try a few rounds, if you would."

As during her first visit, the gunsmith stood a few inches too close to her while she assumed her stance and aimed the revolver. Pop! Pop! Pop! went the .32 pistol. Three neat holes formed a new triangle in the target.

"Feels fine," she said. "Very comfortable, very steady. May I have a closer look at the target?"

"Of course."

Hayward made a lofty show of working the rope and pulley system to bring the cardboard target to the mouth of the tunnel. Vi touched her bullet holes.

"Hmmm," she said. "As I thought. All three are a little to the left. I had a feeling the pistol grip was a millimeter too thick on the right side. Felt as though it was forcing my hand to compensate, you see."

"Wonderful," Hayward said. "I'll carve a little more wood from the finger grooves. Thank you! Say, may I offer you tea? Or a stronger beverage, perhaps?"

Not waiting for her reply, Hayward opened one of the cupboard doors. Behind it was a drop-down bar top as well as shelves displaying a range of liquor bottles and glassware.

"Name your cocktail," he laughed. He pulled a high stool closer to him, patting the seat in an invitation for Vi to be seated.

"I'll pop upstairs for ice."

"No, not for me, thank you," Vi said. "Although you seem to be well supplied despite prohibition."

"Do not tell me you don't drink!" Hayward said, reaching for two highball glasses. "What will you have? Gin fizz? Cosmo, perhaps? Perhaps a martini?"

"You see," Vi said, "it would present a problem for me. Our landlady, Mrs. Spinney, was very strong in the Women's Christian Temperance Union. She's death on alcohol, or drugs of any kind. She might shoot me if I dared to return with gin on my breath! In fact, I am expected there and I'm nearly overdue. Another time. Perhaps."

He sighed and secured the liquor cabinet. Vi thought the sigh sounded like a schoolboy who's been told he can't have dessert until he finishes his vegetables. Recovering his role as genteel gentleman, Hayward insisted that she should precede him up the basement steps. Vi felt his eyes watching her legs and derriere the entire time. Not until she was out of the door and halfway down the path did she allow herself a couple of deep breaths.

While Mrs. Spinney and Eleanor were setting the table and monitoring the supper on the stove, Vi telephoned the Fall River ranger station. No reply. She asked the operator for the RMNP supervisor's office and caught Dottie about to leave for the day.

"Dottie," Vi said. "Sorry to bother you. I've tried to raise Ranger McIntyre on the phone. If you happen to see him or hear from him, would you ask him to meet me for breakfast in the morning? Would it be possible for him to be an hour late in reporting for duty? I need to share some information with him. About the… the deaths. I'll keep trying his cabin, too. Thanks!"

Chapter Eight
What the Detective Saw

"Ever eaten breakfast in the city, Tim?" Vi Coteau said. She and the ranger were sitting at his customary Pioneer Inn breakfast table, the table next to a window with a broad view of the village and towering mountains.

She paused to sip from the china cup she cradled between her palms.

"Down in Denver where I live," she went on, "there are many, many people whose breakfast consists of a glass of juice, a cup of coffee, and a piece of toast. Or a sweet roll. Period."

Ranger McIntyre looked up from his second heap of hash and egg—and cheese—breakfast casserole.

"Really?" he said. "I wouldn't think food was in such short supply down there. No wonder you're skinny."

"Don't you think you ought to change topics right there?" she suggested warmly.

"Yup," he answered. "Here, try a bit of Connie's casserole. Tell me what you've found out."

"Oh, no," she countered. "I'm paying for breakfast. I get to hear your information first. If you can manage it between bites, of course."

"Fair enough," he said, chasing a mouthful of hash with a swallow of coffee. "I'll start at the end and kind of work my way backwards. The latest news comes from Doc Hall... he's the new clinic doctor... he examined Jon Jules here at the clinic because he says the county morgue and coroner are likely to take weeks doing it. And Doc Hall found Jules was shot."

"With one of those lead pellet bullets?"

"No. At the base of Jules' skull there was a hole and in the hole he found a round ball. It looks like a Number Three buckshot pellet, about twenty-five caliber. The body was found downstream from where the car was parked. Wearing waders and a fishing vest. Canvas creel looped over his neck and shoulder. It leads me to think he was already dead, or unconscious, when he hit the water. Otherwise I think he'd get rid of the creel. It would really drag you down if you were trying to get out of the stream. Jamie and I found his fishing rod where he'd dropped it in the water. And we found fresh shoe prints in the willow thicket, plus the victim's footprints on the stream bank. Taking all the signs into consideration, Jamie and I came up with a probable chain of events. It goes like this. Jules left the car on the road and walked a game trail down to the stream. Came through the willows, came out near the stream, tiptoed through the grass, careful not to spook the trout. He stood there, smoked a cigarette, studied the water, got his hook and line ready."

McIntyre drained his coffee cup and set it on the empty plate.

"We think there was a man who followed Jules down to the stream. Couldn't find any tire tracks or footprints on the side of the road—too much traffic. But however he got there, a man wearing leather soled shoes followed Jules down through the willows. While the kid was making a cast, standing right on the edge of the stream bank, he shot him. Maybe point blank."

"Point blank?" Vi asked.

"Yeah, but it's odd. The twenty-five caliber ball hit the poor kid right in the skull. There's an open stretch of grass along the stream right there, maybe only ten, fifteen feet wide, see? It looks like the shooter probably stood at the edge of the willows and took the shot from close range. My theory is when the ball hit Jules in the head he threw up his hands in shock and his fishing rod went flying out into the water. He lost his balance and fell in."

"What's the odd part?"

"The odd part is, Doc Hall didn't find any powder burns like should be there. Even after being in the water, the doc says, at close range there would be burnt powder in the hair, or under the shirt collar. And Jamie and I didn't find any empty cartridge case, nothing. It may have been a revolver, or single shot rifle. Wouldn't eject a cartridge case for us to find. But… it was more like the ball came out of thin air and hit Jules in the back of the head. Or like it came from a slingshot, except I've never heard of a slingshot strong enough to break a skull."

Vi shuddered visibly.

"But Tim, why?" she asked. "Why would anyone stalk a young, innocent kid and deliberately shoot him in the head? It's like Oliver getting shot in the bus barn. No reason for it, none."

"I think there is," McIntyre mused. "Being a detective, you should've seen it. Maybe you need to eat a bigger breakfast. Helps you think. Y'see, Jules' roommate says Jules was the one who guided the group of tourists up into the Mummy Range, the ones who rode up there with Arthur. As they were leaving town, Arthur stopped and picked up another rider. Those three tourists, all we've got is a couple of mailing addresses in Milwaukee. We're trying to contact them, but I doubt they'll remember much about the mystery rider. But Jon Jules would.

He saw the guy who rode up to the trailhead in Arthur's car, maybe even knew him."

"Sounds logical," Vi said. She took a small gold tube and little mirror from her handbag. "Do you mind if I fix my lipstick? Awfully rude of me to do it at the table."

"Heck," he said, "nothing about your lips needs fixing."

"Oh, ugh," Vi winced. "What are you doing, trying to earn your How To Flirt merit badge? You'd better throttle back on your train of thought before it goes off the rails."

"Hah, hah. All right, we're assuming the same mystery man rode back down Fall River in Arthur's car. When Jules heard about Arthur's death, for some reason he didn't come and tell us what he knew. Now there's no way to find out. I'll bet Oliver could have shed some light on it, too. Maybe after the wreck, it was even Oliver himself who picked up the mystery hitchhiker."

Vi replaced the cap on the lipstick and dabbed her mouth with a tissue. It was her turn to share information, but she was mentally debating how to put it into words. McIntyre might take it wrong, her interest in Hayward and Hayward's interest in her. To have McIntyre become jealous might be amusing, but might also stir his highland grumpiness to a full boil. It would be best, she decided, to stick to simple details and say nothing evasive.

"Okay," she began, "only I'm afraid my news isn't as concrete as yours. Or as interesting. First of all, you know the New Mountain driver, John Smith?"

"Not too well. I recognize him when I see him," McIntyre said.

"When Dr. Hayward and I entered his cottage workshop, we walked toward the basement door, which was already standing open…"

"The wolf's lair was ready and waiting, huh."

"…but John Smith came hurrying up the steps. He nearly

bumped into us at the doorway to the basement. All he said was 'thank you' to Hayward and hurried away. And Hayward never did volunteer any explanation as to what Smith was doing in his cottage or why he would say 'thank you' as he left. Like you and Jamie, I tried to make various details match up. All I could come up with was that Smith was in the basement using the target range. Those New Mountain thugs carry guns, that's no secret. But when Hayward and I went down into the basement…"

"Alone. The two of you alone together, I mean," McIntyre said.

"It's not what you mean, you silly ranger, but I'm going to ignore it. When we got down there I didn't smell any gunshot odor. In a place all quiet and without windows, the smell of burnt gunpowder would linger a long time."

"Quiet and private, huh?" McIntyre said.

"It's odd, see? Dr. Hayward has a working relationship with New Mountain. Maybe Smith was picking up a gun Hayward repaired, or getting ammunition. Anyway, down in the basement…"

"The private, quiet basement," McIntyre said.

"Upstairs," she continued, "Hayward's shop is where he repairs guns. Perfectly clean workbench, collection of small tools like a jeweler's, everything in drawers out of sight. No machinery other than a small vice."

"Well, we all have our small vices," McIntyre quipped.

"Be quiet," she suggested. "Back to the basement. He does have a lathe down there and a long machine like another lathe. Very old. Looked to me like it might be used for boring gun barrels. Like upstairs, there was nothing out of place except for three long cardboard tubes standing in a corner. He said there were fishing rods in them. He's supposed to make custom cork grips for them."

"So?" McIntyre asked.

"So this. He says he builds custom guns, like rifles and shotguns. Have you ever seen one? Does anyone in the valley own a gun made by Hayward? If he's selling them via mail order, have you ever seen him taking long, sturdy boxes to the post office? Ever heard anyone so much as mention a Hayward gun? Down in his basement shop I didn't see a scrap of wood, a bandsaw, any metal shavings, no odor of cutting oil, no forge for making gun parts, nothing. Several locked cupboards and, of course, the shooting tunnel. Which brings me to the target."

"Target?"

"John Smith must have heard us coming. At least he left in a hurry. Hayward asked me to try out the grips he carved for his lady customer…"

"…and look at his etchings, right?"

"Tim! If you don't stop with the nasty insinuations…"

"You'll kick me in the shins again?"

"I'll make you pay for our breakfasts. Not only this morning but always."

"Ouch. I'd rather be kicked in the shin. Okay. What about the cardboard target?"

"I took three shots at it. When Hayward brought it out of the tunnel on his cute little rope and pulley thingamajig, there were my three holes, a little bit to the left of the bullseye. There were six smaller holes scattered around, most of them in the black. Two missed the black and left ragged, not perfect holes, like the bullets tumbled in the air before hitting. The ones in the black seemed slightly larger than a .22 but I couldn't be sure."

"A gunsmith testing a couple of guns, one with worn-out rifling. Seems natural."

"Tim, Hayward is meticulous. He wouldn't leave a used target hanging there. This is a man who probably irons his underwear and socks. When he finishes anything he puts it away and wipes down the area. But not the used target. I think John Smith was down there either practicing or testing a gun, and he heard us come into the workshop. Our footsteps on the floor overhead probably startled him and he ran for it."

"Okay, maybe," McIntyre said. "Why didn't you hear him shooting, and where were these guns you say he was practicing with? You didn't hear any gun, didn't smell burnt powder."

"Who's the brilliant detective? Hmmm?" she said.

Vi exaggerated the suspense by pouring herself a half cup of coffee from the carafe and daintily stirring it with a spoon.

"Watch out for your lips," he suggested as she raised the cup to her mouth. "You've got fresh lipstick on."

"Why don't you watch them for me," she replied with a wink.

"Depend on it," McIntyre said. "Go ahead. Spill the beans."

"What a lovely expression," she said. "Okay, the beans can be spilled in just two words. Air rifle."

"Repeat?"

"Air rifle. I'd bet one of those wall cabinets was open and Smith was practicing with an air rifle. When he heard our footsteps overhead he turned off the tunnel lights, put the gun in a cupboard, slammed the door, came dashing up the steps."

"Holy cow," McIntyre exclaimed.

"Watch your language," Vi smiled.

"Huh? No, I was remembering our moonshiner, Leon Counter! A few years back, when I first started with the park and was getting acquainted with the locals, I occasionally came across evidence of how somebody on the ridge, probably Leon, was in the habit of shooting small game for food. Scatterings of grouse feathers, bits of rabbit fur. To try and catch him I'd sneak up toward his place and hide and figured when I heard a shot I'd grab him. One moonlight night I heard a little puffing noise. Sure enough, there he was with an air rifle and dead snowshoe rabbit. Leon's air rifle, believe it or not, shoots a .32 caliber slug hard enough to knock over a yearling deer. Or porcupine or coyote. Very quietly, too. An air rifle could explain a lot about the Oliver shooting."

"You mean the moonshiner did it?"

"No, no. But a man with a concealed air gun, maybe an air pistol, was standing in the bus barn and saw an opportunity to cause trouble."

"What would it look like? Wouldn't it be noticeable?"

"Maybe, maybe not. All an air gun really needs is a tube for a barrel, a place to store the compressed air, and some kind of trigger. If a guy was pretty clever he could build an air gun into something like a telescope. Or maybe a bicycle pump. A bike pump would already have a plunger to compress the air. Come to think of it, if a person was on the road trying to hitch a ride and had a bicycle pump in his hand, you'd assume he'd had a bike accident and didn't want to leave his pump where it could get stolen."

"Seems logical," Vi said.

"And if your theory about the gunsmith's silent shooting range holds water," McIntyre continued, "our charming Dr. Hayward is very, very likely to know the owner of such a gun."

"Which one of us is going to ask him?" Vi inquired.

"The one with the most charm and tact, of course," McIntyre answered.

"Not the one with the breakfast crumbs on his tunic and coffee on his upper lip?" she said, handing him a napkin.

On Saturday evening a monosyllabic messenger from the telegraph office brought a laconic telegram to Mrs. Spinney's house. Early the next morning Eleanor set out for Longmont to meet the Denver train. Eddie Hazard would be on it, carrying news he wouldn't trust to the telephone lines.

"But you know how people are," Eleanor told Vi and McIntyre, "a white person wearing nothing but underwear and carrying a dead cat can get on a train and no one asks why—but they see a Black man in a business suit on the train and right away they need to know where he thinks he's going and what he's going to do when he gets there. Our clever Hazard, though, he persuaded a friend to loan him a hotel porter's jacket and cap, in case anyone should ask him why he was on his way to Longmont. His story was that a businessman staying at the hotel had sent him to bring back some documents."

Eleanor, Vi, and the ranger, were relaxing on McIntyre's porch, the ladies seated in his two chairs and himself sitting on the deck with his back resting against the wall, smoking his pipe. The Colorado afternoon was all blue sky and peaceful quiet, unbroken except for the occasional auto taking a Sunday drive up into the deep and menacing shadows of Fall River canyon.

"Well," Eleanor continued, "I was telling you about Eddie. He can't talk too good of English like us'ns can. I swear, it seems like he makes up new words on the spot. Anyway, as Eddie tells it, he and his fellow jazz tooters and skin men—he's in a jazz band, Tim—they snag a cashy gig for a hoity-toity bash way uptown. Huge palace of a place, three sets of musicians in three rooms big as ballrooms. There's a cat gut tribe—string trio—a board 'n' bugles—piano and two horns—in another room, and Eddie's bunch, they're the only Black guys in the building. He didn't actually see any pointy white hoods, but they got the feeling half of Denver's KKK were there, too."

"In other words," McIntyre said, "Eddie's in a jazz band hired to entertain a bunch of rich white men. Why come all the way to Longmont to tell you?"

"Because," Eleanor said, turning to give Vi a meaningful look, "between the KKK and the Chicago thugs, Eddie doesn't trust the telephone. Or even the mail service. It seems our beloved Senator Speckle was at the party. Not only there, but half stoned and trying his best to be the center of attention. Trying to dance with all the women, groping several of them, yelling his political opinions into other people's faces, laughing too much and too loud and being a general donkey butt. Here's the good part: Eddie says that at one point Speckle got a kind of impish gleam in his eye. He sent one of his subordinates out of the mansion toward where the cars were parked. When the thug came back, Speckle linked elbows with him and the two of them oiled and slithered their way around the room, Speckle acting like a drunk who's trying to make people think he's hiding a big secret. And he's going around slipping little packets into the hands of various guests. Fingers to the lips, 'shhhh' sounds, very hush-hush."

"Interesting!" Vi said.

"Wait until you hear the rest of it," Eleanor continued. "Speckle and the hired clown make their way to a little outdoor kind of balcony. Eddie and the jazz combo are out there taking a cigarette break, okay? Speckle sees the boys. He heads over to them where he mumbles a bunch of slop about loving jazz and how they're a terrific bunch of... well, you can guess the word he used... and he does the finger-to-lip gesture and goes 'shhhh' and has his henchman slip each of them a little envelope."

"Money?" McIntyre asked, already suspecting it wasn't.

"Very small, square envelopes. Powder. Cocaine and heroin. Eddie said the band leader tried to refuse. Bad enough being a Black guy late at night in a rich white neighborhood without carrying drugs on you. The leader says 'ah, we couldn't! Damn generous, awful damn generous. But heck, we wouldn't want to have the party guests run short. Let's let your friends have it, okay?'"

"Good idea, turning it down," McIntyre suggested. "Although the dope was probably worth a lot of money."

"Oh, yeah," Eleanor agreed. "But the band leader tried to turn it down anyway. For a second time. Your Honorable Senator Speckle, he said 'never mind, boys, we got plenty.' Eddie said Speckle winked and... the way a drunk will whisper out loud... he said 'hell if we run out I tell our seven little men t' climb aboard a bus and haul their butts back to the mine for more snow.' That's it, Eddie said. Verbatim. Except the senator went away laughing at his own joke about Snow White and the seven dwarves."

"Wow," Vi said. "A mine tunnel. And a senator-size drug stash. I think we've got him. The Denver D.A., the honest one, this is what he's been hoping for. If we find the dope, we'll be able to collect our fee and be done with the case of Speckle and his crumbums."

McIntyre re-lit his pipe. His eyes were on the mountains and canyons, but in his mind he was revisiting his talk with Leon Counter. The back seat bus rider, the dropped package, the car following, the barricaded mine tunnel—puzzle pieces beginning to form a surprising picture. It could be why whoever was behind the New Mountain company wanted exclusive access to the national park. Like Leon stashing his best moonshine as an investment, a hedge against future uncertainty, the hoodlums must be accumulating a stash of heroin and cocaine. Wouldn't take much of it to make a man wealthy. Ten fifteen, even fifty pounds would be easy to hide. And the park service could be providing all the privacy they needed.

The murders were beginning to make sense to him. During the fatal drive up Fall River road, Arthur Ogg possibly said something about drugs. Or maybe he said it in town. Yes, that was it. He loved his coffee shop chats. He probably said he'd seen a package drop from a New Mountain bus. Maybe he repeated the local rumor about drug dealers posing as tourists. Whatever he said, the shooter overheard him. Thought he'd better throw a scare into him. Therefore the shooter waited at the edge of town and hitched a ride with Arthur. When they were alone during the return trip he shot him. No, wait: when they approached the steep drop-off he asked Arthur to stop. He got out to walk the rest of the way. As Arthur started driving away, the shooter shot the tire, hoping to cause a blowout. It didn't work, so he shot Arthur. In a few minutes Oliver came along in the New Mountain bus. He recognized the shooter and I bet he asked for money to keep quiet. Shooter needed to get rid of him. And finally there's Jon Jules. Jules saw who got into Arthur's car.

"Mine," McIntyre said at length.

"Pardon?" Vi said. "What's yours?"

"District. I think this hypothetical cache of drugs, if it exists, is in my district. I think anyone who goes snooping to find it will be looking to end up as a corpse. If I'm right, these gangsters play for keeps. It means I need to flash my badge at you two and tell you to back away and stay quiet. I'll find Leon Counter and tell him the same thing. No snooping. No asking questions."

"Well?" Vi Coteau said.

"Well, what?" McIntyre replied.

"You're supposed to say 'okay?' to us. Ask us if it's okay with us."

"I already said it, but only inside my head. And you two answered 'okay' in my head. You back away and let me figure out what to do next. If I find this supposed cache, of course."

"I think we should let him continue the investigation," Eleanor said to Vi. "When I was a ranger I saw this lanky character track down a thieving packrat by following it home to its stash. On hands and knees in deep grass. I say we stay out of his way and let him do what he's best at."

"When you say 'packrat' you mean a burglar?"

"No," Eleanor said. "I mean a small rodent who likes to collect shiny objects."

"That's what he's best at? Tracking mice? I think I'm disappointed," Vi said.

"You two make a good pair of comediennes. Just watch your own backs," McIntyre growled. "I'm ordering you not to get killed in my district."

* * * * *

A whispered word, a light tug on the reins, and Brownie halted in the deep shade of an ancient Douglas fir.

There on the trail ahead was a sight to illustrate a cover of the *Saturday Evening Post* or make a railroad poster advertising Rocky Mountain National Park. The trail was blocked by a fallen pine tree, apparently blown down by the wind. There was an axe leaning against the log and most of the branches were lopped off and stacked off the trail. Two young rangers, stripped to the waist and shining with sweat, stood on opposite sides of the trunk, attacking it with a two-man crosscut saw. The log was three or four feet thick but the long teeth of the saw went easily back and forth, cutting the wood away in a steady, strong rhythm. The men pulled the saw, the teeth methodically whished back and forth, and the pile of sawdust steadily grew with each stroke.

McIntyre nudged Brownie to move forward.

"Out of uniform, boys?" said the ranger.

The sawing stopped. Russ Frame, on the far side of the log, picked up his canteen for a long drink of water.

"Hot work," Jamie Ogg said.

Initiative. McIntyre liked the two young men for their initiative. When a hiker reported the pine trunk blocking the Odessa Lake trail, other assistant rangers would probably pass the report to the trail maintenance crew; the crew, however, was busy building a new section of the Bierstadt Lake trail. Taking the initiative when they heard about the problem, Russ and Jamie saddled their horses, collected a crosscut saw and a couple of axes and went to take care of it. They could cut and move the log themselves; they were considerate of the work crew's schedule. Reporting the problem through official channels would only make things more complicated. They saw what needed doing and pitched in to get it done.

Jamie and Russ both appreciated how McIntyre stripped off his own tunic and took turns with the crosscut. Before long the second cut was finished. Using thick tree branches as levers the three men joined forces to roll the log section off the trail. They sat on it and rested. Except for being half naked, they might have been big game hunters posing on a trophy. Doing what he was there for in the first place, McIntyre filled them in on the latest clues and his own theory about a drug cache. He methodically described each aspect like it was a jigsaw puzzle piece, theorizing how one piece would fit into another.

The picture became more and more clear. Jamie became more and more agitated.

"It's like I figured," he said. "One of those New Mountain bastards killed my dad. And the air gun, it makes sense. Hell, one day I was lookin' at Andy Schuel's new shooter's catalog and there's a whole story with pictures about air guns powerful enough that poachers can kill rabbits, badgers, even deer with 'em. Hell, Tim, you remember the big elk killings? The guy with the takedown rifle? I betcha our murdering s.o.b. has a takedown air rifle. Only one in the whole valley, probably. And the snooty gunsmith, Hayward, he likely knows who owns it. I say we brace him. Make him tell the names of anybody who's got a air rifle. Then we go find the shooter and hang 'im."

"Hold on, ranger," McIntyre said. "Hold on. Don't go getting hot under the collar. If you two start any vigilante stuff, more than likely it'll be you and Russ who'll end up in the soup. Besides, like I told the lady detectives, we might be up against very dangerous, very slippery characters. Chicago boys who are used to gang violence. It won't do to go charging into their bus barn to arrest anybody. Nossir. We need to figure out our own advantages. Work out a strategy to get rid of the whole lot of them."

"All of 'em except the one who shot Jamie's dad," Russ said. "He's gonna pay for it."

"Okay," McIntyre agreed. "You two stay quiet, try my plan, and if we prove who did the shooting, you'll have first crack at him. Here's my idea. First we need to make up a ghost story, a real doozy of one, and start spreading it around. Russ, you could spin it out at the campfire talks. We'll bring Eleanor in on it, too, and tell her to pass it on to the New Mountain drivers. Let's meet at my cabin tonight, the three of us. Meanwhile, see if you can think up a couple more scary ideas. Like ghostly bodies with their heads missing, wandering the Fall River canyon. Mysterious fog. Strange crying echoing in the night. Once we've got a good yarn made up I'll tell it to Eleanor and maybe Leon Counter and Andy Schuel. Anyhow, meanwhile, I need to go to the S.O. and make sure Nick's aware of what we're going to try. See you two tonight, my place."

* * * * *

Ranger McIntyre found the wheeled chalkboard in the S.O. supply room and pushed it into Nick Nicholson's office. On it he drew a reasonably recognizable outline of the park, showing the Bear Lake road and a lopsided pyramid meant to represent Longs Peak.

"We already have maps," Nick said. "And you're not much of an artist."

"Part of my plan," McIntyre replied. "I figure I may as well give you the rest of it."

McIntyre drew two small chalk circles, one on the Bear Lake road and one on the leaning pyramid.

"I want your okay," he continued, "and a little money, to buy dynamite and use it to seal shut two old mining holes. One hole's off the Bear Lake road and one's on Longs Peak. We'll say they're hazardous. I'll recruit that guy from the work crew, the one with experience handling dynamite. We'll blow up the openings."

"Safely? You won't shoot rocks through tourists' windshields, for instance?"

"Safe as we can be. No problem there."

"Okay. You messed up my chalkboard in order to show me two mines I already know about?"

"No. I need there to be a map of mines where almost anybody can see it. Remember how we built a barrel trap and trapped a nuisance bear last season? Took him all the way over Milner Pass and let him go? It took a long trail of bait to bring him out of the woods, remember?"

"What I remember," Nick mused, "is the Fish and Wildlife Division telling us we'd dumped our bear into a grizzly's domain, and the grizzly was awful hard on our bear."

"That's the idea!" McIntyre said. "I'd like to run those Chicago thugs out of our park and dump them in another gangster's territory, let them shoot it out. Anyhow, the chalkboard's part of the bait. What I'd like is for you to keep it in your office and keep adding more abandoned mines to it. Oh, and if you could arrange for Eleanor to come to the office… maybe mention to a few people you want to talk about getting her back on the ranger force… when she asks about the blackboard map, tell her how we're starting a project to dynamite all the old mining holes. She can casually mention it to the New Mountain boys, see? She'll know how to do it. She'll tell them you're making a map of the ones to do next."

"Bait," Nick said.

"Bait," McIntyre replied. "And there's one other thing, in case anyone asks. Russ and Jamie and I, plus a couple of dude ranch wranglers, the ones who tell campfire stories at barbecues, are spreading a story, a kind of legend, about a demon animal in the Fall River canyons. Comes on foggy nights, kills livestock, frightens campers, eyes glow in the dark kind of blarney."

"More bait?" Nick asked. "What's the idea?"

"If the drug merchants think people believe the place to be haunted, they'll figure it makes it even better as a hiding place. We'll let them 'discover' there's another old mine there."

"Okay," Nick said.

"We want New Mountain to think their drug cache is being threatened, first of all. And what I think might happen next… well, what does a mountain lion do when her birth den is discovered? She scouts out a new place, a place where she figures nobody will go. She moves her kittens there."

"I've got the picture," Nick smiled. "You're out to see if you can make the drug merchants nervous and confused, scurrying to hide their junk. Seems far-fetched. Catching them in the open with all the dope on them, I mean. Long shot."

"But it might work," McIntyre went on. "I'd hope to pick 'em up one at a time, while they're carrying drugs. Maybe two at a time. One of them is bound to be our murderer, too. Probably the most nervous one."

"Okay," Nick said. "I don't think it has anything to do with rangering, but for Jamie's sake, because of his dad, I'll go along with the chalkboard gag and authorize blasting old mine tunnels shut. Probably ought to be done anyway. But nobody in this building should act like they're aware of anything about drug running or gangsters, at least not officially. Right?"

"Right," McIntyre said.

Chapter Nine
Fall River Gets a Ghost, McIntyre Gets a Tip

The deep, utter blackness of the mountain night surrounding the little group of tourists became palpable and seemed to shrink inward. The humans shivered and tried to squeeze even closer to one another on the logs. All of them, couples, companions, children, teenagers, all hunched forward to be nearer the campfire. They sought the heat of the fire, of course, for a mountain night is chilly, but primarily they wanted the safety and assurance of the flickering light coming from the snapping, crackling firewood.

Tom, Fall River Lodge's head wrangler, was truly in his element. His job was to give each guest an adventure, whether it was leading a trail ride along precipitous alpine routes or pointing out fresh bear sign to them as they rode along clutching their saddle horns with both hands. And possibly the part of the job he got the most kick out of, was spinning yarns around the evening campfires.

"It was a cook's helper who found the horse," Tom went on,

drawing out the ending of his Fall River spook story, "of course we always call 'em a 'camp jack' and back in them days, you see, a camp jack was the one whose job was to go to the creek with a bucket. Not like today with modern plumbing, nossir. Anyhow, this camp jack. He's at the creek where he comes upon a horse. This horse was hiding in the willows, shakin' and tremblin' all over. There was blood on its neck and forelegs and sign on the saddle."

"Sign?" asked one innocent kid.

"Claw marks. Three in a row, like this!"

Tom held up his hand in a claw with three fingers extended. The kids' eyes went wide.

"Across the cantle, down one fender. Those claws tore into the seat, too. Later on, others figured the saddle'd saved the horse's life. Well, come daybreak a search party rode up the road—of course in them days the Fall River road only went as far as Willow Park, y'understand. But all they found was blood spattered on rocks and a whole lot of horse tracks where a horse had been a-spinnin' and buckin' and twistin'. It looked like whatever came outta the night fog attacked the horse and rider from all sides at once."

A shiver ran through the audience, and not from the chill of the air.

"They never found the rider," Tom stated.

"What was he doing up there?" asked one fresh-faced young lady.

"God only knows. Well, once in awhile on a full moon night, sure, it looks real invitin' to saddle a horse and take a moonlight ride up Fall River Road. I've done it myself. I figure that's all he was doin'. Or maybe he'd been fishin' up there at Willow Park and was comin' back when the dark overtook him and the fog come down the narrows."

"Narrows?" one guest said.

"Oh, yeah. It's where it happened, they figure. Drivin' up the road y' probably don't notice, but where the switchbacks start to make the road climb to timberline altitude, if y' look south… this here's kinda hard to make clear. Y' see on a north-facin' slope you find your heaviest forest, mostly short needle trees like firs and spruces. The north slope in the narrows is real thick timber. And lots of downed logs and other deadfall. Nobody ever goes in there. The road, see, it climbs the south slope, across the river. But the north side… the legend starts with a miner, see. This was back in maybe eighteen-ninety or thereabouts. Before they built the road, see. Jus' a track up along the river. This miner, he made his way into the thick forest at the narrows, and he managed to build him a rough cabin. Plenty of trees for logs and y' don't need to drag 'em very far. He began burrowin' into the mountain lookin' for gold. I never saw the hole he dug, but I heard it's more'n fifty yards deep, a tunnel right back into the mountain."

"Did he find gold?" someone asked.

"Never got the chance t' stay there long enough," Tom said. Tom picked up a stick and stirred the campfire, letting the tension hang in the air.

"Nope," he resumed. "One early mornin' he come hurryin' out of Fall River valley all beat to pieces, mutterin' about the fog. There was only a few settlers in the valley then, of course. He stumbled into the first house he came to, incoherent, clothes torn, bare-headed. 'It got my dog the first night, that fog, ripped its throat out,' he told them. 'The second night the fog got my mule, damn near tore its head off. God how the animal screamed in the fog but I didn't dare go to it. Didn't dare.' And the next night of fog, thick enough t' hide the moonlight, there came a clawin' and poundin' on his cabin door. The miner got half crazy, climbed out the window, ran and ran and ran down the trail—this was the river trail, mind you, 'cause there weren't no road, jus' a rough track—they figure he'd run and walked better part of ten miles. At night."

The silence of the black evening, broken only by the crackle of the fire, was almost as nerve wracking as Tom's tale. He waited for a dramatic minute or two, and finished.

"Well," he said, "time to turn in. Long day tomorrow. But I'll leave y' with a bit of advice. You feel any urge t' explore the narrows part of the canyon, I wouldn't do it. There was a honeymoon couple, oh, ten years ago I guess…"

He broke off as if he didn't want to frighten anyone.

"What?" the teen asked.

"We don't talk about it. Young and romantic, see? Lookin' for ways to be alone with one another. Well, they figured t' go and find the miner's cabin, or what's left of it. They'd tied their horses there at the switchback. Various ones of us searched all summer, never found hide nor hair. Vanished. It was thought they might've caught a ride with a passing car, see? Went on over Milner Pass and on to California maybe. Left their luggage behind, though. Strange, right? Anyway, my ol' soogan's callin' to my bones. But, all o' you listen to me. If there's any sign of fog in the valley, you stay at the lodge. Don't go pokin' around up on the north slope. And if the fog comes down, you run and don't you look back."

Ranger McIntyre kept chuckling while Vi Coteau was recounting Eleanor's version about a deadly blue fog and a three-clawed creature haunting the Fall River narrows. Back when McIntyre was a boy, Old Man said trout in a stream have silent, invisible ways of spreading danger signals, prairie dogs who see a coyote can inform other prairie dogs hundreds of yards away, and even the trees of a forest seem to share information. A single honeybee can scout out a bounty of pollen and tell the hive where it is.

"Eleanor's already heard it! Well, I'm not surprised," McIntyre said. "Scare people with a story and they can't wait to go scare somebody else with it. Hey, would you like to bet the New Mountain hoodlums—I mean, drivers—are going to use our blue fog story to drum up more business for themselves? I bet they'll start telling people they'd be safer in a bus with a dozen other people than in a jitney car with one or two people."

"I could bet you a dinner," Vi said, giving him her foxy sideways look.

"Oh, no. No, you don't! I won't fall for your 'bet you dinner' trick again. I learned the first time. If I win I have to put on a tux and have dinner in a swanky Denver restaurant. And if I lose, the same thing happens."

"I have a new evening gown I could wear," she continued. "Satin? Oodles of beads? Cut very low to leave my back showing. The front's clingy… well, let's say I can't carry my pistol while wearing it."

Perhaps you know a woodsman, or a soldier, whose quick, alert eyes never seem to be at rest, eyes alive to every movement however slight. But perhaps you've never seen those same eyes start to glaze over into a faraway stare as his brain goes on furlough.

"So…" McIntyre blinked and finally managed to reply, "you're headed back to Denver?"

"Yes." She smiled to see his reaction. "I want to see how the office is doing, write a few checks. And phone my former boss. I'm certain he'll be more than interested in busting this New Mountain Stage Company scam. He can have a flying squad of federal agents up here inside of twenty-four hours. I'd bet—oops, there's my tricky word again—I'd bet with the new Dangerous Drug Act in effect he'll be eager to make a big drug-related arrest."

"Great," the ranger said. "Tell him it'll take a few days to set it up and work the thing, but at the very least it should be the heaviest haul of dope he's ever seen. The way I understand it, it only takes less than a thimbleful of cocaine, or heroin, to send a man to jail. But I wouldn't be surprised to catch them moving twenty, thirty pounds of the junk. And I plan to have the dealers caught red-handed with it, too."

Although they were on a public street not far from Mrs. Spinney's place, Vi took the risk of putting her hand to his neck and pulling him to her for a parting kiss on the mouth. She kissed him partly because it was simply fun, partly because it was deeply pleasurable, and partly because she wanted to see his eyes go all glassy again. She was unaware of her other male admirer loitering not far off, waiting for her to return to the house. When the stalker saw her kissing the ranger his knuckles went white clutching his hiking staff.

A moment later saw a slightly lightheaded ranger on the move once more, walking briskly in the hope that swinging his legs and arms might bring his brain back into focus.

Quiet, contemplative, and reluctant to leave the village and the mountains, Vi strolled slowly toward the house. She was almost at the gate when she felt something encircling her arm. She looked to see a loop of strong wire tightening above her elbow. Hayward was there, looking her up and down with his cold eyes.

The gunsmith was dressed for mountain hiking, or at least dressed according to what fashion magazines thought was 'in' for hikers, with tweed knickerbockers, polished brogans, argyle socks, a belted tweed jacket and slouch hat. With both hands he held a long hiking staff. Protruding from the end of the staff was the wire loop he had playfully tightened around Vi Coteau's upper arm.

"Clever, isn't it?" he said, drawing her closer to him.

If he'd snared my left arm instead, Vi thought, *I'd have pulled my Colt on him. He'd be limping away with a bullet in one of his brogans.*

She knew to remain calm, although her impulse was to wrench the stick from his grasp and beat him over the head with it. Instead, she would go on the offensive verbally.

"Doctor Hayward," she stated flatly. "I intended to come looking for you. I'm leaving town today and would like to take my little Remington pistol with me. If you've finished with it. Please remove your… bit of wire… from my arm."

The ice in her voice put him on the defense. He would need to account for not one but two ways in which he had offended her.

"Of course," he said, loosening the wire, "very sorry. Only a bit of frolic. An impulse. But I'm afraid your automatic pistol isn't quite available. I've, uh, sent it off to a man in Saint Joseph who can professionally repair the damage on the slide. He will refinish it like new."

"I see."

"But come walk with me," he said. "Let's go take advantage of the bench beside the river, sit in the shade of the narrow leaf cottonwood—*populus angustifolia*. There's a matter I wish to discuss with you."

Vi paused and held out her hand to examine his walking stick, while her brain went flipping through pages of Kate Warne's book *A Guide for Lady Detectives*. The chapter on "Suspects." *Never pass up an opportunity to learn more about any person connected with the case you are investigating,* Warne's handbook suggested.

Hayward rose to the lure. He put the stick in her hand, pointing to a small camouflaged button resembling a knot in the wood. The button rode in a very narrow slot.

"The loop of wire is retracted into the tip of the staff, you see," he lectured, "and if you'll place your lovely thumb upon the button and slide it forward you'll see the wire appear again. Yes, very good. If you'll exert a bit of downward pressure…"

She pressed the button and the wire loop retracted with surprising speed.

"Spring loaded! Awfully handy for snaring small game. Or nasty canines. Or lovely brunettes!" he said. "Anything beyond one's reach, actually."

Vi was reminded of a sales device she'd learned from her father, a successful salesman. If you want to sell a bit of hardware, such as a tool, be sure you put it into the client's hands. Let them demonstrate it to you. Let them suggest other uses for it. In her case he was obviously, too obviously, using his explanation as an excuse to stand too close and touch hands with her. But it also seemed like part of a sales routine. Could it be that Hayward was making and selling these things?

"And it comes with a cap, of course," he continued, taking from his pocket a rubber crutch tip. "Can't have dirt fouling the wire, you see. There. All safe. Perhaps… would you be interested in seeing similar eclectic hiking staffs? Come, I'll show you. If you'd care to stroll toward my cottage perhaps we can discuss the house next door. It's still up for sale, although I have taken an option on it."

"I should tell you," she said, falling into step with him, "another party has suggested I move here and open a ladies' detective agency. They too have a house in mind. In a different location."

She didn't mention how the "other party" was little Gala

Book, the barber's pigtailed daughter. Vi had come up with a hunch by this time, and it was that the gunsmith was somehow part of Senator Roland Speckle's organization, possibly part of the upper echelon. She also had a strong suspicion that the gunsmith's main weakness was jealousy. In her handbook for lady detectives, Miss Warne was very specific on that point: among a male's weaknesses, jealousy goes before even pride and greed. And is far easier to exploit.

When they reached his cottage the gunsmith offered to prepare tea for them before showing her his collection of unusual walking sticks. Vi politely declined.

"Very well," he said.

He led the way down the stairs into his basement work and shooting area. There he unlocked a tall cabinet, one of a half-dozen built into the wall, mused a moment as he made a selection, and finally took out three wooden staffs, propped two of them against the wall, and showed her the third one.

"A possibly useful accessory for a city detective such as your pretty self," he said.

It appeared to be a bamboo, or cane, walking stick approximately thirty inches long. Vi suspected it was a sword cane, and she was correct: Hayward twisted and removed the curved handle to reveal a slender blade.

"A sword cane," she said. "How clever. I admit, at times I've thought of carrying such a thing. Except I'd choose a different design. This one looks like a cane for a man. I'd rather have something more feminine. Perhaps a parasol? And the blade is too long. Unless one were trained in swordsmanship, it would be a clumsy weapon in an encounter. How about a parasol, with a blade of eighteen inches or less?"

"Excellent!" Hayward exclaimed. "I'll write to the manufacturer and see what I can find for you!"

"Oh? You don't build these yourself?"

"No, no. But I have designed a few. In certain Asian neighborhoods of certain California cities there may be found craftsmen who can fabricate almost anything. For a price. Let me show you this other one. It's a unique bit of equipment, you'll have to admit."

When he set down the sword cane and picked up the next walking stick, thicker and longer, she reached for it. But Hayward kept it from her.

"No, let me handle it. I'll show you," he said. "You might get grease on your hands. This is unique, as I said, and quite the antique. There was an old man in California, back in the 1890s, who went about the city with a donkey pulling an ancient Spanish cart. He collected bottles, rags, broken furniture to repair and sell. His cart, being of the type with wooden axle and wooden wheels, squeaked as it rolled along. Out of sympathy, an Asian craftsman made him this walking staff. I don't know who inherited it after the rag man died. I acquired it by means of postal auction. The stick comes apart here in the middle, you see, and you pack the hollow interior with grease. As one screws the top half down, a little at a time, small bits of grease come out of the tip. It allowed the old man to dab a little on his squeaking axle when needed."

"Well!" Vi said. "Imagine! A grease gun in a stick. What a wonderfully subtle way to tell the old rag man he was making a noise. It's a lovely story. And the rubber tip keeps it from leaving grease stains on the pavement?"

"Oh, yes. In fact if you were to lose a rubber tip from any of the sticks in my collection you'd have to be careful not to put the tip down in the dirt. Well, take this remaining one for example. Looks like a gentleman's ordinary evening stick, eh? Quite classy, quite formal? Remove the rubber tip, remove the silver handle, and it becomes a blowgun. Load a poison dart from the hollow handle and you have a lovely assassination weapon."

Hayward went back to the cupboard and brought out one more walking staff, rather ordinary-looking, almost shoulder high. After removing the rubber cap for her, he leaned closer—uncomfortably closer—to point out the metal lever recessed in the wood. He instructed her to lift the lever: a six-inch dagger blade snapped out the end of the staff. Hayward seemed disappointed in her reaction: other girls might have squeaked or giggled in surprise.

"I see," she said in a bored tone. "We have a spear as well as a hiking staff. Could be useful in any number of situations, I suppose."

He retracted the blade and put all the walking sticks back into the cupboard. He began to say there was another one he would like to demonstrate; Vi, however, made her excuses. Returning upstairs, she declined his offer of tea and conversation. He said he hoped to discuss the matter of the vacant house next door, but again she declined. She left him standing in his doorway, watching her walk away.

* * * * *

Denver would have to wait. Vi drove to the S.O. instead, where Dottie gave her Ranger McIntyre's whereabouts. Dottie also let Vi use the telephone.

"Operator," Jane said.

"Number, please?"

"Jane," Vi said. "This is Vi Coteau. I wonder if you could help me with a little tiny bit of deception."

"Probably," Jane said. "Detective stuff?"

"Something along those lines," Vi said. "Could you ring up

Doctor Hayward and tell him he'd had a long-distance call, and he should wait while you get the party back on the line? I need to keep him inside his house for five or ten minutes."

"Gee," Jane answered. "Fun! Sure I can do it."

Vi pointed the Marmon toward the Moraine Park road where she soon discovered McIntyre's official pickup truck parked at a viewpoint where tourists stopped to photograph the vista. She also discovered the man himself, looking every inch the ordinary uniformed ranger performing his ordinary duties. In this instance his duty consisted of kneeling with his hand on a young lad's shoulder while he warned the miniature miscreant not to throw any more stones at the chipmunks.

"Okay," McIntyre was saying. "I want you to go out there in the grass, find every pebble you threw, and bring them back to the parking lot where they belong."

The boy's mother, obviously not unimpressed by a tall handsome man in uniform, gave her son a light spank on the behind and smiled beatifically to watch him scamper out into the meadow. Wearing her most beguiling eyelash-fluttering smile, she turned back, disappointed to discover the slender brunette from the sporty convertible taking possession of the ranger's arm.

Vi led him away from the tourists and described Hayward's assortment of unusual walking sticks, including how innocent they appeared to be, once the trigger mechanism was retracted and the rubber tip replaced.

"We mustn't leap to conclusions, not at this point," she finished, "but I'm beginning to have a rather deep suspicion about the man. More of a sneaking hunch, perhaps. But what if our Doctor Hayward works mostly for the bus company crowd.

Guns, ammunition, repairing guns? What federal investigators call an 'armorer' to a criminal gang—if there really is one—operating under the guise of the New Mountain Stage Company. What if the other cupboards in his convenient basement workshop contain other special-use devices. Like Tommy guns? Browning Automatic Rifles? Maybe grenades or other stuff they wouldn't want anybody to find at the bus barn, but armaments a gunsmith and weapons collector might own."

McIntyre nodded absently.

"Are you paying attention?" she asked.

"I was wondering…" he said, "where in the village you'd go if you wanted to buy a crutch tip."

* * * * * *

Rangers McIntyre and Frame made an early start the following morning because, as McIntyre told his sleepy helper, a low angle of sunlight was better for finding small objects on the ground. They began at the edge of town at the spot where they assumed Arthur Ogg's extra passenger boarded the touring car.

"If we're lucky and have been living right," he said, "the rubber tip of his stick got knocked off when he climbed into the car. Search along the side of the street and down the gutter. Maybe it rolled into the weeds."

No such luck. No crutch tip in the weeds, not in the gravel, nowhere.

The early morning had started out chilly, and became even colder as they went higher in elevation. They drove up the Fall River road switchbacks, skirted Willow Park, emerged at timberline and stopped at the Mummy Range trailhead where Arthur dropped off the party of hikers.

"The hikers got out here," McIntyre said. "Maybe the

hitchhiker did, too. Maybe to stretch his legs, or maybe so another passenger could dismount. You take the other side of the parking, I'll go this way. If anybody comes along and wonders why you're poking around, pretend you've ridden all the way up here and need to find a place to pee."

"I don't have to pretend," Frame said.

The keen alpine air penetrated their wool tunics. Russ Frame searched diligently, but the shivers made his vision jumpy. Nevertheless, there was no sign of a lost crutch tip.

"Back there in the krumholtz I saw a half of a footprint and a smudge like might a walking stick might make," McIntyre said. "But there's been enough rain to wash out most tracks. At least we looked, and didn't find the crutch tip. I don't think he lost it here. Let's go back to the truck."

They drove back down the road, into the glare of the morning sun, back down into the shadowy forest, back across Willow Park, and finally Russ Frame ventured an opinion.

"What a way to spend the government's money, two rangers searching the national park for one lousy crutch tip. Even if we find it I don't think it'd prove anything."

"Sure it would," McIntyre answered. "It's little, but could be part of the puzzle picture. Think about those peanut shells from last summer. How we found fish traps in the Thompson River and a bunch of peanut shells? We figured the poacher kept peanuts in his pocket and munched on them while checking his traps. Murphy's grocery is the only place in town selling 'em, so... look: Hayward showed Miss Coteau a bunch of sword canes and weapons disguised as walking staffs. Told her he was careful to keep rubber tips on them to keep dirt and moisture from fouling the blade or whatever. You see my point? Okay. A witness in town saw a man with a thick walking stick climb into Arthur's car. And we found what could be this same man's tracks where he got out again before the car went over the edge. But we didn't see marks of a stick. None. So what do I think? I think the hiking stick was actually a weapon. Maybe a blowgun. Maybe a new kind of rifle. I'm guessing he lost the rubber tip. He realized it was missing. He got careful not to put the tip down on the dirt. Like you and your Savage .303, see? You wouldn't stick your rifle muzzle in the dirt, would you? No, Russ, I think it's why we didn't see any stick marks in the dirt. I think it's because the shooter lost a little rubber cup. Sure, it's a long shot, but it could link one of Hayward's 'special' walking sticks to Arthur Ogg's Dodge car. But seeing as how we didn't find it, we'll do the next best thing. Let's try to find out where the mystery man might have gone to buy a new one. And when it comes to any kind of hardware, Marley's the man to ask."

They paused at the Fall River entrance station where a temp was dutifully sitting behind the information window. No problems to report, the temp said. In fact, traffic was so light and the routine so dull he'd spent his time lounging in the sunshine beside the building, reading the latest copy of *Uncle Billy's Whizbang*. In other words, everything was calm and normal; McIntyre suggested driving into town for lunch and a chat with Marley.

"Tim?" Russ said as they rolled along.

"Yeah?"

"Mind if I say something?"

"Say away."

"Might be my imagination. You think maybe you're a little too anxious to connect the gunsmith with these murders? What I'm getting at—wish I'd kept my mouth closed—is how everybody in town sees the way he hangs around Miss Coteau and he's a slick city-type bachelor. Maybe I thought you might be eager to pin something on him?"

"Could be," McIntyre replied. "You might be right. I'm probably jealous. And I'm darn sure of one thing."

"What?"

"I don't like him."

They found Marley hard at work, as usual. There was a time when a village blacksmith's shop would be a place of horseshoes hanging on pegs, broken wagon wheels leaning against the walls, maybe a plow blade waiting to be welded. With the advent of motor cars it was primarily fenders, radiators, gasoline tanks and car bumpers in need of repair.

Ranger McIntyre described what he thought the crutch tip would look like.

"Probably bigger than one you'd find on a cane," he concluded. "Would anybody here in town sell heavy duty tips? The druggist, maybe?"

"Maybe," Marley said. "But if you really need one… wait here a minute."

Marley went rummaging through the wooden boxes beneath his workbench and came back holding exactly what McIntyre had described, a large black rubber cup.

"Here you go," he said. "I was salvaging parts from Arthur's Dodge car. Perfectly good tip. Only like you said, it'd be too loose if you put it on a cane or crutch. It was stuck under the back seat, kind of lodged between the seat brace and the side of the car. You can see it's made to fit over a water pipe or a metal leg like those new kitchen tables—nearly two inches across, I'd say. I figured maybe for the end of a brake lever or maybe Arthur'd been hauling a stool with rubber feet on it. Piano stools have those? Anyway, there you are."

"What a relief!" Russ said. "I was afraid Tim was going to have us out there searching the whole national park for it."

McIntyre stepped out into the sunlight to examine the tip. As Marley said, it showed almost no signs of wear. On the bottom, the maker's mold made a circular ridge of the rubber, with a capital letter G in it. Undoubtedly the manufacturer's monogram. The inside of the rubber cup held a faint aroma of shellac, or varnish. If this tip came from one of Hayward's custom walking sticks…

"Russ," he said, "we've got a little more tracking to do. Poke around Hayward's neighborhood for quarter-size circles with a letter G in them. See if any of them lead back to his house."

"Why not go up to his door and ask if it's his?" Russ said.

"It's like fly fishing," McIntyre replied. "You catch more fish if the fish don't suspect you're fishing."

As with McIntyre's trout, not all of his similes were worth keeping.

Chapter Ten

Leon Conspires, Gala Investigates, Coteau Plans a Picnic

"Andy," McIntyre said, "you ever heard of a walking stick that could shoot a bullet?"

Andy Schuel was on a step stool, putting a box of winter mittens on a high shelf behind the counter.

"I guess we won't be needing those for a few more months," he said, climbing down and sliding the stool out of the way. "A stick that shoots bullets, you say. Well, according to a story in the new shooter's catalog, the first guns ever invented, they were like sticks. Little more than tubes with a touchhole. Kinda like holding a small cannon barrel in your hand and lighting the fuse. But I guess a fella could maybe take a barrel from an old muzzle loader and make a walking stick out of it. All you'd need would be the barrel, and the nipple, really. You'd put a percussion cap on the nipple, hit it with a rock and bang! But as a walking stick? It'd be awful heavy. Wouldn't be accurate, neither."

"I guess you're right," McIntyre said. "Heavy. Have to be fairly heavy to take a charge of gunpowder, even black powder. And it couldn't be a repeater, either."

McIntyre described the two separate shots that ended Arthur Ogg's life.

"Oh," Andy said, "you want a repeater? Let me see… I remember reading an article here…"

Andy reached for his annual shooter's catalog, already browsed, thumbed, and dog-eared by half the males in the village. He flipped past section after section of pistols, hunting knives, holsters and scabbards, shotguns, and finally came to the article he was looking for.

"One thing guys like about this catalog," he said, "it's got all kinds of picture articles about the history of firearms and various weaponry. Here's the one on swivel cannons… y' might want to mount one on your pickup, in case you're attacked by an outlaw gang of ground squirrels. Ah! Here's the part we want."

McIntyre tried to read the story while Andy kept trying to summarize it for him.

"See?" the storekeeper said, "mid-nineteenth century. England, mostly. Or in Europe, like Germany in particular. Air rifles made to look like hiking sticks. Heck, they'd go up to what we'd here in the States call a .38 or even a .40 caliber. According to the writer they used a separate air pump. You'd attach the pump, pressurize the air reservoir in the top of the handle—see the picture you got your thumb on? It says the air gun could shoot three nine millimeter bullets without recharging, and hard enough to bring down one of those tiny little deer they got over there, or a rabbit or badger. It'd be great for a poacher, see, 'cause of bein' almost silent. I tell you, those Victorian gunsmiths, they were good at it. Turn the page. See the picture? It's more of a .25 caliber shooter, but the air pump is built right into the stick. You work it up and down, I guess, like a bicycle pump. Helluva gadget, huh? And there's another one on the next page, what they call an alpenstock, with an air rifle barrel inside. Says there under the picture the thing could shoot through a car tire."

McIntyre was listening, but his mind was picturing the bus barn. Oliver, the gasoline can, the blowtorch, the dimly lit gloom of the place… a man with such a device could shoot from the hip at close range, then simply step back into the crowd, or into the shadows, and become a another rider, or one of the drivers, carrying a walking stick. Simple.

Scary, but simple.

* * * * *

"Lemme ask y' a favor."

It was the voice of moonshiner Leon Counter. He seemingly appeared out of the ground like an Irish gnome catching a whiff of whiskey.

"Stay aboard your horse a while," he said quietly. "An' wave your arm around pointin' at stuff like you're askin' directions or somethin'."

"Okay," said the ranger, pointing north down the treeless ridge and south toward distant Moraine Park. "Being watched, are we?"

"You got it, Sherlock," Leon replied. "Them damn dealers from back east, they've put a scout t' watchin' me for the past couple days. He's up in them rocks to the west. Damn idiot didn't think of how his telescope flashes in the mornin' sun."

"You'd think they'd give a hermit a little privacy," McIntyre said with a smile.

"Who you callin' a hermit? I ain't no hermit."

"Y' live in a cave hidden behind a brush hut decorated with smelly animal skins, y' only bathe when you're trapping beaver and fall into a pond, women and kids run away at the sight of you, and when anybody comes up this ridge you chase 'em off. But you're not a hermit?"

"Happens I'm a self-employed enterenpreneur, I am. Anyways, you're here 'cause y' got my message," the moonshiner stated. "I got me a notion your scheme's startin' in to work out."

Ranger McIntyre shifted in the saddle and looked off to the east, his back toward the man with the telescope.

"Leon," he said, "when did you start talking like a hillbilly?"

"I need practice," Leon said. "I got them there Chicago hoodlums thinkin' I'm a dumb hick, but mebbe a useful hick."

"Part of the scheme?"

"Yeah. Two of 'em approached me for information. One wears really dark glasses. Diego's his name. Samplin' my hooch one evening he got really chatty. Turns out he'd like to replace Ladro Topo as foreman. Maybe it'd be a step toward bein' an enforcer for the KKK. In Denver. Interesting info, huh? Th' other contact's not so much of a weasel. More innocent-looking New Mountain kid. John. Comes off as havin' no ambition except to keep his job and be useful, but I think there's lots more to him than that. Anyhow according to him the New Mountain gang, including the Jones brothers, heard your ghost story about a blue mist and three-clawed forest creature. I told him there's this old mine tunnel up the Fall River canyon. And he told me—they both told me—about your project of blasting abandoned mines? You got the Jones brothers nervous. Next day or two I'm supposed to take John and Diego t' see that old mine tunnel. I think I've got 'em convinced that the park service don't even know about it and everybody would be too scared to go near the place anyhow. I might have mentioned it's like the one Dutch Schultz has in his underground distillery. In fact, they might have got the notion I sometimes have dealin's with Dutch."

"Do you?"

"Better you don't know," Leon said. "But we ought not stand here yakkin' much more. Might make the telescope guy suspicious. Tell you what, let's wave our arms around like we're mad as hell at each other. What do you reckon Brownie will do if I slap her on the rump like I'm sendin' you on your way?"

"Depends. She might trot off with me, or she might turn around and bite off your damn hand."

The ranger and the moonshiner ended their act by yelling at one another, waving their arms threateningly. Leon slapped Brownie's rump. As if she understood the charade, the mare broke into a trot as her ranger 'tried' to rein her in. But next time they went to visit the smelly hermit she would remember the hard slap…

With his work day ended, McIntyre spent extra time brushing Brownie. Afterward he changed into civilian clothes, fired up Small Delights and headed for town. According to the temp on the park entrance gate, other than a mid-afternoon bus tour and a couple of locals the only other car he saw was a brown Franklin coupe. It drove slowly past McIntyre's cabin three or four times.

The ranger slowed down for two deer, a doe and her yearling crossing the road. He was satisfied that his visit to Leon Counter made the New Mountain spy both curious and nervous. And the surest way to catch a trout, or trap a rogue bear, was to make them curious and nervous. Sooner or later they need to see what's going on, and they break cover.

He slowed again where the road afforded a view of the deep pool upstream of Rollinger's cabin. He didn't have time to stop and fish, but maybe he'd see a trout rising. One lunker trout in there would go more than two pounds. On several occasions McIntyre teased the fishy brute out of his hiding place, made him reveal his presence. The trick, McIntyre discovered, was to use an outrageously large dry fly and drift it repeatedly along the river bank. Old Mister Trout lay on the bottom, camouflaged against the pebbles, but he finally could not resist going up to the surface to see what darn thing kept floating over his feeding territory.

Let's see if we can make Doctor Hayward break cover, thought McIntyre. *If I ever get a chance to set the hook on him…*

* * * * *

In the back of Book's Barber Shop, Ranger McIntyre sat down on a low stool so his face would be more or less the same level as Gala Book's. He reached out to tug one of her pigtails, but she jerked it away.

"Whatcha got for me?" he asked her.

"More info," she replied, "but it probably ain't worth much of anything."

"Isn't," he said, correcting her.

"Yeah. Well, you know I'm in the metal collecting business."

"Among other things," McIntyre said.

"One of my fish worm customers said he'd heard lots of shooting up behind Prospect Mountain at the old gravel quarry. It made me figure there'll be brass lying around, okay?"

Gala dug into both pockets of her overalls, pulling out a clasp knife, two skeleton keys she'd found, two sticks of gum, several nickels and dimes, a ball of string, a spring hook off of a dog leash… and a half dozen .45 caliber brass cartridge cases.

"I bet there's hundreds of these up there. Or there was. I filled a coffee can. And there's more, if I go back and poke around in the brush and grass. I figure them Chicago men…"

"Those Chicago men…"

"Yeah. I figure they've been up there shootin' with Tommy guns! What you think!"

"Nothing illegal about owning a Tommy gun," McIntyre said. "But thanks. I'm glad you told me about it. Glad to see you, too, 'cause I've got a detective job for you."

Gala's eyes lit up. Being a detective like Miss Vi Coteau was exactly what she wanted to do.

McIntyre took the oversize crutch tip from his pocket and handed it to her.

"Take a sniff of it," he said.

Gala sniffed.

"Alcohol?"

"Close. Try again. Think about those house number signs you make for people. The kind you make out of old barn wood? What do you finish them with?"

"Shellac," she said. "Heck yes. This rubber thingie smells like shellac inside."

"Right," he said, taking it back again. "This is a secret operation, you understand, but I'd like to find out who in the village uses shellac. It can't be too common. Most men use varnish nowadays. Maybe you've seen a shellac can in a trash bin, or maybe wherever you buy yours from, they could tell you who else does. Got it?"

"Sure," Gala said. "I 'spect I can find out by today, maybe tomorrow. My usual rate, twenty-five cents per piece of good info."

"Not a whole dollar like at the church social?"

"Nah. I just did that for fun. Daddy taught me if y' charge extra sorbitant fees y' end up losing customers."

"Maybe you oughta charge by the hour?" McIntyre suggested.

"Nah. I been askin' around and keepin' my eyes open and you know what?"

"No, what?"

"Nobody as far as I can find out ever got rich workin' to be paid by th' hour."

* * * * *

"Hello there, ranger," Dr. Hayward said. He spoke with forced cordiality. "Out for an evening stroll around our village, are you? And you with miles of national park trails to patrol."

"Good evening, Doctor," McIntyre replied. "Matter of fact I came to town for supper. Felt like having a bowl of chili at Kitty's Café."

"Oh," Hayward said. "I thought perhaps, because you stopped in front of my house, perhaps you were spying on me. Or maybe you suspected Miss Coteau would be here?"

"Nah," McIntyre said. "I heard she's gone to Denver. Tending to her detecting business. I'm busy as all heck, too. You probably didn't hear about it, but the park's trying to seal shut a bunch of the old mine tunnels. Public safety and all. Only a matter of time before a tourist decides to explore one and ends up trapped by a cave-in. I don't do the blasting myself, you understand. My job's to pinpoint a hazardous mine to dynamite and send the crew. Anyway, you were curious why I'm here. I've got no interest in your house. No, it's the one next door. It's been for sale and I thought I'd have a look."

"A look? At buying it?"

"Sure. See, if I was to marry I'll need to make a choice where to live. Either the government will let me rent the cabin I'm in, or one of the other cabins in the park, or else they'll pay me a housing allowance to rent or buy a place in town. This house would be ideal. Quiet street, real handy to the stores, and not far from the school. For when we have kids."

McIntyre watched Hayward carefully, the way he would watch a wild dog or range bull for signs it was going to charge. Hayward's neck seemed to be a little more red and his eyes were slightly wide.

"But," Hayward said, "you, uh, should realize… you see, the fact is, I'm considering taking an option on the property. Being next door to mine. Good investment, and I could control who lives there. This talk of marriage, though… ?"

"Nothing definite," McIntyre said. "Later in the season, maybe. Maybe September. I feel I should solve these shootings first, before I pay attention to wedding plans. Arthur Ogg, the bus driver, the kid in the river… all three in my district, see? And the higher-ups want answers. Believe you me, I've got lots on my mind besides real estate and weddings. As if I didn't have enough to worry about, the story got out about a Fall River ghost or phantom or blue mist monster. Headquarters wants me to talk to all the guides and hostlers, ask them to squelch it. Because Number One, we don't want people in the Fall River valley going into panic at every movement in the bushes and racing their cars to get out of there whenever a little cloud shows up. Number Two, the road's not only a major attraction, it's the only route from here to the western slope. Washington doesn't want there to be any legends about it being haunted. And speaking of Washington and the feds, in my spare time I'm supposed to look into rumors of drug trafficking."

"I see," said Hayward.

"Well, right now a bowl of Kitty's chili's calling my name. I gotta go," McIntyre said. "But one of these days we'll talk more about the house. See you!"

McIntyre strolled casually away, whistling a little tune. He was extremely pleased with himself. It was as plain as the nose on your face, as his father used to say: Hayward wore a wide streak of jealousy where Vi was concerned. If Hayward ran true to breed, being a male, he'd do one of two things. Either he'd lose all interest in the woman, telling himself she was fickle and stupid and not worth his effort, or he would spend even more of his time trying to impress her with stories of his financial connections and his importance. Kind of like a sage grouse in mating season, dancing around in the dirt, puffing up all his feathers to impress the hens.

Either way, McIntyre was thinking. Either way suits me right down to my boot heels.

* * * * *

Gala made a good day's haul behind Torgerson's Hardware and General Merchandise. Three feet or more of insulated wire, good for various salable craft projects, a torn leather glove she could cut into a pouch and make a shepherd's sling, and a shoebox-size wooden shipping crate destined to become lashed to the back of her bicycle to carry cans of fish worms.

As soon as the store seemed empty of customers she stashed her findings beneath the wooden steps and went inside.

"Hey, hi Gala!" Torgerson said. "What brings you, this fine day?"

Gala looked at the floor, shyly pulling one pigtail. She liked this store man. He treated her like a fellow businessman and always took interest in her money-making projects.

"Mommy sent me. She'd like a nickel's worth of cup hooks, please. She likes the silvery kind, not the brass ones. I got the nickel right here."

"Comin' right up!" he said, choosing a small paper bag and opening one of the many drawers of hardware. "Anything else?"

"Well, sir," Gala said, "I been needin' shellac. But only 'bout half a cup."

"Oh," Torgerson said. "I'm afraid I've only got the pint cans. And quarts, of course. Too expensive if you only need a dab or two. As I recall, you prefer to buy the flakes and mix it yourself."

"'Cause I get alcohol for free," she said. "From father's supply for barberin'. But I was thinkin'. Maybe you'd know of somebody who bought a whole box of flakes or maybe a can full. Y'know, they'd probably have half of it left over like always seems t' happen with cans of paint, and if I knew who they was—were—I could either hobo it off'n them or maybe dicker for it."

"Man," he said, handing her the sack of cup hooks and taking the nickel, "I guess nobody else in this whole valley would think of that. You're sharp, you are. One of these days I bet we'll see you owning half this village. Well, let me see… Mrs. Foster bought the last box of flakes. Needed to coat a damp place in her wall plaster, but I'd say she used all of it. The hostler from out at Brynwood Lodge bought a small can last week. Doctor Hayward, he bought a pint, too. If I were you I'd probably try him first."

Gala thanked him and, retrieving her materials from under the steps, headed home humming to herself. Two pieces of information. She'd parlay one bit of news into two parts and charge Ranger McIntyre double. One, Doctor Hayward bought shellac. Two, only two other people had. Plus, finding the wooden box for fish worms was a bonus. She'd be able to carry twice as many soup cans up the river to sell to fishermen. Empty cans were free, dirt was free, worms were free, and now she had a free box to carry them in. Pure profit for her. The little girl skipped along, kicked a pebble at a stray cat, and smiled.

* * * * *

McIntyre spent the remainder of his evening on Fall River, fishing the slow-flowing, quiet section meandering through meadow grass and willow thickets. With his pocket pliers he cut the barb from a size fourteen Rio Grande King and began catching trout, releasing the small ones. He called it "choosing his breakfast" and it was more of a game, one he usually enjoyed. On this particular evening, however, he couldn't seem to stop looking upriver into the black mouth of the Fall River canyon. Although distant, the dark shadows taunted him, challenging him to come and find Arthur's killer. He thought about the story of how Ulysses made his crew stop their ears with wax and lash him to the mast so he could hear the song of the Sirens. The fishing was relaxing enough, but he kept sensing the canyon watching over his shoulder, daring him to come and find a clue it was hiding.

Maybe one more time, he thought. *Maybe if I spend a little more time where Arthur's Dodge went over the edge, maybe…*

A pan-size brookie broke surface, grabbed McIntyre's Rio Grande King, spit it out again, and dove for the bottom where it would remain for the next half hour.

"Damn," McIntyre muttered. "Probably spooked every fish in this whole stretch of river. I should've been paying attention."

He reeled in his line and headed upstream. Unbidden and unwanted, images of mine tunnels being dynamited crept into his thoughts. Like one little trout could spook all the other fish into hiding, maybe his crazy mine tunnel plan really would spook the bad guys. Maybe. Maybe he wasn't making much progress toward solving Arthur's murder, but at least he might catch one or two crooks as they relocated their packages of drugs. There was a splashing sound on the far side of the stream and he looked in time to see the ring of water. Another trout broke surfaced, and another.

All afternoon the air was moving uphill very, very lightly, almost imperceptibly. As the sun dropped behind the Front Range and the mountains began to cool, the air went calm. In a half hour or hour a very light little breeze would begin to move downstream. For thirty minutes or more, however, the flying insects would take advantage of the calm and land on the surface of the water to drink. And thus would be ignited the fly fisherman's favorite moment. An evening rise.

He returned to the cabin with four good brookies on his stringer and bits of a Scots ballad on his lips. He closed the door and put the fish in the sink in time to answer the irritating jangle of the telephone.

Down in the village, Jane was working what they called the "summer girl shift" at the telephone switchboard, glad to have the paycheck but nevertheless looking forward to shutting down the board at eight o'clock and going home to bed. From her corner window she saw John Smith approach the telephone exchange building, a brown envelope in his hand, casually strolling along like a man merely coming to pay his phone bill. She got off her stool and stood behind the counter as he came in.

"Help you?" she asked.

"Anybody around?" Smith asked.

"I'm all alone. Can I help you?"

"You already have. The boss appreciates how you tipped him like he asked, meaning how we got to learn there was a convention of Methodist ministers comin' to town. You heard 'em phone for the reservation, we got t' learn from you what hotel and we got the jump on the competition. Four loads! And on the deluxe tour, too! The boss says to give you this."

She knew what the envelope contained. A contribution to

her college fund. And no harm done. Two days after telling Mr. Smith about the ministers' hotel reservation the same news was in the local newspaper.

"Tell me," Smith went on, flashing what he hoped was a disarming smile, "you got any other tidbits for the ol' bus company, hmm?"

"No, not really. It's been real quiet this evening," Jane said. "Well, there was one odd message. Long distance from Denver. You know Miss Coteau? Eleanor's friend? She asked me to try and find Ranger McIntyre and left a message for him to meet her tomorrow because she was coming up to see him on his day off. She said… this is the odd part… she'd meet him with egg salad on her face at the lock lake. For a picnic. What's a lock lake?"

"I should know?' Smith replied.

"Well, when I passed him her message I asked about it and the ranger did say in Scotland a lake is called a 'loch' and I told him it's all she said anyway except she wasn't able to raise him on the phone. However, she asked me to connect her to Tiny's store out at Beaver Point. Maybe she thought he'd be there."

"Okay," Smith said. "Well, listen, thanks kid. You enjoy your cash. An' don't put it all in the piggy bank, neither. You go have yourself a ice cream soda, okay?"

"Sure, okay," she said.

"Good girl."

* * * * *

Dr. Hayward did not take the Smith's report graciously.

"Drive my car over to the bus barn. Fill the gas tank, and check the oil, and tire pressure," he growled.

In his mind's eye Hayward could imagine a scenic lake like the lochs in the *National Geographic* photos, probably high in the mountains, maybe above timberline, and there they'd be, the damn ranger and Vi. Close to one another. Alone. Laughing. Maybe she'd be lying on a blanket beside the lake and she'd be on her stomach and have one foot in the air, kind of dangling her shoe from her toes maybe, and there'd be a little breeze moving her hair. Drinking wine, too, probably. Probably she'd be feeling carefree and happy. She'd take off her shoes and stockings and wade in the cold water. Then lie down again, this time on her back, letting the sun warm her legs, letting him kiss her.

Hayward grumbled his way through a supper of beef and beans. Afterward he went to his basement to make certain his walking staff was in good working condition. And to polish his binoculars.

On the same evening, as it happened, Ranger McIntyre was also polishing the lenses on a pair of binoculars. A new pair, supplied by the government to replace his old army field glasses. Half the size and half the weight of field glasses, the new ones would no doubt be with him more of the time.

Jane labeled Vi's phone message "kinda odd" but McIntyre knew immediately what the words meant. As Mister Conan Doyle would write, it was "elementary, Watson." At the very beginning of their friendship Vi Coteau told McIntyre about her three weaknesses: one she kept secret, one was for nonpareil candies, and the third was for egg salad sandwiches. To her great delight the three hundred pound owner of Tiny's Store & Delicatessen at Beaver Point made mouth-watering egg salad sandwiches. Baked his own bread, mixed his own mayonnaise, collected fresh eggs from his own chickens. It didn't take much deduction on McIntyre's part to realize Vi intended to obtain a picnic lunch at Tiny's.

As for the "lock lake"—it was the site of their very first picnic. One particular road in Rocky Mountain National Park passes through a certain stretch where the forest is especially dense and shadowed. The trees grow close, hiding a seldom-used side road most travelers drive by without noticing. Even if they do notice it, and venture to follow it, about two car lengths from the main road they find a sturdy locked gate and an official government NO TRESPASSING sign with the information "Domestic water supply, no fishing or boating."

For their picnic, McIntyre unlocked the gate one very warm mountain day, locked it again behind Vi Coteau's sporty Marmon convertible, and they drove into the forest. The road, if two overgrown wheel ruts could be called a road, led on through the trees. Vi drove slowly and cautiously lest tree branches might scrape her paint job. There appeared an opening of bright daylight at the end of the shadowed corridor; in a moment they broke out into a mountain meadow where a little creek meandered into an idyllic, beautiful, nameless and quiet small lake. To the park service it was only a water supply for a distant campground. To the ranger it was a private picnic spot. Vi called the place "the locked lake."

Knowing her as he did, the ranger figured she would be there ahead of him, waiting at the gate. With a picnic hamper. What she might be planning to do after their picnic lunch, God only knew.

But, McIntyre was thinking, *if God knows, we'd probably better hope He isn't watching.*

Chapter Eleven

Rusticus interuptus

"What's wrong?" Vi asked. "You look worried."

In the ancient code language of the human female, "what's wrong?" actually means "You are not paying attention to me and you'd better have a darn good excuse." The standard male-talk response, "oh, nothing," may be interpreted as his way of saying "I'm not sure why I'm thinking what I'm thinking but it seems awful complicated and I don't understand it myself. I'm being quiet so I don't end up sounding stupid."

"Oh, nothing," McIntyre replied. "Why don't I grab the picnic basket and you bring the car robe. There's a nice flat, dry spot over here. Unless you'd rather sit in the shade."

"C'mon, silly ranger," she said, folding the car robe over her arm and following him along the shore of the pond. "Out with it. What's put the extra crease on your scowly brow, huh?"

"Nothing, really. Well, I stopped at the entrance station, wanted to tell the temp where I'd be in case of emergency. I was in a hurry to be here by noon. There were two men getting into their car. They were wearing suits. I'd swear at least one of them had a bulge under his coat, like he was wearing a shoulder holster. I didn't have time to follow them, and besides, I wasn't in uniform."

"Feds," she said.

"Feds?" he replied.

"You didn't think you were investigating the dope racket and the New Mountain strong-arm boys all on your own, did you?"

"I thought I was investigating to find out who shot Arthur Ogg. And the other two victims."

"Yes, you are. However, in the process you've succeeded in making the dope runners nervous. And also my spooky admirer, our friend the gunsmith."

"The two heavies carrying armpit cannons into the park, they're feds?"

"Eleanor and I have been in touch with my former boss at the bureau—he's been doing a lot of secret service work—and believe me, the federal agents are very, very interested in this hypothetical drug cache. Not to mention the possible link back to our bent Senator Speckle. They told me a couple of agents would be scouting the terrain this week. If your little trick works, the mine tunnel caper, I mean, they'll probably ask you to set up a roadblock at the top of Fall River road and help them figure out the best spot for scooping the bad guys into their net."

"Holy cow," McIntyre said.

"Indeed," she answered, spreading the car robe on the grass. "Now come sit down and let me tell you what's bothering my own little mind."

"Bothering you?" he said. "Something bothering you?"

"You know—Eleanor once said you can trail a field mouse across a parking lot. And Jamie told me, and I quote, you can follow a deer fly through a chokecherry thicket. So why can't you ever seem to detect it when there's concern in a woman's face?"

"I, uh… because I'm distracted? By how pretty the face is?

Maybe?"

"Horsefeathers, maybe?" she suggested. "But let me tell you why my pretty face has a serious look to it. I have to come right out with it. I'm thinking about the other woman. The one who died in the car accident. You know, before we met each other? You were in love with her."

"Yes," he said.

"I'll go ahead and blurt out what's bothering me. I need to know if you two came here. What I mean is, was this little lake a special place for the both of you? I'd really like you to tell me. It's beautiful. And private. And I love it. But if there's memories here for you… well, it would bother me."

"Sure," McIntyre said "I get it. And yes, we came here. Twice. One time to show it to her. We walked around the lake, followed the creek back into the forest, talked and talked. The second time we came here, I was trying to teach her how to cast a fly rod. And we ate lunch here, but it was one I'd packed by myself. Turned out she didn't care for venison sandwiches, even with horseradish on them."

"Ugh," Vi said.

"We made an arrangement, though," he continued. "We both assumed she'd be moving to the city because she wanted to go into nurse training, or open her own art gallery, have a career besides being a housewife. And we knew I might be offered a chance to transfer to another park, or I might want to change careers altogether. We came up with an agreement. We'd try not to have anything be 'ours'. Not 'our song' or 'our picnic spot' or 'our table' at the Pioneer Inn. If and when it came time to go our separate ways, we agreed there should be as little sentimental joint ownership as possible. Yes, she was here at no-name pond, but no, it wasn't our special place. Satisfied? Can we open the picnic hamper?"

Tiny's picnic assortment included bottles of root beer. Vi went to her car and returned with a bottle of wine instead.

"*Vin ordinaire*," she smiled. "French table wine. Too bad we don't have a table."

He laughed. It was a little laugh, not much of a laugh at all, but the first one in several days.

"We can't serve it at room temperature, either," he quipped. "Don't have a room."

She didn't laugh, but she did smile. And as they ate and drank, using squares of waxed wrapping paper for plates, and paper cups for the wine, they gazed at the mountains, and forest, and reflections of the sky and clouds in the pond. They reminisced about other picnics. Such as the winter picnic at the mine tunnel where they'd built a fire against the rock face, or the other winter picnic in the sunroom of a remote, shuttered lodge, or the time they shared his tent in a small meadow far to the north.

"You showed up unexpectedly and caught me washing myself in the creek," she laughed. "Boy, was your face red! I was in my chemise, remember?"

"Hard to forget," he confessed.

"I bet you'd blush if I said I'd love to go skinny dipping in this pond!" she teased.

"Sure. I'd blush. I'd also arrest you," he added. "Like the sign says, it's a water supply. For a campground. They don't want people bathing in it."

"Pooh," she said, biting a potato chip in half in mock annoyance.

"Let's talk about Hayward," he suggested. "And Smith."

Vi finished her wine and sprawled on her back with her arms reaching toward him.

"Let's talk about you kissing me," she countered.

* * * * *

They lay side by side on the car robe, nearly as relaxed and contented as two people could ever be. The original idea, to find a private place to make a serious, uninterrupted review of the facts in the case, seemed to have lost importance.

"Those clouds," Vi Coteau said, pointing skyward where a few cotton puff clouds drifted aimlessly.

"What about them?" McIntyre asked, shading his eyes to look.

"They don't look like anything. Part of a picnic ought to be looking at clouds and telling each other they look like puppies, or dragons, or lion heads or sheep. But those clouds don't look like anything."

"It's 'cause they're over the national park. Those are government clouds. The NPS mission is to protect and preserve national parks for all future generations. Clouds are required to maintain a natural shape at all times."

The ranger rolled over onto his stomach and extended his arms in a spread eagle.

"What are you doing?" asked Vi, also turning over on the robe.

"I'm languoring," he said. "Lying here in languor. I read about it in a dime novel somebody left at a campground. The hero ate a good meal and went into languor."

"That's not languor," Vi said. "What you're doing is languishing. Look, watch me. I'll show you what languor looks like."

He watched her going through various languorous poses, and he laughed.

"You don't know the first thing about languor," he teased. "What you're doing there is lingering, like when it's your day off and you ought to climb out of bed but you linger. I bet you look like a lazy cat when you linger in bed, I bet."

"Silly ranger," she said. "Personally, I bet you'll never find out…"

She was interrupted by a splash in the lake behind them. More of a "sploop" sound than a splash.

"The trout are getting restless," she said. "Did you bring your fishing pole?"

"Fishing rod," he corrected. "But be quiet. Hush. Keep on languoring, but watch the tree line over there for signs of movement."

"Why?"

"I don't think the sploosh was a trout rising. Didn't sound like it. I think it was something hitting the water. I don't suppose it could be your feds playing games on us. Maybe they followed you up here and tossed a rock to surprise us? Maybe used a slingshot."

There came a second splash. McIntyre spotted the figure moving in the forest shadows.

"He's changing position," McIntyre whispered. "Make for your car! Now!"

The third shot came too late. Vi and the ranger, although both barefoot, crouched and sprinted for the shelter of the Marmon. The third shot smashed through the wicker picnic hamper, breaking a jar of pickles and badly wounding a Golden Delicious.

Vi reached into the drawer beneath the seat of her convertible and drew out her Colt Police Positive revolver.

"You ought to find yourself one of these," she told the ranger. "They're called 'a gun.' Can come in handy."

Ignoring the jibe about seldom carrying a pistol, he held out his hand for the gun.

"I think," she said, scanning the line of trees, "we've already established which of us is the better pistol shot. You go get your own gun."

"Air rifle again," McIntyre said. "No sound. Did you notice the interval between shots? He needed to pump it up each time. And... I think he was trying to hit me but not you. Low power, low velocity, undependable at a distance, danger of hitting the wrong person... small wonder his shots went wild... Oops! There he goes! Heading through the trees for the gate!"

Vi leveled her revolver and took the shot. The moving shape stopped momentarily and then hurried on through the trees.

"What was that for?" McIntyre said. "He was way too far away to hit him with a pistol."

"Incentive," she said. "I didn't think he was running fast enough."

They heard the automobile engine starting up, followed by a whine of clashing gears as the car backed up, turned around and sped away. Even if McIntyre had been wearing his boots it would have taken him time to start his pickup, then stop to open the gate. His Small Delights would never have the power to overtake the shooter's car.

Vi moved the basket and picked up the car robe, one corner damp with pickle juice.

"This is sure a great personal secret picnic spot," she said.

"Yeah," he agreed. "I'd guess he's been watching one of us. Probably you. Followed you out here, discovered what we were up to. Saw an opportunity to throw a scare into us, but didn't have time to go home for a real rifle. Had his poacher's air gun with him."

"The question is," Vi said, "who was it? And why?"

"He drove off in Hayward's car. Seems likely it was either him, or the man I figure to be his so-called 'silent partner' from the New Mountain outfit. My money's on Hayward since he's the one who follows you around. Reminds me of an egg-stealing weasel trailing a chicken. He's jealous of me, see? Probably because I'm good looking. Also, I think he'd like me out of the picture because he thinks it would stall the mine tunnel blasting project."

"When you're through telling me how good looking you are, fill me in on what else you've been thinking," Vi said.

She reached into the wounded picnic hamper and brought out a small, unharmed pie.

"Do you have any immediate plans?" she asked. "Anything to do with a nice single girl, a blanket, and wine?"

She didn't see a smile, but the mischievous glint in his eyes did not go unnoticed.

"Well," he said, "like I told Hayward the other day, I plan to apply for a mortgage loan and buy the little cottage next door to him. I'll fix up a corral and stable in the back yard for Brownie. Might even have the bedroom painted and prettied-up so when we're married…"

For a slim woman with small fists, Vi Coteau could put a bruise of surprising size on a man's shoulder muscle.

"I mean today, you moron," she said, setting down the pie in order to show him both fists clenched. "Or have you already forgotten somebody took a shot at us? What do we do at this particular moment?"

"Oh. Well. You wanted to go swimming in your birthday suit. I was thinking you could dive into the lake and search for those bullets."

"Phooey," she said. "You want them, you doff your own duds and jump in the lake. On second thought, don't. The sight of a naked ranger would make the trout die laughing. Besides, one slug went through the hamper. It should be right around here somewhere. C'mon, I found two forks. Let's sit down and have the pie. And share information, why we came here? Private, remember? The big bad sniper's gone, we're still alone, and I need something better to think about."

"What's the poem the Arabian guy wrote? 'A jug of wine, a piece of pie, and you…'"

"You want a bruise on your other arm? Tell me what's really on your professional tree cop mind, and what you really plan to do."

There's nothing like a few bites of tasty apple pie to trigger a serious, meditative mood and set a man's mind back on the track.

"Okay," McIntyre said after swallowing. "Mostly I'm concerned about Jamie. And Russ, too. They're upset, and rightly. I'm worried they might strike out on their own and get themselves in trouble. I need them both to be patient while I gather up more details, more evidence. They're only going about their duties and waiting because I told them I've got a plan, sort of, to trap the guy or guys who did the killing. It's why I've been looking at footprints and gas cans and crutch tips."

"Sounds to me like you're building a problem for yourself… hey!" Vi said abruptly. "Wait a minute! We didn't see any car, the one the sniper got away in. Why do you think it was Hayward's?"

"It was Hayward's. Same way I can tell when it's your coupe coming up the road. The sound of the engine. See, I've been living in the woods long enough…"

"…you've got moss behind your ears?"

"…I pay more attention to sounds than a city woman like you would. Even at the aerodrome with Uncle Sam's Flying Finest in France we learned to recognize whether an approaching airplane was a Nieuport, a Spad, a Sopwith, or a Folker."

"Watch your language," she said. "Okay, you recognized the sound of his sedan. So what? You can't arrest him, obviously."

"No. Important thing is one of them took a shot at me. It means Hayward's broken cover. This is good pie, by the way. Anyway, he's broken cover, he's showed his position. He's apt to be wary and nervous. Sooner or later he'll be nervous enough to make a mistake and show himself."

"Eleanor and I are hoping for the same thing in the case of Senator Speckle. In fact, according to Senator Blume, who doesn't want to be involved, Speckle has already become a little careless of late."

"Careless how?" McIntyre asked.

"Women and parties, mostly. When he first got elected he played the part of a family man, always showing up at ribbon cuttings with his wife and kids. But nobody's seen them with him lately. However, he has been seen with cute young flappers and good-time girls. Also, he used to hold quiet little dinners for business executives and politicians. Now he throws wild parties with jazz and dancing and imported champagne. According to rumor, even the anti-alcohol KKK zealots are upset with him. Like Senator Blume told Eleanor, it's as if Speckle has no interest in his own political future. Like he's inherited a fortune or made a killing in the stock market and has no worries about the future. He still does his wheeling and dealing in the senate and still schemes how to make himself more powerful, but they say most of his free time is taken up with carpe whoopee diem."

"You still think he's connected to the drug dealers?"

"Heck, yeah," Vi replied. "He's got a huge investment this national park bus monopoly, and he owns a share of a wholesale fruit and vegetable operation. You can't buy your way into those kinds of schemes with mere cash. Or even with bootleg booze. No, it takes drugs."

"Drugs?"

"It's the way of the world, Tim. Before the war a man might

save up some money, or inherit it, and buy into a small business and work hard to attract steady customers. But now it's all about greed. Buy stocks and bonds and your money will double in no time. Get a drug connection established and everyone you meet will see you as their ticket to the millionaire's club."

McIntyre raised his eyes to the high mountain peaks, beyond the man-made lake, past anything created by the hand of humans, up to the loftiest forested slopes and beyond to the jagged granite summits tipped with snow. To Vi Coteau it seemed as if he was listening to the unbroken silence.

"And people wonder why I'd rather live in a log cabin in the woods," he said.

"Maybe," Vi said, "if Speckle goes down, he'll take Hayward with him. Everything is starting to point to Hayward being one of Speckle's enforcers. No proof, but…"

"But it wouldn't make Jamie feel any better. Hayward having to leave town, or maybe going to prison, I mean. Not enough for Jamie."

"I know," she said.

"Well, we'd better pack up. Strangely enough, whenever I'm shot at it tends to spoil the picnic. Heck, even those little ants there are having more fun than us."

He pointed at the ant hill Vi avoided it when spreading out the car robe.

"I wonder why ants strip away all the grass around their mound?" McIntyre mused. "To clear the area for construction? What's really fascinating? Ants build a mound ten, twenty times the height of a single ant and do it one grain of sand at a time. One grain! There was an article in *National Geographic* about the pyramids in Egypt and this archaeologist was saying how nobody could figure out how the ancient Egyptians managed to stack up all those blocks of stone. But right here we've got an ant pyramid and they built it one tiny grain of sand at a time. Each ant brings one tiny piece."

"Nice," Vi said.

"Ants?" he said.

"No, silly. You. The way you can have huge, complicated issues on your mind and still be distracted by tiny little things like ants. Or bugs landing on a trout stream. I think if I ever married you it would be mostly to follow you around and see what you'd think up next."

"Marrying me would make you quite a change from going at life doing sixty miles per hour."

"Nothing wrong with a little speed," she smiled. " And change can be good for you."

"Don't let my Scottish ancestors hear you say it," he answered. "They even wore kilts to avoid wearing underwear that would need to be changed."

* * * * *

The following day found Ranger McIntyre in full uniform, tall boots polished, tunic brushed, flat hat set square on his head, striding toward the supervisor's office. Widow Mildred Small, shopping bag hanging from her arm, stopped him in mid-stride to invite him to come see her latest dry fly creations; Andy Schuel also stopped him, again, but only long enough to inform the ranger that it was a beautiful day, something the ranger was already aware of. Just as McIntyre came abreast of the post office he nearly strode into a collision with Dr. Hayward, who emerged from the building carrying a long, narrow box.

"Ranger McIntyre," Hayward said. "Good morning."

"Yes, it is," McIntyre agreed. "Looks like you've ordered a fishing rod."

He saw the glint in Hayward's eye. It reminded him of an illustration from a children's book, a picture of a sly fox confronting the naïve hare.

"Quite interesting, actually," Hayward said. "Quite interesting. Here, let's sit down and I'll open it. I'm eager to see if they live up to the seller's description. No, no. You've got time. Come, sit."

The postmistress, like store owners up and down the street, provided public seating benches outside her building. She did it primarily to keep village loiterers from standing and gossiping inside the limited confines of her patron lobby.

"Okay," McIntyre said. "I've got a minute or two. But I'm expected at the S.O. Busy day, busy day."

"Oh?"

Hayward unfolded a pocket knife to cut the string, but decided to first try untying the knots. He handed the open knife to McIntyre.

"Hold onto this a moment," he said. "I think I can slip the knots."

It was an ordinary folding knife, with one longer blade and two shorter ones, a black handle molded to look like bone. Turning it over in his hand, McIntyre noticed a little white powder in the hinge at the base of the longer blade, as if recently jabbed it into a tin of talcum powder or powdered sugar. Maybe a bit of talc found its way into his pocket.

The gunsmith methodically removed the string and wrapping paper from the long box.

"You were saying you had a busy day ahead of you," he said.

"Typical waste of time stuff," McIntyre replied, snapping the knife shut and handing it back. "They're bringing in an old lady—and would you believe it, a couple of character witnesses for her—to interview her about how she acquires feathers and fur from park birds and animals. She's the one who ties dry flies."

The ranger was fibbing. True, the widow Small was summoned to the S.O., but only to be asked to take on a couple of house guests. House guests who were actually federal agents.

"Widow Small," Hayward said. "Dry flies."

"Right," McIntyre said. "Ridiculous waste of an hour. I'm also supposed to meet with a politician from the state government and waste a couple more hours showing him how we've been blasting abandoned mine tunnels."

"I see. Ah! Look here! I knew this would interest you! They've sent me both sticks in one package! Let me take them out and show you, this longest one should be…"

He removed wrapping paper from a thick, lengthy, sturdy staff. Hayward made a close examination, running his fingers over every inch of the wood.

"Ash," he finally said. "Very strong. Fine. Unless I'm mistaken, or unless they've sent the wrong one, there should be a little surprise when I lift this lever. See it? Here in the upper part, almost invisible, embedded in the wood. Here, you hold the end cap."

Hayward removed the rubber tip, larger than the average crutch or cane tip, and gave it to McIntyre. The bottom of it showed two raised circles and a capital letter G.

"Gaynes Rubber Company," Hayward remarked, noticing McIntyre's interest in the object. "Tips, bumpers, chair leg protectors, excellent quality. Ah, I see how the stick works! Look, you press one end of the lever down, like this, and the other end of the lever pops up like a concealed trigger. Here we go."

Hayward worked the lever and three sharply pointed prongs emerged from the end of the walking stick, spreading apart as they came. Each prong featured a nasty-looking barb at the point.

Hayward laughed to see McIntyre's puzzled expression.

"A fishing spear," he said. "Let's say you're out hiking and you come upon a quiet bit of water and there are fish in it. Simply extend the prongs and presto! Fish for supper!"

The man's as cool as a cucumber, McIntyre thought. *Calmly sitting here showing me what he bought, when the last time he saw me he tried to shoot me. Or sent his pal to do it.*

The second walking stick, shorter but equally thick, turned out to contain three hidden glass tubes. The handle unscrewed and the tubes slid out. Each was fitted with a rubber stopper.

"According to the maker," Hayward said, "one could hide eight to ten ounces of brandy, or whiskey, in his walking stick. I mean, imagine if you were on a picnic with an attractive lady and wished to offer her a bit of alcoholic refreshment…"

McIntyre caught the allusion. Hayward was smug, full of self-confidence, very full of himself for openly telling the ranger how a walking stick need not be a walking stick at all, and then referring to a private picnic when he probably damn well knew about the one with Vi.

On the Thompson River, underneath the bridge at the High Drive crossing, there lived a lunker of a trout, a bold, smart old fish. Whenever McIntyre made a cast into the shadows of the bridge, the monster seemed to delight in taunting him. The fish would rise lazily toward the surface, let himself be seen, nudge McIntyre's dry fly with his nose, and drift down toward the river bottom again. This would happen several times, until with a loud splash of its tail to spook all the other trout the thing would be gone.

"Well," Hayward said, folding the wrapping paper and rolling up the string, "I do need to be getting on. Don't blow yourself up today! As for myself, I may go see if Miss Coteau would like to try a spot of spear fishing. Just to test this new gadget."

"Before you go," McIntyre replied, "and while we're talking

about weapons, you don't happen to know of anyone local who owns a rifle with a silencer, do you? Maybe you've been asked if you'd ream the bore of a gun and tap it to screw in a silencer?"

"No," the gunsmith said. "Probably illegal, anyway. Why do you ask?"

"A guy took a couple of shots at me and I didn't hear the report."

"Who was it, do you think? A poacher you once arrested?"

"Not sure. Brown sedan, slouch hat. Left footprints smaller than you or I would. You take what, a size eleven shoe?"

"And a half. But a brown sedan?"

"He got away in one. I only caught a glimpse of it, but I've found two other people who saw a brown Chevy on the main road, heading for town and going fast. One of them thought the driver looked like one of the New Mountain drivers but never knew his name. I think a couple of them use fictitious names anyhow. I mean, 'John Smith'? 'Joe Jones'? Whose leg do they think they're pulling?"

Hayward's nervousness was becoming obvious. He seemed anxious to end the conversation. Like the Ol' Lunker, McIntyre thought. Keep annoying a fish long enough and he'll attack the lure.

"Couldn't be John Smith," Hayward said. "He was here. He was showing me how to clear a blockage from my own car's fuel line. Nice chap. Friendly. Familiar with engines."

McIntyre hadn't told Hayward when the shooting incident took place. But instead of asking Hayward how he knew when it happened, he decided to cast his lure in a slightly different spot.

"I guess I need to go back and look for more footprints," McIntyre said. "It's funny what you find when you really look. There was a shooting at the Small Delights Lodge once, and guess what? I found the tree limb where the shooter steadied his

.303 rifle. Knocked bark off, see? Oh, wait a minute. I've still got your crutch tip here. But speaking of tracks and tips, it's kind of odd how they mold the bottom of it."

He handed the rubber cup to Hayward.

"What do you mean?" the gunsmith asked, looking at the bottom of the tip.

"Oh, I was just noticing the letter G molded into it. Meant to advertise the company, right? Shouldn't it be a symbol instead, one people would remember? Maybe a diamond or a crown or a star. But let's say you happen to notice where a man has been walking with a stick and left little pokey places in the dirt with a G in them. It wouldn't make you think of a company name starting with G, would it? It'd just be a plain and blurry letter. But anyway, I can't keep you here yakking. My supervisor's waiting for me. Need to arrange for more dynamite. And find out where the boss wants the boys to set off the next blast."

"Not near the village, I hope?"

"No, no. Probably do the one in Black Canyon next. The one on Longs Peak afterward. One of our rangers suggested the hole on Mount Chapin, above Fall River, but it's in solid rock and shallow, more like a cave. Not dangerous. And remote. There's no point in blasting an even bigger hole in the mountain. We'll leave it alone, along with the so-called 'haunted mine' on the other side of the valley."

The trout cautiously rose toward the surface, eyeing the dry fly.

"Oh?" Hayward said. "Haunted?"

"Supposedly. I've never seen it. It's way up a north-facing slope, in heavy timber. One old-timer said he stumbled across it and there was a moaning noise coming from inside. But nobody goes there. Hardly anybody even knows it's there. If we ever did decide to blast it closed, it'd be the last one on our list. Well, gotta go!"

And the ranger left the gunsmith standing on the sidewalk holding both of his clever walking sticks in one hand, looking at the incriminating letter G on the rubber tip he held in the other. He seemed to be thinking that he should warn Smith to do a better job next time.

Chapter Twelve
From a Free Meal to a Federal Case

Jane, the summer hire telephone operator, read the ranger a message written on a page from a pocket notebook. Folded in half, it was slipped under the door of the telephone exchange and was marked "Message for Ranger McIntyre." It looked like a man's handwriting.

Breakfast on me, it said, *Seven A.M. your usual place.*

Jane was a teenager who took her summer job seriously. A few minutes before six o'clock in the morning she unlocked the door, found the note, opened the switchboard, and rang up Ranger McIntyre at his Fall River cabin. Being one of several girls with a crush on the handsome bachelor ranger, her voice quivered a little as she apologized for waking him. But no, he said, he had been up for over an hour. Starting to think about breakfast, in fact.

McIntyre was only too happy to abandon his planned breakfast of fried corn meal mush, syrup, and sausages. He donned his tunic, boots, and hat, and headed for town.

By seven o'clock he was seated at his favorite table, drinking in the magnificent vista of the mountain peaks washed in brilliant morning sunshine and gazing into the translucent depth of a glass of chilled orange juice. It was a rare treat, as fresh oranges seldom found their way to Colorado's high country. He gave his food order to Connie, although she already knew what it would be. One plate of pancakes heavy enough to ballast a two-masted schooner, with syrup, unless waffles were available. Then he'd have those, and one large plate of eggs over easy, the runny yolks contained with a surround of bacon slices as thick as a man's belt.

"And a couple of those sausages," he added.

The tall man in the double-breasted suit who entered the Pioneer Inn looked all around the dining room, nodded to Connie, and walked directly to McIntyre's window table.

"Mind if I join you?" he said. "This table has a great view of the mountains."

"Help yourself," the ranger replied, pointing to a chair.

"Helluva morning, huh?" the stranger continued. "Awfully quiet. And mountain air! Pure enough you're not aware you're breathing it."

Connie came with the coffee decanter and cups. The stranger ordered the day's special, a steaming bowl of oatmeal with fresh strawberries, brown sugar, fresh cream, accompanied by thick toast with locally made chokecherry jelly.

"Better than the Holy Wall café, huh?" McIntyre asked.

His allusion was to a crowded, greasy café in the shadow of one of Denver's downtown churches, a place frequented by workers in the federal building because it was nearby, not because the food was any good.

"I guess you've made me, if you know the Holy Wall cafe," the stranger smiled, sipping his coffee. "Coteau said you were clever that way."

"Tailored suit, snap brim hat, shoulder holster bulge. And an expense account. Gotta be a fed."

The point of their meeting, federal agent Will Sutter told McIntyre, was to see whether the park service and the federal drug and alcohol control bureau could coordinate their efforts with regard to the New Mountain Stage outfit.

"So far we've elected to leave them alone since the only drug traffic tied to them has been among Denver's elite. Mostly it's stuff supplied for a social gathering or used as payment for political favors. But what's changed is there's been two murders and an attempted murder of a government officer—meaning you, y'understand—so my partner and I are going to be asking questions and generally making the bad guys nervous until, maybe, one of them decides he'd be better off by cooperating with us. Might eventually help us catch a few of them with their hands in the cookie jar."

"What do you figure's in the cookie jar?" McIntyre asked, forking a chunk of sausage into a puddle of syrup.

"How the hell can you eat a half ton of breakfast and still function all day?" Sutter said in reply. "Amazing. Anyway, our sources out of New York and Chicago tell us one of your state politicos and more than one of the charming KKK elites have been getting shipments of dope. Heroin, cocaine. The Klan likes to brag about 'purifying' society, but they've found out that drugs are more effective than money when it comes to bribery. We think the stash is probably in fairly small packages, the kind you could carry in a lunchbox or in the pocket of your overalls. Or in your case, a fishing creel."

"You seem to know a lot about me," McIntyre said.

"Let's say my wife and Vi Coteau occasionally meet for lunch. Anyway, we think the dope distributors are stockpiling the stuff. And in this area right here. It might even be a major stash. The eastern gangs are moving, see, expanding their territories westward. Anybody—probably the senator's at the center of it—with a stockpile halfway between the east coast and the west coast stands to make a million bucks."

McIntyre excused himself a moment and came back with one of the national park maps Connie kept at the cash register for tourists. Opening it, he showed Sutter the location of the old Moraine Park mine tunnel, the location of the one with a new, heavy, padlocked door.

"Interesting," Sutter agreed. "Remote, safe, dry. Probably they keep a sentinel posted to watch it. But I see no way to tie it to any one person. In fact, maybe a guy with no drug connection at all got hold of it legitimately—bought the original mineral claim, maybe—and put the door on it so as not to be sued in case a hiker might wander in and get injured. Nah, raiding your mine tunnel wouldn't help our case any. We need a way to catch somebody important, carrying the stuff in or out of there. But let's talk about your attempted murder. I've got information to share with you."

"Could we call it an incident, or anything other than attempted murder? Murder has a final sound to it."

"Okay. Incident. There's a vacant house next to the one owned by the gunsmith, Hayward…"

"I know the place," McIntyre said.

"There's four feds in town. Me and my partner took a room at the widow Small's place. Besides us there's two more. Man and woman. They're masquerading as a married couple, a professor collecting local anecdotes for a book about F. O. Stanley and a biologist interested in snakes. They persuaded the owner of the house next to Hayward's to rent it to them for two months, see? They're keeping an eye on Hayward. They put a tap on his phone line, too. The other evening they heard him giving hell to some other party for 'missing the damn tree cop.' I assume it was you. And yelled 'nearly wrecking my car to boot' which I take to mean he'd loaned the sniper his sedan. And there's more: the agents heard enough to be certain it was one of them—Hayward or the man on the other end of the line—who took the shots at the jitney driver, the one who went off the road and died."

"Arthur Ogg," McIntyre said. "It fits. But four agents on one case? Seems like two would be enough."

"You can lay that to your little friend in the pigtails. The barber's kid, Gala Book?"

"What's she done? Started printing her own money?"

"Nah. Me and my partner went in for a haircut. Mostly we wanted to see how good a contact the barber might turn out to be. Little Gala was in the shop. She made my partner right away, said 'you're a policeman, aren't you?' She'd caught a glimpse of his weapon, and asked if it was a .45 auto."

"She's nosy, for sure," McIntyre agreed.

"Good thing. She went skipping out of the shop and came back with a small paper sack. Empty .45 casings. Said she'd been scrounging them and maybe we'd be interested in buying them. To reload, see. The way she pitched it to us, we could save the government a penny per bullet by reloading and she'd only charge us half a cent. Turns out she picked them up…"

"Let me guess," the ranger said. "South of town, on the side of Prospect Mountain, where the New Mountain drivers practice with their Thompson."

"Bingo. We sent the shells to Denver, to our weapons expert, who sent me a telegram yesterday. The marks left by the firing pin, and by the extractor, match up with brass found at a murder scene on Market Street. Our chief of bureau told us to turn up the heat on the whole tour bus operation. One Tommy gun isn't much of a connection, but it's enough to start asking questions. I'd love to catch those hoodlums with drugs on 'em. At their trial we'd make the murder connection, see?"

"Speaking for the national park service," McIntyre said, "we suspect they're moving drugs with the buses. The locked mine could probably be their cache. We could raid it, sure, but all we'd net would be a hole in the mountain and a bunch of dope in it. Maybe we'd arrest one thug if he was standing sentinel, possibly get him for carrying a gun inside the park. So instead of organizing a raid on the cache we came up with the blasting idea."

McIntyre went on to describe how a two-man team was dynamiting old abandoned mine tunnels, using a random pattern so the New Mountain thugs wouldn't be able to anticipate the next tunnel on the list.

"We keep a map of it at the S.O.," he said, "and detective Pedersen keeps the New Mountain boys informed. They think she's their spy, see? They think she comes to the office on a phony pretext and gets a peek at the map. She tells them the next couple of mines we're going to blast. They trust her. They figure she's in it to get even with the park service for firing her and also make herself a share of the dope money."

"Right," Sutter agreed. "Your plan seemed a little too dramatic at first, but we're in touch with Pedersen. We've already worked out a way for her to alert us if the gang starts to make a sizable shipment. Like, for instance, if they should clean out the cache and put all the dope on a bus or truck. Problem is, she'll only have one shot at it. She'll need to tip us the word, then steer clear of them, and quick."

"As it happens," McIntyre said, "I've got a lookout of my own, too. On a ridge above Moraine Park. A couple of the New Mountain drivers are customers for his product, but he wants them and their dope gone. He'll get in touch with me if they begin a move."

"You're talking about your moonshiner pal, Counter," the fed said. "We know all about him."

* * * * *

It wasn't Leon Counter, however, but rather two young assistant rangers who lay in hiding halfway up the Fall River road, using binoculars to watch the other side of the valley. There was plenty of moonlight and the air was cold and still. So still was the air, in fact, they could occasionally hear groaning noises and cusswords coming from the old mine as the criminals struggled with heavy, rough timbers.

"Ooops!" Russ Frame whispered to Jamie. "I just saw the little guy trip on a rock and drop his end. He don't look too happy in his work!"

Ranger Frame was correct. Ladro Topo was not at all happy to be lugging the uphill end of a heavy mine timber. He felt shooting pains in his back, a blister on one foot, and multiple slivers in his palms. Antonio was berating him for slipping and dropping his end of the timber. Ladro grunted loudly as he picked it up to resume the uphill struggle. He silently thanked various deities for making it the last of the long, heavy timbers. Two more trips, one to lug the thick door up the hill and one more to bring the hardware. Then he could enjoy a stiff drink and a good night's sleep. Hauling lumber and building a door frame in the dead of night, in a haunted freezing canyon, was not his idea of a good time even if it meant a share of the drug money once the new cache was finished.

It was Antonio's turn to complain when he rammed his head into a protruding pine branch, causing him to drop the end of the timber on his toe.

"The guy cusses real good," Ranger Ogg whispered.

"Is even cussing in English?" Ranger Frame whispered back.

"Dunno. But we've seen enough. Let's slip back to the truck and head for the barracks."

During the following evenings the two young rangers, sometimes including Assistant Ranger Don Post, took turns using their off-duty hours to monitor the old mine tunnel on Fall River. At times it was entertaining to lie there and watch while the city thugs hauled planks and timbers up the heavily forested mountainside, using different routes each time. They tried hauling the door, but when it proved too heavy and awkward they were forced to take it apart and carry a piece at a time.

"Trying hard not to leave a trail," Post whispered. "I bet they don't realize they're leaving a dozen tracks all leading to the same place."

Finally all activity ceased. For two evenings in a row, Dan and Russ arrived in the early twilight hours and saw no signs of movement. Cautiously, rifles in hand, they made their way down the hillside, crossed the road, found a place to cross Fall River, and climbed up the wooded slope to the mine tunnel. All they found was a thick door set into a crudely fashioned framework, hidden behind a screen of freshly cut spruce branches.

"Can you believe it?" Russ said. "What'd they do, figure those branches would stay green? When they dry out it'll turn into a brown pile and stick out on the hillside like a sore thumb."

"How do you like their sign?" Dan asked.

The hand-lettered sign on the door said STAY OUT EXTREAM DANGEROUS. The heavy iron hasp below the sign was secured with an equally husky padlock, however, the hasp was installed with the screws visible.

"Should we go back to the truck for a screwdriver, you think?"

Dan said.

"Nah. There's nothin' in there 'cept an empty hole. Let's head on down. We can stop off at Fall River Station and tell Tim how the so-called bus drivers have got their cache finished."

"I sure hope he finds out who shot Arthur Ogg. And soon," Dan said while they were on their way down the mountain. "Jamie doesn't say much about it, but you can tell he's startin' to strain at the leash. If he finds out who the shooter was there's no tellin' what he'll do."

"I know what I'd do. But Tim'll figure it out," Russ replied. "Trouble is, the ranger's got a lot on his mind. Needs to get this whole drug problem straightened up, see about catching them with the stuff. And there's the dynamite project, people are asking questions about why the park is wasting money doing it. Oh, and a lady asked me the other day when we were going to hunt down this blue mist ghost of Fall River and get rid of it. Said she didn't feel safe driving up here."

"Speaking of ladies, what about his cute friend, the lady from Denver? I bet she's giving him stress about whether to marry her. Boy, I'd ask her to marry me in a second, believe me!"

"And do what? Move to Denver and apply for a job rangering at the city zoo?"

"Well, if our ranger wanted to marry anybody, he'd find a way to do it. Like he always says about jigsaw puzzles, real often it only takes finding the one piece to have it all make sense."

The New Mountain driver calling himself John Smith, or J.D. Smith, held to his own philosophy about rising higher in the organization. When he got started he was nothing but a money collector for the gang, but he soon saw how becoming friendly with the 'customers', instead of threatening them, could lead to better opportunities. When a deadbeat trucker offered him driving lessons in lieu of a couple of one-time payments, Smith took the deal. Learning to drive a heavy truck, or a bus, would put him ahead of the other boys in the strong-arm racket. They could collect payments, but he could collect payments and take over a shipment if the driver didn't pay. One or two risky deliveries of bootleg whiskey and he was "in" with the Jones Brothers. They needed a man like him for their 'tour bus' company.

Other drivers saw Eleanor Pedersen as someone to be avoided. It was best not to talk to her at all, in case you might accidentally give the ex-ranger information she shouldn't have. Smith, however, saw it the other way around: Eleanor might be the key to another door of opportunity. He was therefore disappointed when he suggested they take a long lunch hour, along with a bottle of wine, down by the river behind the bus barn. She politely turned him down.

"Sorry," Eleanor said, "but my roommate and I already planned to share our lunch today. We thought we'd meet at the little table you boys built behind the barn. Near the river."

He knew the place, all right. A bunch of creekside aspen for shade, a rustic table with benches, right against the barn wall so if a boss yelled for you while you was out there having a smoke, or takin' a little hit, you'd hear him. It was spitting distance from where they'd smashed the wall boards to let the light in.

He knew the place. When the two ladies arrived with all their chatter and laughing and sandwiches, John Smith was already sitting inside the barn. The gloomy corner smelled of burnt oil and charred wood, but it was nice and cool. More important, from the gloomy corner he could hear every word the women said.

"You and I never got a chance to talk," Eleanor was saying to Coteau, "I mean, I wasn't sure we should say anything real personal in front of Mrs. Spinney, but you never told me how the picnic with Tim McIntyre went."

"Let's say it was interrupted," Vi answered. Beginning with the gunshots and subsequent suspicion that the shooter was either Hayward or one of his goons, Vi described her afternoon with the ranger. As girls will do, she even went into minute and irrelevant details because she was, herself, re-living the romantic moment.

"I wore my pale blue frock, the one with the dark navy ribbon around the hips. Well, it's not important. Oh, but he more or less suggested I take it off and go for a dip in the lake!"

"He didn't!"

"Indeedy-o he did," Vi said. "It cooled him down on the idea when I suggested he strip and go first. Let's see, there was also the ant pile. He got very philosophical about the ants and how they build mounds one grain of sand at a time."

She went on to tell Eleanor about McIntyre's philosophical observation about ants. Eleanor laughed because McIntyre's ants had triggered a memory for her.

"Say," Eleanor said, "when you were old enough to be interested in boys, did you ever go to a party where they played the peanut and greyhound game? My goodness it was fun, searching the lawn for peanuts. And one time... maybe you read about it in the papers... there was this librarian in Denver? She needed to move all the books, thousands of them, from one building to another one. A new building. Well, they weren't budgeted for it. She and a friend began driving the books to the new building, one box at a time. But one day they came up with a brilliant idea. They got the newspaper to run a story about their problem, and in it they urged all citizens to come and check out four or five volumes from the old library, then return them to the new one. Would you believe it, inside of a month almost all the books migrated to the new location! People even thought it a great lark, bragging to one another how many library books they checked out and returned."

John Smith listened with interest. The lady ex-ranger's story, it could be the key to his boss's problem. Yeah, she'd dropped it right into his lap! This was going to earn him a share of the dope, maybe enough cocaine to set himself up in a distribution racket of his own. "Yeah," he imagined himself telling the boss, "it's a slick idea for sure but I don't want no pay raise. I'd rather have, say, maybe a brick of the product. Or half of one. If my idea works, that is. Otherwise all bets are off."

No more doing Hayward's dirty work. Snooty bastard.

He was supposed to go to Hayward's place right after work for more target practice with the hiking staff air gun. But Smith changed plans. After the other drivers locked up and went to supper, he'd stay behind and talk to the boss. It was time to show them he was an idea man, not just a foot soldier in the gang. In his mind was the germ of a scheme to move the drugs, and it was dead certain to move him a few rungs up the ladder. It was time to make his move.

Evening once again in the mountain village.

Supper dishes were washed and dried and put away. Parents gave kids permission to go out in the streets to play stickball, roll hoops, play jacks, or run around doing hide-and-seek. Cribbage boards and checker boards were brought out. In a few cottages there were villagers leaning near their Zenith or Westinghouse radios to listen to the Denver radio station. All up and down the sidewalks, through the streets, up the hill to houses, the long twilight brought a sense of timelessness, a pending quiet calm as if, if people moved very slowly and made little noise the pine-scented evening would go on and on and the darkness would be held at bay.

Vi Coteau and her friend Eleanor were sitting on Mrs. Spinney's porch, Vi in the rocking chair, Eleanor on the porch swing, waiting for Ranger McIntyre.

"They're careful not to let me hear anything," Eleanor was saying. "They put on an act like they believe my cover story, all the while keeping their eye on me. I'm supposed to see the whole operation as legit. But it's awful obvious how this tunnel-closing scheme of your ranger has 'em nervous. Plus, the sneaky deliveries to their Moraine Park cache, they've all but quit doing it. Smith still occasionally rides with me on my bus, acting like a supervisor. I think he's looking haggard here of late. Edgy, see?"

"Sure," Vi replied. "Let's not push it, though. Not take any chances. I think McIntyre might be right—don't ever tell him I said that!—if we can make the bunch nervous enough and desperate enough, it's real possible the Denver ring leaders will hear about it and send an enforcer to see what's going on with their investment. McIntyre thinks the senator himself might come. Tim says the senator reminds him of a dominant buck deer in mating season, trotting everywhere to keep an eye on all the does even if he doesn't want to mate with them."

"Sounds like one of Tim's homey similes, for sure," Eleanor agreed. "I wonder how he'd survive in the city with only squirrels and house pets to compare people to. The darn guy's got more animal stories than the *Outdoor Life* magazine."

"Maybe that's where he gets them," Vi suggested. "But speaking of our dear ranger, here he comes."

"Did you say 'dear' ranger, or 'deer' ranger?" Eleanor asked.

McIntyre parked his Small Delights, shut off the engine, and wondered what the two women were giggling about. Vi was all smile and charm, coming down the porch steps to meet him.

"Should we drive," McIntyre said, "or walk?"

"Let's walk. Such a beautiful evening."

Arm in arm, the two strolled into the next street. The village could boast of no more than three real streets, four if one counted the dirt track generally referred to as "the alley." It would become a street once the city fathers got around to naming it.

While they appeared to be meandering in the direction of the vacant house next door to Hayward's cottage, they concocted a simple plot and agreed how to play the scene.

Act One: McIntyre gallantly opens the garden gate for the lady.

"What about the federal agents?" Vi whispered.

"I already checked. One's at the barber shop playing chess. The other one said he'd be in the basement fiddling with their new two-way radio."

"It looks like Hayward's home," Vi said. She nodded very slightly to indicate the kitchen window at the rear of Hayward's cottage. The light was on.

"What the hell… I mean, what the heck kind of curtains are those?" McIntyre whispered.

"Café curtains. They hide what you're doing, but you can see out over them."

"What kind of real man would have café curtains?" McIntyre said.

"Never mind," she said, taking his arm. "Tell me, what are these bushes? We're supposed to be a loving couple looking at a house we intend to buy, remember."

"Should I kiss you?" he said.

"Only if you want me to step on your foot. Pretend to explain this bush. Then make it seem like you want me to look at a rock or a patch of dirt or whatever."

"Okay. My goodness, look at the rose bush there. Not like you city folk have. This is a wild rose. Smaller little flowers, lots of thorns. And next to it," he said, pointing elaborately, "is what most people call a wild currant. It has a kind of berry fruit in the fall. You can eat them, after they turn deep purple, but they're mostly seed."

She gripped his arm with dramatic affection, gazed up into his face admiringly, and said three little words.

"Isn't that rhubarb?"

"Yep. Locals call it pie plant. You find it in a lot of old mining towns especially. Most cabins have it growing wild. Fruit trees don't thrive up here in the mountains, but pie plant does real well, after it's started, and you can use it for pie or jam. You can even make wine out of it."

Vi continued to hug his arm as they strolled about the property. She chattered on about picket fences and window awnings, about flagstone walkways and vegetable beds, about whether the lawn was large enough for croquet. She kissed him, twice, pecking him on the cheek the way girls in love do in the moving pictures. All the while, both she and McIntyre were fully aware of Hayward watching from behind his café curtains. He was watching and he was fuming. His plans did not include McIntyre. His plan was to have the lovely Vi Coteau living alone next door where he could watch. Where he could drop in for tea, or ask her to join him for supper. His wealth was certain to increase dramatically, once the Denver boss decided it was time to liquidate the dope stockpile, and with enough wealth and a beautiful woman at his beck and call he would be living a life many men would kill for.

Kill for.

Two days later, Agent Will Sutter contacted Ranger McIntyre. Something must have happened, he said, and it seems to have upset the drug gang's apple cart.

"That oily character, the New Mountain driver named John Smith? He was over at Hayward's place again," Sutter said. "Usually he heads for the basement. You can hear him slam the basement door. Sometimes there's gunshots, like he's practicing with a pistol, maybe. Anyway, the last time he was there he and Hayward got into a helluva ruckus, a real brouhaha. Our associates heard Smith yell 'No!' four or five times, and once Smith shouted he was done doing dirty work. He told Hayward—they heard him 'cause he'd opened the back door and was about to stomp out of the place—told Hayward to damn well do it himself."

"Any idea what?"

"Couldn't tell. But it was like Hayward told him to do take a large risk, and he was saying he'd done enough already. Oh, and he yelled he meant to leave and said first he'd take his share, but Hayward said he couldn't."

"Probably a share of the drugs," McIntyre said.

"Probably. What about the risky job?"

"Well, if Coteau's plan worked, Hayward probably asked Smith to kill me."

"So… Coteau wants you dead?"

"You'd think so, wouldn't you?" McIntyre replied. "I sure do present complications to her free and modern independent professional woman lifestyle. Strictly between you, me, and the doorpost, I get a kick out of it."

"You mean you sometimes toy with her affections? Vi Coteau, the lady with the concealed pistol?"

"Yeah."

"Boy," the agent said. "And here I was, thinking being a g-man was dangerous."

Chapter Thirteen
Mr. Smith, A Blonde, and McIntyre's Complicated Theory

Supervisor "Nick" Nicholson explained that the Mesa Verde national park was in need of experienced rangers, following his explanation by suggesting that Ranger McIntyre might want to stop hanging around the village and spend time actually patrolling his district. Taking the hint, wearing his full official uniform and driving the official pickup truck, McIntyre went about checking campgrounds and talking with tourists. As an added measure of job security he made certain his assistants were also taking care of park business.

Strictly not by accident, lunch hour found him pulling up in front of Tiny's store at Beaver Point. And by arrangement, not accident, there sat the bright yellow Marmon convertible owned by one Miss Vi Coteau.

"We've got a delicate question to ask you, Tiny," McIntyre began after seating himself next to Vi in one of the two booths at the back of the store.

Tiny shoehorned his three hundred pounds into the opposite

side. The sight of the couple enjoying his sandwiches made him grin with genuine delight.

"You want me to cater your wedding reception!" Tiny said. "Consider it done! I wonder if I could make an egg salad wedding cake in Miss Coteau's honor?"

"You're very kind," Vi said, reaching across to pat Tiny's huge hand, "but this is about a telephone call."

"Oh?"

"We don't mean to pry into your business," McIntyre said. "But it might have to do with this drug case. We learned about it from little Gala Book. The other day she was practicing her detective snooping—trying to emulate Vi—and Gala came up with two interesting points of information. She charged me for them, by the way. A dime apiece, or two for a quarter. She's made friends with the summer switchboard girl, Jane, who flirts with the young repairman, who tries to impress Jane by letting Gala collect scraps and bits of discarded copper wire. It makes him look like a kind fella who loves kids, see. Well, during their chat Jane answered and transferred a couple of long distance calls from Denver, plugging wires into the board and talking into the mouthpiece. Gala overheard Jane connecting one of those Denver calls to you. And here's the part we're curious about. Jane remarked to Gala that the caller was the same as the one Mr. Smith phoned a few times previously. You know, a kind of 'hmm what a coincidence' kind of remark."

"Sure," Tiny said. "Miss Coteau, would you care for a nice crisp dill pickle with your sandwich? A new batch came in."

"Thank you, but I don't think I will."

Tim McIntyre, she thought, has enough on his mind without watching me bite into a dill pickle.

"Okay. Well, it's simple," Tiny went on. "Another catering job. A secretary of a senator—a real senator, mind you!—phoned me right out of the blue. Said she got my name from the New Mountain Stage Company. The senator wants packed picnics for fourteen people, everything wrapped in butcher paper, unlabeled, in separate paper bags."

"When?" McIntyre asked.

"They're going to let me know. Meanwhile I've ordered extra heads of lettuce and a couple of hams. Why?"

"Did they say who the picnic was for?"

"Oh, sure. Let's see. It's called the Ladies Hiking Club or Hiking Women or some such thing. A group of females, anyway, with plans to go for a day hike in the park. I think... I got the idea... this senator is coming along but as a secret guest, see? I'm not supposed to know it. Don't tell anyone I told you."

"Secret guest?" McIntyre replied. "On a fresh air outing for wayward girls? It sounds like a publicity stunt. Why would he want it secret?"

"Hanky-panky with attractive young ladies?" Vi suggested. "If Speckle's the secret guest, he's got a reputation as a lech. In fact, women and liquor are his greatest weaknesses. Maybe he'll persuade the girls to hike to a lake for skinny dipping. For that you could arrest them!"

"Our lakes are way too cold for any bathing, nude or otherwise. But I wonder... Tiny, did the person on the phone mention liquid refreshment to go along with the picnic lunch? Did they order bottles of pop, root beer, anything wet?"

"Nope. I thought of that. Just sandwiches, salad, chips and stuff."

"Okay," the ranger said, "what if they're carrying their own drinks? Better still, what if this senator—we're assuming it's Speckle—brings a supply of liquor for the picnic? Could be wine, champagne, gin, even rum. What if we catch him with it in the park? Charge him with transporting liquor. Might not be enough for an arrest, but we could tell the newspaper about it."

"Let me see if I understand," Vi said. "You want to sneak around, spy on a senator, invade his privacy, maybe take covert photographs, try to catch him with his pants down or the cork out of a gin bottle, and tell it to the Denver newspapers."

"You don't think I should, huh?"

"No! I love it! Tiny, I'll try one of those pickles after all."

* * * * *

When she casually asked about John D. Smith, who had not been around the bus barn for several days, Eleanor learned he drove to Denver on some "personal business." On the day before his departure there was an altercation between him and the gunsmith, Dr. Hayward. And Hayward, according to the undercover feds using the rented cottage next door, was starting to look nervous and mentally preoccupied.

"Looks like things are about to get interesting," McIntyre said.

He was back on Mrs. Spinney's front porch sharing the evening with the three ladies. He was not sharing his ranger-size slab of apple pie.

"Maybe we've stirred things up," he continued. "Reminds me… "

"…of trout fishing?" Vi said oh, so very sweetly.

"Yeah. Last summer, on a real calm stretch of Fall River in the Beaver Meadows. I'd already caught my supper, so I decided to experiment. There was a hatch going on, mayflies all over the surface, and the trout were having a feeding frenzy. I thought I'd see whether I could spook them into hiding, see. I cut a long willow and stirred the water with the leafy end of it. Guess what happened?"

"Okay, I'll guess. The brookies dove for cover, the mayflies drifted on downstream, and you arrested yourself for cutting a government willow," Eleanor suggested. "Great story, ranger. Next you oughta tell Vi and Mrs. Spinney about the time you were playing a trout and you tripped and fell into an ant hill."

"You're a hoot, Pedersen," he replied. "No, those fish were frenzied to the point where they even attacked the willow branch. They…"

"Threw caution to the wind?" Vi Coteau suggested.

"Who coined that phrase?" Eleanor asked. "Shakespeare?"

"Aristophanes," Mrs. Spinney replied, "but he actually said 'throw fear to the wind.' He may not have spoken it, but he wrote it. In Greek, of course."

McIntyre scraped the last crumb from the pie plate and set the plate on the step next to him.

"Boy," he said, "a good storyteller doesn't have a chance with you women, does he?"

They laughed at him, but they'd seen his point. First it was Hayward acting nervous, then Smith acting mysteriously. Now the senator was coming in person and risking exposure of his connection to the New Mountain gang… tension seemed to be in the air because of McIntyre stirring things up with persistent questions. And dynamite. There was a difference, however: brook trout don't usually carry guns and kill people.

The next morning Ranger McIntyre was summoned to Supervisor Nicholson's office.

"Bad news, Tim," Nick said.

"I'm being transferred?" McIntyre said, turning his flat hat around and around in his hands. "But I'm doing the job alright. I've even kept up with the weekly paperwork. Well, the previous week's worth, anyway."

"No," Nick said. "It's not about your reports. It's about your boys Jamie and Russ. Our undercover married couple of feds took a hike up Roaring Fork the other day. They ran into Jamie and Russ fixing the old log bridge on the trail. They all recognized one another, of course, and stopped to chat awhile, and the woman agent happened to mention how their investigation led them to solid evidence about who shot Arthur Ogg. Jamie's dad."

"Oh, God!" McIntyre said.

"You said it. It's not her fault. She simply thought it would make him feel better to learn they were making headway on his dad's killer. But now that she's spilled the beans to Jamie I'm worried as hell. If your scheme succeeds in stirring up the suspected drug dealers, and Hayward, we'll need to move fast and move smooth. Our two young men could skewer the whole affair. Figure some way to rein in Jamie and Russ. Make certain they won't take a shot at the murderer and queer our whole drug trap. The feds are ready, it looks like this female hiking party is our chance, and we don't need a couple of mavericks with rifles out there looking for revenge. Got it?"

"Got it," McIntyre answered.

McIntyre ate lunch at his card table, searching for one or two pieces of his new jigsaw puzzle, the one or two bits needed to finish part of the picture. In a way he was rather hoping not to find them. The puzzle's border was finished, there were segments of puzzle already assembled, and when it was completed it would be over and done with. But he enjoyed the doing of it more than the finishing. Finishing left a little void, left a man looking around to find something more to do. Maybe glue the pieces together and hang it on the wall…

Lunch and puzzle were both interrupted by a temp who

scurried up the hill to tell him there was a call for him on the emergency telephone. McIntyre followed the kid back to the entrance station.

"Ranger McIntyre," he said to the mouthpiece.

"Counter." It was the moonshiner of Moraine Park.

"Problem?"

"Nuthin' urgent," Leon said. "But I figgered I'd better hike over t' your emergency phone and tip you off. They've moved another good-size packet of stuff. Same as before, a White bus come up the road. A while later it come back down. A rider on the back seat dropped somethin' out. Looked almost like a small brick wrapped in paper."

"And?"

"Guess what? While I'm watchin' your fancy-pants hiking dude, he popped outta the woods. The townie what wears scent you can smell a mile away? He gloms onto the package. Stuck it inta his haversack and hit the trail toward town."

"Good, thanks. See anything happening with the Fall River mine tunnel?"

"Nah. Not since they finished the door. They ain't been here for any more bottles of my product, neither. Personally, I got a theory. I got a theory they've tumbled to the fed agents and they're layin' low. Not movin' drugs, except for that one package. Not transportin' illegal liquor, nothin' because they know they got the agents watchin' 'em."

"Okay," McIntyre replied. "Leon, I owe you. Much appreciated."

"What y' can do for me is make dead certain your bomb squad don't blow up the old tunnel up behind my place. I got me more'n twenty gallons of product aging in there."

"Consider it safe," McIntyre said. "I'll tell everybody on the force where your stuff is and to leave it alone. I'll even put a notice in the newspaper."

"McIntyre," Leon said, "there's some things we don't make jokes about."

Private detective-*cum*-tour bus chauffeur Eleanor Pedersen was the next person to realize she was looking at a final piece of the puzzle. It came in the shape of a peroxide blonde doll with pneumatic breasts, a sporty type obsessed with her appearance and comfort. She came to the village a day early to locate—and secure—the best available hotel room. The other female hikers would arrive the following morning. Let them squabble over single and double rooms and closet space and bathrooms. She and Mister S. would be quite comfortably established.

She of the shining crimped hair and fashionable pumps did not give the hotel her real name, of course, and when she crossed the street, walking like a model coming down a runway, to inspect the tour bus establishment, she gave no name at all to Eleanor, who was in chauffeur uniform and cap, sitting in the driver's seat of the open touring bus parked outside the bus garage.

Eleanor was fiddling with the petrol mixture, trying to tune the engine's loud popping sound to a steady roar. When she became aware of the blonde standing there watching, however, Eleanor shut off the ignition.

"Good morning," Eleanor said, politely.

Looking the blonde over from pumps to hairdo, Eleanor was tempted to ask her what time the burlesque show was going to start, but she quenched the temptation.

"Well!" said the other. "A lady bus driver! Who'd have thought of it? How much does it pay, dear? And do you meet a great many wealthy gents this way? I'd imagine lots of your riders are rich, since it costs rather a wad for a gentleman to vacation in the mountains, take time from business and all. How are the tips? Good, I'd guess! Especially if a girl… except in a bus driver uniform, well, a girl couldn't actually show… anything… to get larger tips, I mean."

"Are you interested in taking one of our tours?" Eleanor asked, trying to ignore both the blonde's balcony and the term 'tips'."

"Tomorrow," peroxide replied. "Well, or maybe the day after. Anyway! A hiking group. We're being hosted by…"

The pause was as obvious as was her bosom.

"By a… let's say an important dignitary. He's providing an excursion for us, you see."

"What's the name of your group?" Eleanor asked. "We were told to expect you, to have a couple of buses ready, but there was confusion as to what the group was called."

"Well," the blonde stammered, "the, uh, ladies club for hiking. Girl mountaineering group. See?"

"Sure. This will be a day hike, I gather? No camping overnight?"

"Yes, one day hike. Sen… I mean Mister S, he has ordered box lunches. Have you ever been to a box social? Well of course you have. All of us have. Ever so fun. Each girl is going to be given her own backpack, see? And… get this… inside her pack are two box lunches! Two, see? One is for her. The other's got a number on it! Isn't it too exciting? The plan is, we set out on a forest trail or path. They'll have a guide I guess for us, and after we make it to a certain spot there will be men. They haven't said how many. If there's not enough to go around it doesn't bother me since I've got it all over those Olive Oyls who think they're some kinda sheilas. Anyway the senator promises we'll be in a perfectly romantic place in the woods and these men will have wine or gin drinks with them, and each one will have a number and the lucky girl who's carrying the box lunch with the number will share with him, see? Like a box social in the woods, only the men won't have to bid money on the boxes!"

I'll bet they won't, Eleanor thought.

"Well, toodle-oo," the blonde said, swiveling her rear differential to head in the direction of the door marked "Office."

Incredible, Eleanor thought. She restarted the White's engine and resumed tinkering with the fuel mixture, but her mind was making an image of the whole picture. The drug drops, the blasting of mine tunnels, the careful way the Jones brothers kept everything looking legitimate, more mines being dynamited. Smith has an argument with Hayward and Smith hauls himself off to Denver. When he comes back to the bus barn almost a week later he's looking as smug as the Siamese who just ate the budgie. Next thing you know a troop of girl doxies shows up to carry backpacks through the forest.

Eleanor decided to risk it. She would make a visit to the RMNP Supervisor's Office on the pretext of checking to see whether the map of the dynamite project targeted any more tunnels. She told Jones she would try to wangle more information out of Dottie, or Nick. She was on the schedule for a two-hour tour, but afterward she'd pretend to drop in at the S.O.

"After all," she said, "we're old pals, the office girl and me. Now that I'm driving tours I ought to know where there's going to be any blasting going on, so I can keep my customers away from it. See?"

Jones was a little suspicious, but went for the idea anyway. After she got her bus ready for the next day, he said, she could take a couple of hours off. Providentially, while Eleanor was fueling her White tour bus and cleaning the windscreen, little Gala showed up. Gala was making her usual rounds, her shoulder bag holding a few pipe tobacco tins of fishworms to sell along the river behind the bus barn, her bright eyes alert for any economic opportunity from a pop bottle worth two cents at Murphy's Grocery to a stray dog she could catch and return for a reward.

Gala stopped and sized up the tour bus, with its tires almost as tall as herself.

"I'm glad I don't have to wash a bus," she said to Eleanor. "Take all day."

Eleanor agreed with her, and invited the girl to step up on the running board with her.

"Got a job for you," she whispered. "See if you can contact Ranger McIntyre and Miss Coteau. Tell them to meet me at the S.O. after lunch, say one o'clock. Top secret, okay?"

"Sure!"

"Okay," Eleanor said, reaching into her trousers pocket, "here's a couple of dimes and a nickel in case you need to make a phone call—although knowing you, I imagine you'd con a free phone somewhere—and here's a dollar for your time. Good enough?"

"Holy cow, you bet!"

Gala was almost about to start off on a dead run when she realized she was on a secret detective mission; with a casual wave of her hand she went strolling off in the direction of the river. Fishermen had worn a path along it, and the path made a nice private way to get from one end of the village to the other.

* * * * *

Even before Eleanor had finished informing the assembled sleuths about the premature blonde and the box social picnic,

McIntyre was cutting sheets of typing paper into fourths and scribbling notes on them. Vi Coteau and Nick Nicholson, even Gala Book asked questions and suggested a few theories, but McIntyre kept on putting pieces of information on bits of paper, pushing them here and there on the conference table.

The others finally fell silent and watched him. After a few more minutes of scratching his chin and rearranging the notes, the ranger looked up like a man who had suddenly realized he was not alone. With an apologetic grin he got up and turned the portable blackboard around. He picked up the chalk.

"Vi," he said, "you alert the feds and the sheriff and tell them to make certain they've got enough transportation for a half dozen prisoners. I'm sure all the jitney drivers will be willing to help haul crooks, if we need them to. Eleanor, it's up to you to convince the Jones brothers and John D. Smith that the park rangers don't suspect a thing, that they're all doing their usual routines, except for the dynamiting crew. Gala? Can you figure a way you could hang around and watch the Creagdhur Lodge? We need to be alerted when the group of girl hikers leaves for their so-called picnic. Think about how to do it, okay?"

He moved two of his scraps of paper, scratched at his chin again, and nodded as if agreeing with himself. He turned again to the blackboard.

"Here's what I think we've got thus far," he said. He wrote names and places on the board, circled them, connected the circles with arrows

"We thought New Mountain was selling cocaine and heroin by dropping it off the back of their touring buses. I asked two of the jitney drivers to hang around and keep an eye on the bus barn. Every week the same plain black car, same license plates, would arrive. A man would get out of the car, carrying what looked like a camera bag, and climb into the bus, sitting on the back seat. Leon Counter's been watching the old mine tunnel on the moraine, mostly because our suspected bad guys have a sentinel watching it. Plus, Leon's been selling his highest grade hooch to various New Mountain fellows. You ever watch the little pikas storing grass for the winter? That's what it reminds me of. Dope is coming in, one package at a time. A prearranged signal tells our famous hiker, Hayward, to be near the road at a certain time. On foot or in his car. He picks up the dropped parcel. When the coast is clear he stashes it in the cache. Smith, Ladro, probably even one of the Jones brothers, they're also stockpiling pint jars of Counter's liquefied corn. Probably intend selling it, or having a party later on.

"Let's assume we've got them worried their cache will be broken into, inspected, then dynamited. But they've heard about another tunnel, one nobody knows about, and it's in a haunted canyon where a deadly monster comes out of the fog. They'll need to relocate their packages of dope. Their problem is if they put all their eggs in one basket, or all their drugs in one truckload, and the rangers, or the sheriff, intercepts it, there goes the whole investment."

"And the personnel," Vi suggested. "The whole moving crew would go to jail."

"The Jones brothers don't care," McIntyre said. "They don't care who they use or what happens to anyone else, as long as their dope is safe. This brings us to the subject of the ladies who like to hike."

"Before we talk about the hikers," Nick interrupted, "do you remember the kid named Dwayne? Works at the Creagdhur Lodge? It was his car John Jules borrowed to go fishing the day he was killed. Nice young man. Dwayne stopped in here yesterday because he's been hired to guide the female hiking club on their outing, and he wanted to find out whether he needed to register as a guide with the national park. Very conscientious of him, I thought."

"Ah!" said McIntyre, scribbling the word "guide" on the blackboard and putting a circle around it.

"The fact that they need a guide is a clue to the route they'll probably take. Knowing the route, we'll be able to deduce where to set up an interception."

"Maybe," Nick said.

"Judging from what the garish blonde early bird said," McIntyre went on, "and judging by the probability that it's the senator who's sponsoring this whole hiking scheme, I think it's safe to guess they are young, single, and not serious outdoorswomen. Apparently they don't even own backpacks. The senator has a reputation for spending time with females who like easy money and a good time. They aren't housewives. They do have occupations where they can take off a week. Probably not showgirls. Showgirls they need to be there for every performance, but possibly hostesses or dime-a-dance types. Maybe these 'ladies' hang out in nightclubs or speakeasies, where they fell under the eye of Speckle and his shady associates. If they're that sort of women it brings us back to the question of how far they could hike, how much they could carry, and where the guide would plan to hike them to."

"You shouldn't end a sentence with a preposition," Vi Coteau observed.

"Right at the moment," he answered, "grammar ain't what I'm up to."

"You did it again," she remarked.

"Be quiet," he recommended.

Ranger McIntyre crossed the conference room to the large topographic map.

"Okay," he continued, "whoever, or 'whomever' organized

this hike, why didn't they have the group stay at the Stanley or the Livingston? The Creagdhur is okay, but the place is starting to show its age, the rooms are smaller and darker, and the food is nothing to write home about. Are they staying there because it's cheaper? Expense doesn't seem to be an issue with the sponsor. After all, he's hiring buses and providing backpacks and buying box lunches, not to mention hiring a guide. But what's unique about the Creagdhur? Its location."

"You shouldn't begin a sentence with a conjunction, either," Vi said.

He picked up the long, pliant pointer stick and showed it to her before using it to point to the map.

"With any other hotel in town you'd need to drive through the village if going to Moraine Park. But look here. But from Creagdhur you could take this back road past a few scattered summer cottages, drop down to the river here, and end up right at the Thompson entrance to the park. And early in the morning there wouldn't be anyone on duty at the entrance. It greatly reduces the chance of anyone seeing a couple of busloads of women and getting suspicious as to what they're up. To."

He traced the theoretical route, continuing to Moraine Park and the site of the barricaded mine tunnel, indicating the road.

"Unloading passengers here would look curious," he went on. "No trailhead, no parking or turnaround area. Not even an outhouse. Eleanor, what's the next normal bus stop on this road?"

"Well," she said, "up the road about a half mile is the Wolf Lake trailhead. From there to Wolf Lake is an easy hike, not terribly scenic."

"Perfect," McIntyre said. "If I'm right they'll unload there. And the guide—what's his name? Dwayne?—I'll bet a week's wages whoever's behind this all-girl hike has instructed Dwayne to lead the group, bushwhacking downhill through the trees, skirting this cliff you see here on the map, down to the mine tunnel where they're going to pick up the stuff."

"Stuff?" Gala said.

"Sure. We don't believe the yarn about a box social, do we. Don't ask me what's going to become of Tiny's delicious box lunches, because I don't know and it doesn't matter. What happens is, the bad guys believe the park service is about to break into the drug cache and blast it with dynamite. But they've found a new hiding hole in a haunted canyon, a hole practically undiscovered. They need to move their stuff quick and quiet and in one operation. The longer it takes them to move it, the more steps they have to go through, the more danger there is of being discovered. Or have something else go wrong. This is what I think they'll do: a couple of New Mountain toadies will meet the girls at the first cache where they hand each girl two fairly heavy parcels, each wrapped nice and tight and secure in brown paper and cord. Might offer the ladies a few nips of booze, even if it's early. A few drinks'd leave them all giggly and excited. They'll never suspect there's no picnic."

"So the women's hiking group will transport the heroin and cocaine bricks over to the new cache!" Nick said.

"Right. You've got it. It's a mule train. It's a string of ants carrying grains of dirt. Eleanor, I'll bet you almost any amount of money you and another driver will be assigned to drive up Fall River with empty buses and pick up the hiking club when they come stumbling down the hill. And they won't be happy girls, either."

"Because there was no box social picnic. No new men to meet."

"Mostly unhappy because the feds and the rangers are going to be waiting. Right about here…" he indicated a spot along the route from cache to cache, "…and that's as far as the dope is going. The ladies will be made to leave names and addresses with the marshals and agents. We'll send them with Dwayne to meet the buses at Fall River. They'll glad to be the heck out of there without going to jail."

"You're sure they'll take the route you think they will?" Nick asked.

"Real sure," McIntyre said. "Think about it. City girls, good time girls? I'm betting whoever started this hiking club, told them it'd be a real lark, a whiz of a fun time."

"Whomever," Vi said.

"Pardon?"

"You should say 'whomever', not 'whoever'."

"The whom who told them whatever probably told the girls how they'd stay in a mountain lodge, go on an easy hike, and rendezvous at a picnic with outdoorsy men. Being female," he said, looking straight at Vi Coteau, "I expect they'd go shopping for new hiking shoes and snazzy new outfits, likely to be impractical for bushwhacking. The guide, Dwayne, recognizing their inadequate footwear, opts to lead them around the steep parts. He'll avoid the thick part of the forest and stick to the easiest slopes he can. He knows his destination—the bosses told him and maybe showed him on a map—but he'll choose the easiest route, depend on it. A young man leading young women? He'll do all he can to keep them happy."

"Why's he hire all these young women you're talkin' about?" Gala asked. "Couldn't they rent a truck? Like Mr. Whortle's Reo Speedwagon f'r instance. Do it in one load. He'd only ask, I dunno, ten bucks for the day? Gas extra?"

"It's about illegal drugs, Gala. Whoever's hiding the drugs and selling the drugs can't afford to be caught holding them. They need flunkies to take the risk. And they won't pay them to do it, because that would look suspicious. Some guys to go to the Moraine cache and wrap the drugs. Those same guys pass the packages to the hikers, then clear out. They'll be clean and innocent, not carrying anything themselves except maybe a flask or two of moonshine. The fed flying squad intercepts a bunch of women innocently carrying drugs. They don't have any criminal records, don't really know what's going on. Whoever's with the mule train, hopefully it's our dear senator, can be searched from here to kingdom come and the federal agents won't find any drugs on him. He'll tell the feds he only sponsored a hiking club of girls who'd like to get out of the city for a day. He'll admit coming along to have fun with the girls, to relax, blow off steam and so forth. He'll blame the drugs on the flunkies who were supposed to bring box lunches, those guys. He ordered box lunches and can prove it. He'll say he saw the girls pick up their box lunches and put them into backpacks and haversacks. No, he'll say, he didn't see inside any of the boxes. Plus he had no idea where their guide was going to lead them. Somebody else, he'll say, arranged the hike. No, I'm afraid your crooked senator will be able to walk away from the whole dirty deal."

"Nick," Vi said, "do you ever worry about employing a ranger who thinks like a criminal?"

"Almost every day," Nick replied. "But this time it might work out. At least according to McIntyre's imaginary scheme the federal boys stand to capture a huge haul of dope. Some drug dealer somewhere will lose a very large amount of money. I actually like the part about letting the hiking club ladies escape. Think of all the paperwork there'd be if we arrested them. And think what they'll be saying about those men and the senator back in the city."

"I'd still like to nail Senator Speckle," Eleanor said. "And Hayward. And Smith. All three give me the crawly creeps."

Chapter Fourteen
The Tangled Webs Our Minds May Weave

Supervisor Nicholson hosted a small gathering. In his office. Included on his guest list were himself, Ranger McIntyre, Assistant Rangers Jamie Ogg and Russ Frame, and Dottie Milner, his secretary. Nicholson had been sleeping poorly of late, lying awake worrying about what McIntyre was planning to do about the transportation feud, the killings, and the possibility of drugs being hidden in his national park. If he was ever to get a good night's rest he needed a clear, complete account—and he wanted it written down—of exactly who would be involved in McIntyre's scheme to trap the drug dealers. Entrapment was a dirty word among lawyers and district attorneys and in court it simply wouldn't wash to have a park supervisor say "I didn't know about it."

"It's not a trap, really," McIntyre began. "Here's our version, the story we'd present to a judge, if it comes to that. We had taken notice of a suspiciously barricaded old mine tunnel near Moraine Park. When it became general knowledge that we were dynamiting dangerous old tunnels and shafts in the park, persons unknown began construction of a heavy door on a remote and little known mine tunnel up the Fall River road. Hearing a rumor that a large transfer of heroin and cocaine might take place between the two locations, I, uh, I deduced a logical route the drug carriers might take. With federal assistance I went ahead and set up surveillance. The feds have further evidence of a bunch of drugs involved."

"Okay, okay," Nicholson said. "We'll make sure the judge understands it wasn't a trap. Tell me the names of all the 'assistants' who'll be involved. I don't want any surprises, and I don't want my bosses to say I didn't know what was going on."

"Sure," McIntyre said. "Well, I'll be there, and Brownie."

"Forget the horse," Nick snapped. "Start with the feds. Who are they, how many?"

McIntyre took out his pocket notebook and read off the names of the four federal agents, added Vi ("full name Violet") Coteau and Eleanor Pedersen, the county sheriff and his deputy, and finished with a roster of rangers and assistant rangers he expected to recruit.

"The rangers are mostly for safety," McIntyre said. "Same reason we'll have Brownie and other horses. See, if the women from the hiking club break and run for it, we'll need to round them up and make sure nobody falls over a cliff or ends up lost in the woods. If I'm right…"

"Stop saying 'if'," Nick growled.

"If I'm right, they'll be carrying the drugs but won't know it. We'll need to seize the dope, but we can't charge the women with anything, at least nothing to stick. We'll herd them toward the nearest road. And believe me, by the time they're back in Denver they'll no longer feel friendly toward the senator and his circle of friends."

Nicholson took the list from Dottie, read it carefully.

"You make certain," he said, "make certain the bad guys don't think Dwayne was in any way part of your trap. We don't want him—or anyone else—getting killed."

He sat back in his chair.

"Not happy," he said. "All these agencies, all these people with guns running around in my park. Dope dealers with Tommy guns, people with silent air rifles that look like walking sticks, bus drivers who are really detectives, or gangsters… no sir, I'm not happy. All I've got is a vague inclination to trust you. Again. But let's move on. Jamie, Russ, I think Tim has another matter to discuss. About your future assignments."

"Oh, no!" Russ exclaimed. "No, Nick, really! It was my fault anyway. Don't have Jamie transferred on my account! I didn't think it would do any harm and it was so dang hot that day and we'd been sawing away on the log… well, there was another log across the trail before that one… and like I said, it was so dang hot and we didn't see nobody the whole morning, so I figured it would be okay to take off our shirts. Wouldn't y' know it, a lady and her husband showed up with their darn Kodak camera. Probably they're the ones who complained about rangers half naked, huh. But you can fire me, only it was all my idea. Jamie shouldn't get…"

"Quiet," Nicholson said. "You've got the wrong end of the stick. McIntyre, tell them."

"Okay. Russ, Jamie, to be honest, I don't want you two taking part in the drug bust. It would make me nervous. I'd be distracted, wondering if you were going to fly off the handle and start shooting They told me you found out it was either Hayward or his toadie, John Smith, who did it. Responsible for Art dying, and the poor kid in the river, and probably the sabotage and attempted murder and all of it. We'll catch them both, but legally.

If they're not with the women being used to move the drugs, we'll find another way to arrest them. But I can't be wondering if one of you is going to shoot them."

Russ Frame looked relieved. Jamie looked angry.

"You want us to stay in the barracks and sit on our hands doin' nuthin'?" Jamie said.

"Nope. I still need you on site. But not where you'll be tempted to shoot at Hayward and Smith. As soon as we find out what day it will all go down, you two will take your rifles and go up Fall River. Hide your truck up or down the road. Sneak up to where you can watch the mine tunnel they're going to use as their new drug cache. The way I figure it, the Jones brothers will post a couple of tough guys at the mine to guard the drugs. Probably pile the stuff inside, make sure all of it all arrived. I'm not sure how they plan to separate the drugs from the ladies' hiking club, but they're bound to have one or two flunkies waiting. Your job, your official assignment, is to watch and make certain they don't leave. I'll join up with you as soon as I can and we'll deal with them. And only then. Got it?"

"Got it," Jamie grumbled.

"And we need to be sure it won't be entrapment. Let's say I was making a routine patrol up Fall River road and heard suspicious noises, hammering and like that, coming from the direction of an old mine tunnel. I sent you two up there to set up a surveillance. You saw armed men, it looked like they were getting ready to engage in illegal prospecting. We had reasonable cause to find out what they were doing up there."

"Okay."

"Dottie," McIntyre said. "I forgot one person to put on the list. Norman Duggin. He's a news reporter. I think Vi told him what we're up to. He might bring a photographer."

Supervisor Nicholson put his face down onto his folded arms, doing a convincing impression of a man having a headache. Weakly, he waved one hand at the group.

"Go away," he said softly. "Go inspect outhouses. Go tell tourists not to feed the chipmunks. Go do anything. But just go away."

* * * * *

The criminal opposition held a strategy meeting of their own, in the windowless offices of the Jones brothers. Very few living people ever saw inside the secure little suite. Anyone who happened to notice a plain wooden door off to one side of the dingy bus barn assumed it to be a storage room. Dr. Hayward, ever the courteous gentleman and ever the obsequious, escorted his important guest and one of the guest's bodyguards from their sedan to the office door.

Senator Speckle was dressed to the nines to play the part of a mountain hiker from the upper classes, from his jaunty wide-brim hat down to his heavy brogans. He looked like a man eager to be on the trail. Being a professional politician he wore a more or less permanent smirk, an expression he assumed to be a warm, ingratiating grin. Except his eyes did not smile. They looked as cold as a Hubley patented icebox.

Lou Jones offered to take the senator's hat.

"Be careful with it," the senator said. "Brand new. Imported. You got everything ready? Did the girls arrive safely?"

Jones hung the hat on the hat tree.

"All set," he said.

"Go over it for me," Senator Speckle said. "Start to finish. Every detail. Oh, and by the way, there's rucksacks for the girls in the trunk of the other car."

"Awful handy, owning a military surplus store. Probably a

gold mine, huh," said Joe Jones. "Maybe we oughta open one up here. Sell surplus packs and tents to campers. Get 'em a dime apiece from the government, sell 'em for two bucks."

"Maybe," Speckle said. "About the operation?"

"Sure. Well, we start early in the morning. Two buses pick up the girls at the Creagdhur hotel, along with the guide. One car with three of my boys will be waiting at the old cache already. Well, not at it, of course. Parked in a parking lot up the road. Same place we stop the buses."

"Listen, Lou," the senator said, lowering his voice to a whisper, "I'm kind of worried about what I heard about there being a couple of hotdogs in your gang. I'm told they're the ones who stash the stuff and keep track of it."

"Sure. Hayward here. And Smith."

"They needed to eliminate a couple of witnesses, I understand."

"Yeah. No problem there."

The senator's gesture clearly dismissed Hayward from the office. The gunsmith left without a word, closing the door behind him.

"Hayward bothers me," Senator Speckle continued. "He's too much of a toady. I think he's a little too smart. Too cagey. Wouldn't be surprised if he's dipping into the product. I don't trust Smith, either. Looks like he does whatever Hayward tells him."

"Maybe. What do we do about it?"

"Not sure. Until we have the product shifted, let's put 'em where we'll know where they are."

"We need a couple of men at the new cache. To collect the packages and stash them. There's a real low side tunnel, nice and dry, doesn't go back but about twenty feet. We plan to stack the packets in it. If we pile a bunch of rubble, it'll look like there was a cave-in, see? Nobody'll want t' go in. Nobody'll see the stuff when we're done."

"Yeah, yeah, good. Spare me those details. If we put Smith and Hayward there, they can't shoot anybody. They can't start any trouble. And they wouldn't dare leave the junk unguarded. Yeah, let's get them up there and tell 'em to stay until we send word they can leave."

"They can have some of those lunches!" Lou Jones laughed.

"Tell 'em to take their own food. And blankets."

* * * * *

The Scottish transplant who built Creagdhur Lodge had chosen the north slope, the thickly wooded side of the mountain. Many trees would need to be cut down to make a clearing, but the lumber from them could be used for the lodge and cabins. Most of the stumps were removed except for a few that were large enough guests could use them as outdoor tables. The lodge manager gave Gala permission to set up shop on one of them, providing she agreed to stay out of people's way and to clear up all her stuff when she finished.

Gala removed her inventory from the bicycle basket and arranged it on the stump, tobacco cans of fishworms and handmade cellophane envelopes containing dry flies and wet flies in various patterns. She considered which of her hand lettered signs to set out: one said "Fish Worm Wrigglers 15 cents Can Included" while another offered "Guaranteed Dry Flies 5 Cents Each, 4 for a quarter." However, there was her market to consider. Folks with enough money to stay at a lodge probably didn't buy stuff at bargain prices. So she decided on the sign reading simply "25 Cents." One can of worms, one envelope of four fishing flies, all one price, no haggling.

Gala's early morning business was good, especially for the

worms. For some reason worm fishermen like to hit the river in the early hours and don't want to waste time digging for worms. One man dumped Gala's wrigglers into his own bait can, one that he could hook on his belt, and he gave her back the tobacco tin. "Keep it," he said. Profit for me, Gala thought. While waiting for her next customer she thought up ways to fix her worm cans to carry on a belt. It could double her asking price, probably.

The sun hadn't risen high enough above the forest to shine down on Creagdhur Lodge when a White fifteen passenger bus came grumbling up the road and pulled to a stop. Eleanor Pedersen descended from the driver's seat, took off her gloves, and opened the hood as if to check the engine. But with one hand she signaled Gala to come to her.

"No," Eleanor said loudly when Gala came to stand beside her looking into the engine compartment. "No! You can't ride along for free. I've told you before. Besides, you're too darn curious for your own good."

And, in a whisper, she added, "Quick as you can, but be casual about it. Go to the S.O. Tell them me and another driver have been told to take two buses and go park on Fall River Road, above Chasm Falls. We're to wait there. I'm supposed to pick up the creepy Smith guy, and Hayward, and drop them off along the way. I'm not sure where. It looks like today's the day. You need to get to Nick and tell him. Tell McIntyre, too."

"Another driver and I," Gala said.

"What?"

"My mom and my teacher and Miss Coteau would say you oughta have said 'another driver and I' have been told."

"Girl," Eleanor said, "you're beginning to sound like Miss Coteau."

"Oh, good!" Gala said.

"Not necessarily," was Eleanor's answer.

A door slammed and one of the senator's bodyguards came down the steps from the dining room, picking his teeth. Gala kicked one of the bus tires, shouted "okay, darn it!" and scurried back to her stump to pack up her merchandise.

"What're y' doin' here anyway?" the man demanded of Eleanor.

"Picking up two riders, I was told," she said, latching the engine hood. "Coming up the road it felt like I was getting a vapor lock."

"Your fares are down at the bus barn, you dumb dame. You're blockin' the drive. We got two buses and a limo comin' for these hikin' club broads. Get your rig the hell outta the way."

It was all Eleanor needed to know.

Mounting to the driver's seat once more, she fired the engine into life, did an expert three-point turnaround in the parking area, and rumbled off to wait at the bus barn for 'fares' and further orders. If Gala pedaled straight to the S.O., Dottie would mobilize the rangers and federal agents and McIntyre's plan would be underway. If McIntyre had figured it wrong the park service would have a goodly amount of egg on its face.

The city-dwelling ladies of the hiking club greeted the mountain dawn with a chorus of grousing and bitching that would put an army barracks to shame. However, once the hot breakfast was consumed, and after the senator's men added shots of high-grade gin to the orange juice, group morale improved markedly. One girl said she hadn't heard that much giggling since the day her grandmother served homemade wine to the quilting circle. The ladies joked about how they looked alike in their jodhpurs and white shirts with clever skinny little neckties. They swapped hats with one another and tried them on in front of the hat stand mirror, laughing and chattering until the chorus of female voices had become a cacophony causing the entire dining room to vibrate.

Whether he was at a governor's dinner party or in the parlor of a bordello, Senator Speckle enjoyed being among swarming females, but only up to a point. He circulated, complimenting a blonde, pinching a brunette, smiling gratefully from a kiss on the cheek, nodding at one feminine face after another while surreptitiously edging his way toward the door. Once outside where the early morning air smelled of pine and wood smoke rather than lipstick, lilac talcum powder, and *Eau de Fleurs* he took a deep breath and thanked himself for coming up with this mountain outing dodge. He needed to get away from back rooms and cigar-chewing hustlers, needed to rub elbows and other anatomical features with happy girls for a change. And he felt he deserved it. It would relax him. It would relax him even further when he could be certain that his investment in dope had been moved to a secure place,

The senator's thoughts drifted into a fantasy featuring the swaying caboose of a cute brunette, the one with the walking stick. The fantasy, however, was broken off in mid-debauch by the sound of a tour bus engine climbing the grade into the parking lot. To the senator's surprise the oily Doctor Hayward and his fox-faced sidekick descended from the bus and came toward him. They wore ingratiating grins, wiping their palms on their pants in case the senator should offer to shake hands. Hayward, carrying a tall walking staff, appeared ready to follow the females up the trail.

"I thought you two were supposed to be at the new cache," he growled.

"It's all set," Smith answered. "We're leavin' our car behind so's nobody'll be suspicious seein' it parked along Fall River Road. Arranged so the detective dame's gonna drive us up there, see? T' the wide spot in the road, acrost from the new cache. We'll climb out so's t' hike down t' the creek an' up the mountain. Tell her she's t' wait there. Just wait. Tell 'er th' other bus'll show up, too. See, it'll keep her out of our way all day long."

"How do you plan to make it back to town? The plan is for the buses to haul the broads back to the lodge. After they do their hike. You two need to stay with the cache and help bury the dope with mining rubble."

"Very simple," Hayward interjected. "We merely instruct Miss Pedersen to drop off the ladies and return for us."

"You'd better be going," Senator Speckle ordered.

"Yes, of course," Hayward said. "Before we go, though, I would like to present you with this."

He handed the walking staff to the senator. It was a thick one, made of polished dark wood, separated into four sections with wide bands of brass.

"One of my imports," he explained. "A special European design. As you will discover—when you are away from prying eyes—the top is removable. Inside you'll find glass vials containing a bit of liquid refreshment for yourself, and perhaps for a fortunate young lady."

The senator acknowledged Hayward's offering with a curt "thank you" and dismissed the two men.

Well, he thought, *at least I won't be tempted to cut a walking stick along the way. Wouldn't want to deface government property and have any trouble with the rangers. It's quite an elegant-looking thing, actually. Quite suitable for a leader and gentleman.*

* * * * *

Eleanor drove the White bus up Fall River Road, stopping where one of the thugs told her to.

"We'll dismount here," he said. "You drive on up until there's a place t' turn around. Then come back here and park. Pretty soon one of the boys'll be along with another bus. Orders are for th' both of you t' wait here for the hiking club, see?"

"Then we drive them back to the hotel."

"Right. And come right back for us. Be sure y' got enough fuel and come straight back, no lollygaggin' around anywheres."

"Got it," Eleanor said.

Eleanor drove up the road to do her U-turn. She was approaching the rendezvous site again when another New Mountain bus came growling by, also headed for the wide turnaround. In the driver's seat was Antonio, the company's self-styled ladies' man. He waved to her, flashed his well-rehearsed charming smile, and signaled that he would return to her—lucky girl—as soon as he could turn around.

After parking his bus behind Eleanor's, Antonio he came to sit next to her on her running board. He was reasonably trim, reasonably muscular, and unreasonably fond of stroking the ends of his black mustache.

"I thought you'd be with the girls on the hiking club picnic," Eleanor said.

"Not for me," he replied. "Let the other boys wear themselves out, chasing skirts through the mountains. From what I heard, Mister Topo only needs a couple of men anyway. For show, see. Make the women believe there's more waiting for them at the end of the hike. Big surprise! Ask me, I'd tell you we're spread thin. Two shooters at the old cache, to load the rucksacks, they won't do anything but head back to town. Two at the new cache. And me, sitting here waiting. With very pleasant company, I will add. But it doesn't leave very many men to keep an eye on the girls."

"Ah," Eleanor said.

She stood up.

"Are you going for a stroll?" Antonio inquired. His voice held a hint of surprise as if he could not imagine how a lady could distance herself from his magnetic presence.

"Actually," she replied, giving him a sly look, "I think I need to use the emergency telephone. If you know what I mean."

Antonio answered with a generous wink of his eye and a lecherous elevation of his left eyebrow, bowed, and gestured toward the woods along the river as if he were sweeping a door open for a lady. Such a gentleman!

What Antonio thought Eleanor was going into the trees to do, however, was not exactly correct. As soon as she was certain to be out of his sight, Eleanor located the wire strung through the trees and followed it to a wooden box containing an emergency phone. It rang through to the S.O. where Dottie picked up the receiver.

"Dottie," Eleanor said. "Eleanor. I'm on Fall River Road. It's all going down. Senator and floozies are probably in Moraine Park getting outfitted with rucksacks. He's got a bodyguard and a driver. Two more gun-carrying freaks are at the cache. Ladro and two others probably mean to hike with the women. Hayward and Smith are at the new cache, Antonio's stuck here with me, waiting for the hikers to find their way back to the road. Got it?"

"Got it," Dottie said. "You okay? Armed?"

"Goes without saying," Eleanor replied. "In these baggy driver uniforms you could hide a machine gun and several hand grenades."

Now, the next job's to deal with Mister Terrific, Eleanor thought while climbing the slope back to the buses. She was more than pleased to see Casanova sprawled unconscious along the back seat of his own bus, obviously a man unaccustomed to waking in the hours of dawn. She tiptoed closer. He was breathing loudly, his mouth wide open. His coat, also wide open, revealed the butt of a Luger semi-automatic sticking out of his shoulder holster. Eleanor cautiously mounted the running board, careful not to shake the bus.

"Naughty," she said to herself. "Carrying a pistol in the park. Not to mention careless for letting it show."

Reaching over, Eleanor deftly squeezed the magazine catch and slid the full clip out of the pistol. If the situation should come to a shootout he would have but one bullet, the one in the chamber and she'd have six in her own gun. One bullet only if he was stupid enough to carry an automatic with a live round under the firing pin. She put his cartridges in her pocket and threw the clip into the forest. When he discovered it missing she'd tell him she once heard Hayward say how the spring catch on a Luger was undependable. German engineering. Antonio would likely spend an hour searching under the bus seats for the clip.

These cool, fresh early mornings in the park made her nostalgic for her former job, the life of a uniformed ranger, the uncomplicated pleasure of driving a routine patrol up the road in the hours before any bunches of visitors arrived. She wondered whether Jamie and Russ were going to do the Fall River dawn patrol, and if maybe they'd come along and stop to talk a while. Had Eleanor driven her bus fifty yards further, a short way past the turnaround place she would have spotted their pickup truck half-hidden in the trees.

Ranger McIntyre was also thinking about a former job, in the army flying corps during the Great War, flying his Neiuport biplane over German lines to take photographs of trenches and gun positions. Right now he could really use some aerial photos of the terrain. Heck, he'd settle for a detailed map.

"Don't let me start worrying about what we need and don't have, old girl," he said to the horse, more or less under his breath. "Let's just get on with the job."

Brownie flicked an ear at the "old girl" and kept walking.

"This whole thing's beginning to look like a snipe hunt," he continued. "Like to guess who could end up holding the bag? Me. Clever ol' me. The pine tree patrolman who tried to act like a big detective and deduce which route the phony hiking club might follow across the ridge. A route with no trail. If they don't go where I want them to, if they wander off, I'll have a bunch of men hiding in the woods for no reason. No, that's wrong. There's a reason. The reason is that good ol' tree cop McIntyre told them to."

As a ranger McIntyre often worked alone, riding for days through valleys and canyons and up over ridges of forested mountains in search of a lost hiker, a wandering child, or following a report of smoke or poachers. He found it awkward and difficult to be in charge of others. He put on a big show of confidence while showing them where to wait, positioning the federal agents out of sight, suggesting to the mounted rangers how to make their approach to the hikers, figuring out for the umpteenth time where in hell he himself should be when the trouble started, generally working himself up to a stiff neck. And getting a headache right between his eyes.

Mostly he was worried about where Senator Speckle would end up. Would Speckle go on the hike with the women? If he did, would he be in the lead along with the guide, looking like he was in charge, or would he be behind, looking at the view? The view he'd be looking at wouldn't include trees and mountain peaks. Vi Coteau—and Eleanor—very much wanted Speckle caught with drugs. The best situation would be to confront him away from anyone else, separated from the herd, so to speak. But would he be hiking in front of the women, the bunch of cackling hens following him through the woods? Would he be among them, with his armed bodyguards, where the women would become shields in a gunfight? Or would he stay well in the rear where he could keep an eye on his investment. And on the covey of female derrieres.

Detective McIntyre was fairly sure of one thing, based on experience. Large groups of hikers, say eight or ten or more, tended to become strung out into small groups and singles. There were always a few fast walkers and a couple of slowpokes. Some would wander off course to look at flowers or butterflies. However, at the steep parts where the going got strenuous, they would probably drift back into a bunch. It was human nature, when the going gets difficult, to form a herd.

At the crest of the ridge the hikers would be gathered again, probably. And they'd all be drawn toward the one single open place, the only grassy clearing among all those towering pines. They were sure to stop and rest, McIntyre told himself. Right there where the rangers and feds could surround them.

"Let's don't forget the sheriff and deputy," McIntyre reminded Brownie.

And don't you forget to duck under that tree branch right there, Brownie thought. *I'm not about to climb over a bunch rocks to go around it.*

The ranger dodged the pine branch and they continued on. He rode here and there around the ridge, much like a forest fire boss inspecting a fire line, checking on his crew, looking for potential problem spots, making certain everyone was where he wanted them, all the while worrying about every decision large and small. The tension that had been meandering up and down his stiff neck was now going at a gallop. It became even worse when he began imagining other things that could go wrong. The newspaper photographer might pop out to grab a picture and ruin everything. One of the feds or an assistant ranger might go to sleep. Or worse, decide to light up a cigarette and one of the drug caravan people would smell it. Over on Fall River, Eleanor could get bored. Would she start investigating the terrain on her own, to relieve the monotony? And what if Jamie or Russ, or both, saw suspicious activity at the mine tunnel and got trigger happy? What if they tried to make an arrest based on nothing but suspicion?

McIntyre came around a stone outcrop and stopped. Fifty yards up the hill he could see Vi Coteau and the sheriff right where he had positioned them, behind a massive fallen ponderosa. It gave them a wide view of where the cocaine caravan would most probably stop to rest.

Vi Coteau, he thought. What a gal. For two cents he would go grab her and carry her away from all this trouble and worry where they would have nothing to do except maybe go to the Pioneer Inn for breakfast, or maybe go fly fishing in the beaver meadows. All alone, the two of them. No crooks, no cops, no drugs, not a thing in the world to watch out for except maybe his grammar.

"Unless she'd bring up the 'should we plan a wedding' thing," he said half out loud.

As usual, Brownie had no idea what her ranger was talking about.

Chapter Fifteen

Just a Walk in the Park

"Oooh!" exclaimed a young, almost illegally photogenic female, "look! A real ranger! Ginger! Oh! Isn't he just the bees knees? Look at the sweet horsie! Isn't he too cute!"

Ranger McIntyre dismounted slowly, moving deliberately with dignity in order to make the uniform and badge look impressively official. He was also conscious of looking strong and masculine. Not from ego: the feeling came from wearing the uniform.

"This is Brownie," he told the pair. "And he's actually a her. A mare. I'm District Ranger Timothy McIntyre. How do you do? Enjoying your hike in our park, are you?"

"Oh, gosh, it's swell!" she chirped. Her hand went to her fluttering bosom. "I'm Daisy Mueller. My parents named me after a book somebody wrote but I never read it. This is my friend Ginger. Ginger Tweeton? It's what we all call her because of her ginger hair, but it's not her real name of course. Can we pet your horse?"

Ginger now stepped forward, accompanied by a young man.

"This is Wayne," she said.

"Dwayne," McIntyre corrected her. "We've met. How are you, Dwayne? Guiding the girls on a hike, huh? Nice day for it."

"Sure is, wow. I'm supposed to be guiding a dozen or more. But they've got themselves all strung out back there. There's a bigwig with them, too, plus a couple of gangster-looking types. A few women hung back with the males. Or they're hanging onto them, if you want the truth. Kinda disgusting, if you ask me. A lot of the group already have sore feet. There's a couple of them who keep stopping to take photographs of each other and pick flowers. They're a long ways behind us. Probably take 'em a quarter to a half hour to catch up."

"My parents wanted to name me Anastasia," Ginger said, apropos of nothing whatever. "But I like Ginger. Alice is around here somewhere."

"I see," McIntyre said.

McIntyre had two reasons to feel he'd hit it lucky. These young women hadn't seen the half-dozen rangers and federal agents hiding down in the trees. Secondly, here was an opportunity to find out if they were carrying drugs. He was aware of the fact he didn't have a search warrant or any legal cause to search the packs, just as he was aware of what would happen to his career if a judge found him guilty of entrapment.

"I noticed your rucksacks," he said.

"What's a rucksack?" Ginger inquired.

"An army term. Means a backpack, like that one of yours. I saw enough of them during the war. In fact, if I had to guess, I'd guess yours are from the army surplus store. You've got the army style canteen hanging on yours, and Daisy's pack still has the shovel pocket."

"Gee whiz," Daisy said, sliding the pack off her shoulders. "What kind of pocket did you say I have?"

"The wide flat pouch on the back. It's made to hold a trench shovel. The shovel handle hangs down out of the hole there. But if you don't need to carry a shovel the pocket's just extra weight. Lot of guys took them off their packs. It's held on with steel clips, see."

"Weight's the word, Jack!" Daisy said. "They gave us these back at the truck with lunch in 'em. And a little blanket, they said, for us to sit on once we arrive if we ever do. It must be one snappin' heavy lunch, though. My shoulder hurts!"

"Daisy!" Ginger said. "Girl! Guess what! You made me think of it! There must be oodles of picnic in these packs! Mine's heavy, too. What say we sneak a little nibble? While we wait for the others to catch up? I don't know about you, but I'm awful peckish. Half a sandwich would put me right again. C'mon, what do you say?"

"They told us not to. Each lunch has got a number, remember."

Daisy stepped close to McIntyre to explain. "It's like blind dates! Golly, there'll be a man apiece for each of us and each man's got a number, too, and the lunch is to share with him, see?"

The ranger took a step back and said nothing.

"Sure, sure," Ginger said. She knelt to unbuckle her own pack. "I'll tell my picnic partner, whoever he turns out to be, I got hungry and took a bite of one sandwich. Or maybe there's a donut in here. A donut'd do me."

Ginger stopped and looked up at McIntyre.

"Oh, Mister McGregor! Oh, I'm sorry I'm so rude! It's I'm awful hungry, see? What I mean is I ought to be polite and offer you some, but if too much of the lunch is missing when we get to the picnic meadow, well…"

"Name is McIntyre," he said. "I'm fine. I've got bread and jerky in my saddle bag. Thanks for the thought, but you go ahead if you like."

"Okey dokey," Ginger said. She flipped back the cover of her rucksack. Right on top was a folded army blanket, or half of one, to be more precise, dyed in the strangely distasteful hue of greenish gray found only in military equipment. Beneath the blanket were two parcels. Ginger drew one out and frowned at the way it was triple wrapped, in both directions, with heavy cord. The cord was tied with more knots than a child's monkey puzzle.

"Let me have a go at it," Dwayne said, kneeling beside Ginger.

McIntyre almost sighed with relief. He was afraid she was going to ask him for his knife. He didn't want to be anything but an innocent—okay, mostly innocent—bystander when the packet was opened.

"Say!" Dwayne exclaimed. "This thing's awful solid for a box lunch. Listen, I'm gettin' a bad feeling here. Instead of unwrapping it, let's poke a hole."

The blade of young Dwayne's pocket knife easily penetrated the paper wrapping. It came out showing white powder.

"Powder?" McIntyre asked, with pretend innocence. "For a picnic? Talcum in case of sore feet, you think."

"Yeah," Dwayne said. "But four, five pounds of it? Too weird. Jimminy honkers! Lemme see the other box lunch!"

White powder again. Dwayne took a tiny taste and spit it out.

"Ranger, I swear to God they didn't tell me anything about this!" Dwayne protested. He hurried to replace both bundles and buckled the straps.

"Drugs?" McIntyre said.

"Oh, geez!" the boy cried. "We been duped like dopes! Oh, man! Those goons, those two with the senator, they're gonna kill me if they find out I've seen their happy sugar. What're we going to do?"

"Listen, ranger," Ginger said, her voice trembling and

seeming to have lost much of its innocent sweetness. "You're all wet if you think me and Daisy knowed anything about any drugs! I mean, once in awhile at a night club there's a slick who brings out the nose candy, but… honest to God! Here's how it happened. We're sitting in this nightclub, see? And there's a nice man buying drinks and we're having a whee of a time and he says 'say, a buncha lively broads are startin' up this hiking club for young women. Fresh air, fun. And there's goin' to be these outdoor type men to meet. Blind dates, like. Got a sponsor to pay for excursions, what ya' say, and I swear this is our first time with this gaggle, honest to Pete. Oh, Daisy, we're in the soup!"

A little teardrop made its way down Daisy's cheek.

"It's okay," Ranger McIntyre said. "Listen—give me those two rucksacks—Dwayne, they instructed you to lead the bunch cross country to the wide clearing up ahead of us, right? Okay. You take the girls, head for the meadow, but when you get there, keep heading straight north. The woods are thick down there but at least it's all downhill. At the river, find a place to wade across. Somewhere along the road, on the other side of the river, there's supposed to be a couple of buses waiting for the group. You'll be safe there. I'll take care of the rucksacks. Get moving."

"What about the others?" Dwayne said. "Ought'nt we go back and put them wise, too?"

"They'll be okay," McIntyre assured him. "Listen, don't look around and don't say anything, but I'm not alone. There's other rangers with me. Out of sight. We know about this whole mule train operation and we intend to arrest the men responsible. I'll separate the girls from the gangsters and assign a ranger to lead them to the bus rendezvous. The girls aren't who we're after. Tell the bus driver to wait for the rest. Okay? Go on, go."

Early in his career as a mounted ranger McIntyre had noticed how ninety-nine percent of human females, from those who totter in diapers to those who teeter along on canes, have an affinity for horses, some sort of a mystic bond between equines and humanoid females. Whenever he rode into a campground or came upon a hiking party, it was the females who came to stroke Brownie's neck and share apples or carrots with her. It wouldn't surprise him to learn that back in the stone age it was the female women who actually domesticated the horse.

Whatever the explanation, being aboard Brownie was possibly going to be the key to the next step in his 'plan'. As he retraced the route Dwayne and the girls had followed between the trees and boulders, he crossed his fingers and hoped he wasn't wrong.

Glancing off to his left he caught a glimpse of uniform hiding in the trees. Fifty to a hundred yards ahead was the clearing. The trap was cocked and ready. He reined in at the clearing to wait; he wouldn't be waiting long, for he could already hear the high pitch voices coming toward him. That was another thing about women, McIntyre mused. It seemed impossible for any two of their sex to walk together without keeping their mouths in constant motion.

The ranger had chosen a good site for an ambush. To the females struggling up the mountain the grassy clearing presented itself as the ideal resting place. Several shrugged off their rucksacks and sat down on the nearest flat boulder or fallen log. Two also rid themselves of their burdens and then sprawled unladylike on the grass. A half dozen spotted the tall ranger standing at the shadowed edge of the clearing casually holding the reins of a horse.

"Oooh!" exclaimed one, tugging a folding camera from the

pocket of her plus fours. "Alice! Come take my picture with the ranger!"

"Oh," echoed another, hurrying toward McIntyre and Brownie, "such a handsome boy! Mind if I pet him?"

"The horse? Or the ranger?" quipped the aforementioned Alice. "But Ginger and Daisy? They expect me to catch up with them!"

"I mean pet the horsey, silly! Do snap my photo! It'll only take a second."

"Okey doke, but drop your ugly backpack first. It makes you look like the hunchback of Notre Dame."

McIntyre held Brownie's headstall while 'he' and the ranger posed for pictures and while 'he' tolerated a flurry of female fondling. Beneath the shadow of his flat hat McIntyre's eyes flicked back and forth, sizing up the situation. And the situation was sizing up very nicely, thank you. All but one of the girls, the one sitting alone on a rock rubbing her foot, had become separated from the 'box lunch' rucksacks. The senator and his men stood bunched up in the shade of a towering pine, sharing nips from a hip flask. Even better, one of the bodyguards was carrying his jacket over his arm, openly displaying a shoulder holster and automatic pistol.

"Gotcha," McIntyre said to himself. "Carrying a loaded gun in a national park. That gives me grounds to search the rest of them for weapons. Hah!"

McIntyre glimpsed a shadowed figure moving among the trees down the slope, behind the resting hikers. The feds and the sheriff were beginning to surround the clearing.

"Alice?" McIntyre said. "That's the name, right?"

"Right," she replied. "What's yours?"

"Tim," he said. "Tim McIntyre. Hey! You know what would be really neat? A group photo. All you gals in it. The whole club.

You could all stand in front of Brownie here, while I snap a few pictures for you."

"Say!" Alice said, handing him the Kodak. "Keeno! You're swell to think of it! Ginger and Daisy can wait. I'll round up these other tomatoes into a bunch for the group shot, okay?"

Alice did pause to look around for Daisy Mueller and Ginger Tweeton. But not immediately discovering them, she proceeded to skip from hiker to hiker, pulling them to their feet and hauling them toward the horse and the ranger.

Good enough thus far, McIntyre thought. *At least we've got the women out of the line of fire, should there be any gunplay. I hope Agent Sutter is watching. Hope he recognizes it's his cue to make his move.*

McIntyre took his time aiming the camera while the group of women bustled around giggling about the best way to arrange themselves for a photograph.

Kneeling in the shelter of the pines, Agent Sutter whispered to Sheriff Abe Crowell.

"Looks like he's done it. He's got the girls out of the way. He'd make a helluva good cutting horse."

"You talking about the mare? Brownie?"

"No, the ranger. McIntyre'd make a good cutting horse. Look how he's got the suspected packs all in a pile and the women bunched up out of the line of fire. And as for our dear senator and his thugs, they're standing close enough to our own boys I bet they can smell 'em."

"Better not let Coteau hear you call her one of the boys," Crowell suggested.

"You ain't talking applesauce, as they say," Sutter replied in a whisper. "Maybe you know about that pistol she carries somewhere on her person. Not that she'd even need it if she ever decided to clean my clock for me. First time I met her was with a couple of agents taking a break? At a Joe and sinker joint on Glenarm Street. The young kid behind the counter, the biscuit shooter, he says 'what will you guys have' and Coteau almost tore off his head and handed it back. She takes her sex seriously."

"I wouldn't mind taking her sex seriously myself, except my wife wouldn't like it."

"Let's make our move," Sutter suggested, taking a whistle from his pocket. "McIntyre's fixed us up as good as we can hope for."

The whistle blew. The senator and bodyguards looked around in surprise, women grabbed the arm of the nearest woman, and from three sides of the small clearing came several men in ranger uniforms, other men in business suits, and one classy-looking female in a spiffy hiking outfit. There were no guns actually being pointed, but neither did the new arrivals display any shortage of firearms.

The senator's thugs wisely kept their hands empty and in full view.

Ranger McIntyre, having told Brownie to stand and wait, hurried across the clearing to confront the coatless bodyguard. He looked him straight in the eyes while relieving him of his .45 automatic.

"Loaded?" McIntyre said, jacking open the slide. "Yup, it's loaded. Against the law. It'll be a hundred dollar fine."

McIntyre really had no idea, not a clue what such a 'fine' would be, nor who would administer it, but it sounded good.

The other thug moved his right hand toward his left lapel. McIntyre thumbed the slide release on the .45, chambering a live round. With a resigned sigh the bodyguard opened his coat and allowed the ranger to remove a .38 Police Positive from its shoulder holster.

"Well," Sutter said, "I believe you've given us ample reason to search the whole bunch of you for illegal weapons. Abe, Sam, you want to help me here?"

With all the guns confiscated, hidden and not well hidden, it was time to talk about the rucksacks. Assistant Ranger Don Post retrieved one from the pile, ostensibly to be emptied and used to carry the confiscated pistols. He undid the straps and dumped the contents at the feet of Agent Sutter.

"Should be big enough to hold all the guns," Sutter said. He picked up one of the wrapped parcels.

"Ranger McIntyre told us about you ordering box lunches," Sutter said. "Seems the ranger's a frequent customer for Tiny's sandwiches. But say! This is one solid packet, for a lunch. One of your employees picked 'em up from Tiny's place, did he? Stashed 'em in rucksacks donated by your army surplus store? Handed them out to the girls?"

"You are correct," the senator blustered. "I never touched one of those."

"Awful heavy lunch," Sutter continued. "I hate to be the one to say it, senator, but it's possible you got hoodwinked. This might be nothin' but an old brick wrapped up nice and tight so's you wouldn't open it beforehand. Hard to believe it came from Tiny's delicatessen. I don't want to say Tiny might be a four-flusher, but if he is, we don't want him doin' business next t' the entrance of our nation's national park, do we? 'Course, none of your employees would try to trick the girls, either? I mean givin' them plain ol' buildin' bricks wrapped up t look like sandwiches. Would they. How about we open this one and see?"

"Further up the trail little bit ago I ran into two other girls," McIntyre remarked. "They were hiking ahead of the group. While I was talking with them, one got hungry and began to open hers, but instead of a sandwich she found white powder.

The package was identical to the ones you've got here."

Without reply, Agent Sutter opened his pocket knife and thrust the blade through the kraft paper. It came out dusted with white powder.

"Wow!" he said, sniffing at it. "Smells kinda like vinegar. Ranger, sheriff, what do you think?"

McIntyre wafted his hand over the powder and sniffed.

"Mountain lion," he remarked. "When a lion marks out his territory, this is what it smells like."

"I'd guess cocaine," Sam Bartlett said. "Or heroin. Either way, it sure isn't ham on rye."

A more thorough search of Senator Speckle's aides-de-camp turned up two hidden pistols and a couple of dangerous knives; three rucksacks contained authentic box lunches from Tiny's store. Official steel bracelets were produced and employed before the thugs were invited to relax in the shade and chat with a couple of the rifle-carrying rangers. Meanwhile, Will Sutter jotted down names of suspects and witnesses. Vi Coteau assisted by making notes toward a later account of the incident, notes she asked each of the officers sign and date. It was a procedure recommended by Kate Warne's handbook for lady detectives.

To the consternation of both Vi Coteau and federal agent Will Sutter, the crafty crooked senator had made absolutely certain not to have touched, seen, or even suspected the presence of drugs. He was being very forthcoming with details, telling how he had happened to meet a few of the young women in Denver, how they had expressed a wish to escape the city and breathe fresh mountain air once in a while, and how he had come up with the idea of a hiking club for young females. And had agreed to sponsor the necessary transportation and equipment.

He did admit to a political motive. The generous sponsorship would certainly bolster his image as a public servant, true. He found it awfully disconcerting to imagine how voters might react if they thought he was in any way connected with partytime drugs. As for his formerly trusted bodyguards, they would be severely dealt with. But he himself had never touched the stuff. As previously stated, he had not even suspected. If he was free to go, he would return to the Moraine Park road and find a ride to town. From the hotel a car would drive him to Denver.

Vi and Sutter withdrew to discuss the situation. McIntyre couldn't hear what they were saying, but he recognized Vi's angry way of standing, her way of stamping one foot when enraged. Senator Speckle, calmly leaning on his walking stick and wearing an expression of cooperative innocence—he looked like a man politely acting patient even though anxious to leave—took out a cigarette and asked whether Ranger McIntyre might have a match.

Like Shakespeare's Hamlet, McIntyre felt his gorge rising.

"I don't smoke," he lied, then stalked away.

"Dammit," he muttered to himself. "All this time and trouble, Eleanor working undercover and everything, and this smug misbegotten potbelly porkbarrel politician can meander back to Denver, hire another batch of toadies to replace the ones we've arrested, and go on like before. If only we could've waited… maybe watched him until he had his hands in the dope."

The dope. The stuff on the knife blade. White powder. There was something about it, some other place he'd seen it but couldn't remember. Trouble was, he had too many niggling little questions chasing each other through the dark cells of his brain. Like, where would they hold the senator's henchmen, once they got back to town, and how to transport the drugs and where to keep those, and where to find food for his stomach. There was jerky in his saddlebag. As he walked toward Brownie, the mental merry-go-round began to slow down until he could focus on one image.

Hayward's cottage. He'd almost forgotten about Hayward. Standing in Hayward's spotless, orderly workshop, McIntyre had been able to see past Hayward and into the kitchen, where one thing was out of place. Like most people, Hayward kept a set of metal canisters on his kitchen counter. Hayward's were lined up in order of size, with the labels facing outward. Orderly, organized. Order. Except between "Coffee" and "Flour" there should be one labeled "Sugar." Probably it was in a cupboard or on a shelf. He noticed, but it didn't matter.

Downstairs in Hayward's basement work area, the one with the shooting range tunnel, McIntyre had seen an oversize boring machine, a kind of specialized metal lathe. Only Hayward claimed not to make his own guns or his own 'custom' tricky walking sticks.

"Out of order," Hayward had said, casually. "Motor burned out. Haven't gotten around to finding a new one. Should sell it, really."

The machine's motor, McIntyre noticed, was a large one. The drive belt was missing. As for the light spatter of white powder beneath the machine, McIntyre simply took it to be plaster dust, or hand powder. In warm weather, target shooters might put talc on their hands.

"Except," McIntyre said, talking to Brownie while chewing a chunk of jerky, "what if a man had heroin, a pound or more of it, and had to hide it, and had a sugar canister with a tight lid, and could gut the works out of a old electric motor and hide the canister inside?"

The ranger signaled for Vi and Agent Sutter to walk back to Senator Speckle with him.

"This is going to be a long shot," he told them. "Will, could you kind of cajole Speckle into thinking we're about to let him go home?"

"Well, Senator," Will began, "We're about ready to move out. Do you have a ride back to the hotel?"

"A car waiting for me," the senator replied. "Back at the trailhead where we started. I, uh, arranged it in case I had to quit the hike unexpectedly. Duties of office. You understand."

"Sure. Well, we've got it wrapped up here. It's a shame, Senator, how everybody tricked you. You and the ladies. I guess you can't trust nobody these days, huh. You know what? I think even the doctor guy, Hayward. The gunsmith? I think he's a killer for one thing. Him and his pal Smith. I wish they'd been here. Fact is, we think maybe they're supposedly guarding the new hideaway where these drugs were headed for. Pity is, the drugs didn't get there. It means those two won't be caught with the goods, see. They might get away clean, darn it."

"I suppose you're correct," the senator said. "And I believed in Hayward, I really did. Ah, people these days. I'll be leaving, then. Rather a long stroll back to the car."

"I see you've got the proper boots for a hike, though," McIntyre said. "And a really sturdy stick. Lots of hikers cut them in the woods, which isn't a very good idea. But a stick does give a man better balance, saves the legs from fatigue on a hike. Come to think of it, I've seen one like yours before. The top part unscrews, doesn't it."

"Oh? Oh, yes. Rather a novelty, you see."

McIntyre simply stood there with an innocent, expectant look on his face.

"A gift," the senator went on. "From a… uh… constituent."

"But it belongs to you?"

"Yes."

"May I..." McIntyre reached for the stick and began unscrewing the handle. When he inverted the stick, out slid a slender glass tube. McIntyre pulled the cork and sniffed.

"Whiskey, I'd say."

"Nothing illegal about it!" the senator protested. "I know the law. I'm a lawmaker after all! The 18th amendment clearly prohibits the manufacture, sale, or transportation with intent to sell, alcoholic beverages. It does not prohibit the private ownership of same."

Like an overconfident chess player who has shouted "check!" Speckle took the glass tube from McIntyre and helped himself to a sip of the contents.

"Anyone else care for a belt?" he said. "Ladies first?"

It stands to reason, McIntyre was thinking. *Hayward gave Speckle a fancy walking stick to curry favor. It stands to reason he'd include a nice little surprise, like excellent whiskey. Maybe more than whiskey.*

If the trace of white powder and missing sugar canister meant anything suspicious, it would mean Hayward had been helping himself to the heroin cache. And if he was bent on being a total sycophant, what better bribe than expensive drugs? They'd be the senator's own drugs, but he wouldn't know it.

"Let's see," McIntyre said, jiggling the stick to make the next two tubes slide out. "More alcohol in the second tube. But this third tube... why, Senator Speckle! You appear to be carrying powdered sugar with you! I'd say there's more than six ounces of it in this tube. Or is it talcum powder for your new hiking boots?"

He handed the tube to Agent Sutter, who opened it, smelled it, tasted a tiny bit on the tip of his pinkie, and returned the tube to the ranger.

"Surprise!" he said. "Why, sir, you're carrying illegal drugs! Got another surprise fact for y', too. Perhaps you've heard of the new lab we have, the one you voted the funding for, Mister Speckle? Wellsir, they got a chemist there who can run a few tests and I bet he'll be able to prove the dope in this tube you've been carrying exactly matches the chemistry of the junk in at least one of those box lunches. The ones you arranged for the girls to haul for you. Tell me something: how you like them apples?"

Chapter Sixteen
All Fall Down

It made quite a parade: the senator and his bodyguards, in handcuffs, were followed by Sheriff Cowell, three federal agents, and two assistant rangers who carried rifles. All the scene needed was a brass band playing and drum majorettes twirling batons. As they were hiking along, the news reporter asked Agent Will Sutter to comment concerning Senator Speckle's legal fate; all the agent would say, however, was that the politician was rumored to have support from the Denver KKK. The Klan, and other important groups, should become very annoyed with Speckle for associating with drugs and young women.

"Or," Sutter said, "annoyed with him for getting caught at it."

Vi Coteau would catch up with the procession later, since her Marmon convertible was parked with the other vehicles. She wanted to stay behind a few moments for a word with Ranger McIntyre.

"You've got a long ride ahead of you," she said, stroking Brownie's nose.

"We'll take a shortcut," McIntyre told her. "We don't need to go back to Fall River road. Jamie and Russ can handle everything there. They'll use an emergency phone to check in with the S.O. I'm afraid there's nothing we can do about Hayward and Smith, though."

"I've got a peachy idea!" Vi said. "A kind of celebration meal! How about when I get back to the village I go over to Murphy's grocery, once we have the villains and evidence locked up, and buy a couple of steaks and a few potatoes and we fix late supper at your cabin? Hmmm?"

"Sounds terrific," McIntyre said. "Except you'd better not stay too late. Mrs. Spinney might not want you to be coming in after she's gone to bed."

"Actually," Vi said, "I was thinking of staying the night at your place."

"These modern women," McIntyre said to Brownie. It was not the first time the mare had heard him say it.

Ranger and mare were bushwhacking their way down the mountain and through the forest, heading toward the flat beaver meadows where McIntyre knew of a wide, shallow place where they could wade across Fall River.

"Staying the night," he muttered.

Three simple words he wasn't able to dislodge from his mind. Three or four miles riding off-trail terrain and "staying the night" was all he could think about. He rode in a daydream, mechanically dodging tree limbs. Random thoughts and images wandered unbidden in and out of his mind: he was happy he had washed his tablecloth, glad he had filled the oil lamp—supper in the light of an oil lamp would be awful nice. He remembered having changed the bedsheets two days ago, reminded himself to be sure and fill the hot water reservoir on the cookstove, thought about unplugging the darn telephone, wondered if he'd have time to wash up and grab a shave.

They waded the stream, crossed a willow-fringed flat, crossed the road, and were coming up the last slope to his cabin when McIntyre saw another government pickup parked beside his.

Two assistant rangers lounged on his porch. One was smoking a cigarette. They said nothing, merely got to their feet when they saw him coming and followed him around to the stable where he unsaddled Brownie to give her a rubdown. Jamie carried fresh hay to her feed trough while Russ pumped water for her. With the chores done, the three uniformed men returned to the front porch. Very few words had been exchanged thus far, but now that the horse was properly cared for the men could get down to a full discussion.

"Find the trouble?" McIntyre inquired.

"Magneto," Russ ventured. "Or maybe fuel line."

"Yeah," Jamie added. "Engine started cuttin' in an' out, about halfway down the road. Lucky we made it this far."

"Lucky," the ranger reluctantly agreed.

"Thought about leavin' it here and takin' yours to barracks," Jamie went on. "But decided against it. Gettin' too late. Same with tryin' to phone somebody at barracks to come get us, I guess. They'd either be at supper or already in their racks."

"And tired, too. They had a long day chasing thugs in the woods," McIntyre said. "Not to mention herding a flock of women."

"Boy, talk about being tired!" Russ said. Apparently their discussion of the pickup's mechanical trouble had fully run its course. "We were up all last night watchin' the mine hole. And hungry, boy, I could eat a horse. Not like Brownie, I mean, but sorta figurative horse."

McIntyre sighed, went inside, and telephoned Murphy's Grocery.

"Mabel?" he said. "Hi. Tim McIntyre here. Listen, Vi Coteau'll be coming into your store pretty soon. Would you please tell her she needs to get enough steaks for three hungry men? That's right, three. She and I were planning to eat alone, but now there's two assistant rangers here who think they need to assist us. Thanks, Mabel."

Russ brought firewood and kindling to the outdoor fire circle and got a blaze going. They'd want a bed of hot coals when Miss Coteau got back with those steaks. McIntyre heated coffee on the stove. Shedding their tunics, all three men sat down on logs surrounding the fire where they tossed pine cones and twigs into the flames, sipped their coffee, and waited for Vi Coteau's return.

"So?" McIntyre asked. "What about Hayward and Smith?"

Instead of answering, Russ got up and walked to their ailing pickup truck. He returned carrying a walking stick and a sleek automatic pistol, nickel plated with mother-of-pearl grips.

"They're dead," Russ said flatly. "This is what they were armed with. The stick's got a air gun mechanism in it. Big caliber. Me and Jamie think it's the same as they killed Arthur with."

"I know that pistol," McIntyre said, "it belongs to Miss Coteau. She left it with Hayward for repair. Probably couldn't bring himself to let it go. Both men deceased?"

"Yeah, both dead." Jamie said.

"One of you care to tell me how it happened? Maybe?" McIntyre said.

"We didn't do it," Jamie replied. "Listen, here's what happened. Me and Russ…"

"Russ and I…"

"Yeah, Anyway, Russ and me, we snuck up the mountain, through the woods, until we saw them two sittin' right there at the mine entrance. They're just sittin' there. Like they're waitin' for something. So I went off t' the left and Russ, he went to the right and we got ourselves down behind logs and rocks where we had clear shots with our rifles, see. Long time, nothin' happened. After awhile of waitin', Tim, I started gettin' upset all over again. Antsy, know what I mean? I needed for somethin' to happen. And I kept thinking, one of those two killed my dad. And the bastard was just sittin' there all smug and relaxed. So I lost patience and I ups with my Winchester and snapped off a shot over their heads, see.

"Well, didn't they dive into the tunnel! They got real quiet… heck, you tell it, Russ."

"Sure," Russ said. "Well, after Jamie fired the shot they hid in the tunnel where we couldn't see them. And after a bit one of them, he crawled forward on his belly far enough to take a shot at us, or at least he shot to where he figured we were. He called out 'who's there, show yourself' and I called back 'Rangers! Toss out your weapons or else' but he snapped off another shot and snaked back into the shadows again. He yelled, from inside, 'what do you want with us? Leave us alone! We're only lookin' around in this old mine is all! Go on, we're okay!' You've got no call to start shooting at us anyway!"

"That's when I chimed in," Jamie added. "Probably shouldn't have, but all I could think of was my dad in the wrecked Dodge down off the cliff. So I yelled back at him, 'listen we got proof one of you killed a man and he was my father! And killed a poor kid at the river, too! Y' hear me? We got proof!

"All of a sudden I got a idea. Boy, was my blood up. I yelled again, 'look we only want the murderer. The other guy, he can go. He can walk free, we won't stop him.' I looked over to where Russ was and he was givin' me a fish eye, but I went on anyway. 'The first one of you t' come outta there, unarmed,' I said, 'he can go. The guy who didn't do it can come out. Then if the other one of you, the killer, if he surrenders we'll take him to the sheriff. Deal?'"

Russ told McIntyre that he had seconded the offer, shouting

how they would let the innocent one come out unharmed and walk away.

"I yelled that they were surrounded, with more rangers on the way, and if the guy who wasn't guilty didn't come out we were gonna take them both back to town dead or alive and let the law sort out which one was a murderer," Russ said.

What came next, according to both young rangers, was a long silence followed by the sound of arguing coming from within the mine. Seeing their opportunity while the villains were busy arguing Jamie and Russ crept closer, near enough to hear Hayward and Smith yelling at one another over who was going to go out. They heard the muffled 'pop' as if an air rifle had gone off, quickly followed by two sharp pistol shots.

"We waited a long time," Russ continued. "When we finally figured it was safe we went in and found both of them cold, dead. Oh, and we took their wallets for identification. They're in our pickup. And in case anyone might happen along afterward, we took the guns and shut the heavy door. Used their own padlock on it. So that's where they're at, Tim. It'll take a crowbar or some bolt cutters to get the lock off."

"Alright," McIntyre said. "I'll go back up there tomorrow. With a crew from the trail gang, probably. Take pictures, make sure several other men get a good look at the scene. As witnesses. We'll need stretchers and a truck. Say! Listen! You two hear that? That's a Marmon Eight coming up the road with steaks in it. Coming fast, too. Coteau drives like she thinks she's Barney Oldfield. Let's hope she brought plenty of food."

The steaks were still sizzling when they hit the plates, Mrs. Murphy's potato salad was creamy and thick, like the coffee. Soon there were four people sitting on the logs, balancing plates on their laps, mugs of coffee next to them on the ground. They smiled at one another, watched the flames dance among the pine logs, and they were content.

The aroma of roasted meat reminded McIntyre of Robert Burns' Selkirk grace: *"Some hae meat but canna eat, while some can eat that want it. We hae meat and we can eat, and sae the Lord be thankit."*

"Amen," said Russ Frame, slicing into his steak with his sheath knife.

Being rather more delicate, Vi Coteau applied a kitchen paring knife to her meat. Between small, polite bites she pressed the young rangers for more details about the deceased villains.

"For one thing," she said, "and don't take it as an accusation, are you certain they shot one another? What I mean is, if you had to swear before a judge, could you say the bullets did not come from either of your rifles?"

"Yes, ma'am!" Jamie said. We checked. It must've happened real quick, 'cause we heard the shots one, two, three, like that. From where they was laying we guessed Hayward must've said he was the one who was goin' out first. Sounded like he said he'd get away clean. Leave Smith to face the music. But Smith had hold of the air gun and shot him. Hayward, he must've fired next because Smith had a bullet hole kinda stomach-high, only off to one side. Hayward's got a bullet hole in his chest, but we turned him over, see, and it didn't come out the other side. That walkin' stick's at least thirty caliber. The ball's still in there, if the coroner looks. Then Hayward must've got off a second shot. From all the blood on him we figure it got Smith in the lungs or heart. The second slug never came out, neither. Most likely it's still in the body."

"That's a good point," Russ Frame added. "If we'd have shot them with our deer rifles, my .303 or Jamie's .30-30 Winchester, both corpses would've shown exit wounds."

"Could we talk about something else?" McIntyre said.

"Sorry," Russ apologized. "Hey, I know a different subject! Rumor is you two are thinking of buying a cottage in town! Looking at a wedding one of these days?"

McIntyre looked at Coteau. Coteau looked at McIntyre. The question was, to say the very least, awkward.

"Marriage," Vi said to Russ, using the serious tone of voice a mother might employ while telling a toddler not to consume candy before supper, "is a serious step. It's not only a lifetime commitment, but getting married can spoil all the fun of a long-term romance. I went to the theater this spring, to see a play by Oscar Wilde. *The Importance of Being* Earnest? Have you seen it? He has a wonderful line in the first act. Marriage makes everything so certain, the character in the play says. 'The very essence of romance is uncertainty,' he says. I'm sure Tim would agree."

She was expecting him to come up with a witty remark about marriage, probably. But the ranger was chewing a slice of steak at the moment, so he merely nodded. Besides, her remark about romance took him by surprise. Sitting at a rough campfire with two other men, he hadn't expected the conversation to turn to romance. McIntyre was not a great lover of surprises. And not liking surprises, he sometimes wondered why he found Vi Coteau so darn fascinating. She managed to spring one on him almost every time they met. It was like holding a stick of TNT, fascinated by the sparkly fuse, unable to tell whether it would go off or not, uncertain what would happen if it did. And knowing it would be wise to throw it away and run for his life.

"Although," Vi teased, "that sweet little cottage would be convenient. It's only a short walk from your boss's favorite breakfast."

The boys grinned and shuffled their feet. McIntyre tried not to choke on his bite of steak.

While washing dishes Vi kept teasing McIntyre with sly little glances. He washed and she dried. Russ Frame and Jamie Ogg had gone to have one more attempt at starting their government pickup. The engine coughed, it belched smoke, on full choke it ran, but so roughly as to make the whole truck shake like a wet dog, and the two young men finally gave up.

"Gettin' dark," Jamie said, coming into the cabin. "I was gonna ask could we take your truck and tow ours back to the barracks, but without the engine it wouldn't have any lights. Besides, we're fagged out. If it's okay by you, Tim, we'd like t' help ourselves to a couple of cots and blankets from the truck shed so's we can camp on your porch for the night."

McIntyre looked at Coteau. Coteau looked at McIntyre.

"Yeah," the ranger said. "Go ahead. Come morning, we'll tow the truck to Marley's place."

"Jamie," Vi said, closing the window over the sink and drawing the curtain over it, "if there's an extra cot in the shed could you bring it in here for me? Maybe you'd set it up for me, right by the stove where it'll be warm all night."

Jamie having left to look for folding cots, McIntyre turned to Vi with a puzzled frown creasing his forehead.

"You've already got a room," he said. "At Mrs. Spinney's? Besides, your car's working fine, and it's only four miles to town. Wouldn't you rather be in a nice soft bed, instead of an army cot in a dark ol' cabin?"

"Silly ranger," Vi replied. "I only asked Jamie to bring a cot and set it up. I didn't say anything about anyone sleeping on it."

Glossary
The Language of the Locals

"Alk": a local pronunciation. See **"Elk"**. (Besides mispronouncing the word, locals also refer to the pointy things sticking out of an elk's head as "horns" and have gone so far as to name Estes Park's main street "Elkhorn Avenue" when everyone knows the pointy things are actually not horns but are antlers.)

"Alpine": no spruce trees, no fir trees. ("All pine," get it?) Locals think "alpine" means no trees at all. Not much air to breathe, either, since much of Colorado's alpine region is two miles above sea level. In winter, alpine blizzards are horizontal, while summer's unmitigated sunshine up there makes exposed human flesh look like overcooked bacon. (Europeans, on the other hand, use "alpine" to mean picturesque high mountains where men in leather Bermuda shorts stand around yodeling while the little girls do the goat herding.)

"Altitude": far enough up a mountain to brag about it, as in "we were hiking at altitude," or as in "we were camped at altitude." Usually above the tree line (see "timberline"). "Relative Altitude" is a local real estate concept. As in "Sure, the front yard is covered with rocks and the slope is steeper than a barn roof, but there's a million-dollar view!" A view which will be added to the price, so you may as well enjoy it.

"Antelope": it is extremely confusing when locals say they drove to "the valley" and saw herds of antelope. In the first place, there is no "valley," only the western edge of the Great Plains. In the second place, the only antelope in North America are in zoos.

The animals the locals saw are known as pronghorns. No doubt the confusion stems from all the locals having read the journals of Lewis and Clark in which Captain Lewis compares the odd new animals with African antelope. Of course he also refers to them as "goats," "sheep," and "gazelles." In reality, pronghorns are not related to any other mammal family in North America. They are distantly related to the giraffe and the okapi, but never attend the *Giraffoidea* family reunions in Africa. They would like to, but they are afraid of flying. This fear apparently extends into their everyday life, for it is popularly believed that pronghorns cannot jump. They can run at fifty miles per hour, but can't jump a fence when they come to it. Which is also true of Volkswagens.

"Aspen": slender leafy tree with chalky bark and black spots that look like eyes. It has a short life span, can't be successfully transplanted, tips over easily in the wind, burns rapidly, can't be climbed nor used for structural lumber. But it's the only deciduous tree we have. No ash, oak, maple, locust, laurel. You might find a few cottonwood in the park, but they have almost as few uses as do aspen.

"Back East": in spite of all the hours in grade school attempting to label various states on a blank map of the U.S., most natives of the Rocky Mountain states have only a dim idea of what the nation "back east" looks like. They are reasonably certain where Kansas is, because they believe that if you can't see the mountains you are actually IN Kansas. To natives, New York and Chicago are adjacent to one another. Washington D.C. is within spitting distance of Maine. No one knows where the heck Pennsylvania is, but it is "back east." A relative once went there and saw the Liberty Bell, but was disappointed to discover that the Statue of Liberty wasn't in the same town.

In order to get "back east" you need to cross the Mississippi River and cross those other two states on the other side and you're there. Unless you take a wrong turn and end up in Virginia, which is "down south" or Ontario, which is "up north" somewhere.

"Belay": (1)A safety rope used in climbing. (2)The act of holding one end of a rope while your partner climbs the cliff, as in "don't be afraid to let go, I will belay you." Safety tip: if you rely on your partner to belay you while you climb, it's better if you are below him or her. If you climb above your belay and you slip, remember to wave as you plummet past. (3)Part of a pirate's vocabulary, as in "Belay that scuttlebutt, ye swab," whatever THAT means.

"Bowline": a rope knot used to make a loop that doesn't slip. Very handy for hauling people up out of perilous places and also for securing a boat to a dock. Like a "line" on the "bow" of the boat? With a loop to drop over the bollard on the dock? Get it? Now you need to go find out what a "bollard" is. Learning to tie a bowline knot usually involves a story about a rabbit, a tree, and a hole in the ground. Come to think of it, so does a story about a girl named Alice.

"Cabin camp": a collection of tiny cabins, a step up from a tent camp. A slight step. A typical cabin camp consisted of five or ten one-room non-insulated 10x12 cabins, each furnished with one or two beds, a wood-burning cookstove, a single light bulb hanging from the rafters, and a small table with two chairs. If advertised as "rustic," it meant that the outhouse was up the hill and the water tap was in the middle of the parking area. "Semi-modern" meant there was a community bathhouse with hot and cold showers and maybe a flush toilet. Having a cold water tap inside the actual cabin itself was considered a luxury. "Modern" got you a cabin with a bathroom inside, unless that particular cabin had already been rented, in which case you got semi.

(Historical note: in 1925 an enterprising Californian nailed a string of cabins together, thus creating a line of walk-in sleeping rooms for motorists. He named it a "mo-tel" as an abbreviation for "motor hotel." Within a year the idea of motor hotels and motor lodges had caught on and the rest is profit… I mean, history.)

"Chimneying": climbers enjoy finding a cliff with a long vertical crack that looks like a chimney with one side missing. The challenge is to put one's spine against one side of the chimney and one's feet on the opposite side and squirm one's way upward until the top is reached OR until one's muscles become fatigued. In which case, see "gravity" in the glossary.

"Chinook": a warm wind, often called "the snow eater." The phrase "chinook wind" is regarded as redundant and makes you sound like a tourist. It is permissible to say "it's chinooking" even if it makes you sound like a non-English speaker. A chinook becomes most noticeable in winter when warm air sliding down from the Divide turns the snow sloppy. In a matter of hours a ski slope can go from three feet of packed powder to twelve inches of slush. Some skiers do not like chinooks.

"Chipmunk": countless scientific man-hours have been spent cataloging the characteristics of this pointy-nose little rodent. Thanks to all those generations of intrepid biologist and illustrators, we can now say with confidence that a chipmunk is not a ground squirrel, gopher, prairie dog or marmot. Some tourists, however, fail to appreciate the difference and gleefully send Junior to give peanuts to the "chipmunks" which actually turn out to be black bears.

"Cornice": any treeless ridge above timberline is a candidate for a cornice, which is a shelf of crusted snow that begins at the crest of the ridge and extends outward. It is formed by wind carrying snow up and over the ridge. As the wind hits the top of the ridge and is deflected upward, the snow falls and gets plastered against the lee slope. Basically a cornice is simply a snowdrift hanging off a cliff. If you walk out onto one, chances are very good that you won't walk back again.

"Creek": In the Rocky Mountains, any dribble of water that appears to be moving can be labeled as a creek. But it must have an unimaginative name. Thus we have Willow Creek, Beaver Creek, Rock Creek and Pine Creek. If those seem too daringly descriptive, you resort to calling them North Fork, Middle Fork or Miller's Fork. "Fork" of what is hardly ever specified. When a dribble grows too deep, too wide, or too turbulent to wade across it is termed a "river" much to the amusement of out-of-state visitors who live near real ones.

"**Crevice, crevasse**": being primarily granite and suffering extremes of heat and freezing, the Rockies are prone to cracking. Any crack may be called a "crevice," mostly for dramatic effect as in "wow, would you look at that crevice." The exception comes when the crack is in an ice field (which locals erroneously refer to as "glaciers"). In an ice field the term becomes Frenchified into "crevasses." Be careful: if you fall into a crevasse, crevice, you won't care what it's called.

"**Clearing**": for reasons no one has adequately explained, forests sometimes have expanses of open grass, usually flat and fertile, where no trees, or only a few trees, grow. Some clearings are created with chainsaws and bulldozers but will revert to forest if left alone long enough, for reasons I can't adequately explain either.

"**Creagdhur**": from two Scots words, meaning "dark crag" or "black rock." In our mountains the north-facing slopes have thicker forests, mostly fir and spruce, so north slopes tend to be shady, chilly, sunless, and generally inhospitable. Build your mountain hideaway on a north slope and what you save on air conditioning you'll spend on furnace fuel.

"**Creel**": an outward symbol showing that you are a true fisherman. Also, a symbol of overreaching expectations. (1)A large inexpensive basket woven of willows, used by peasants to carry bread, coal, harvest items, and small children. (2)a small, ridiculously expensive basket carried by fisherpersons, largely for show. A fish creel has a secure hinged lid to keep people from seeing that you haven't caught anything.

"**Divide**": the Continental Divide, an imaginary line running along the top of the Rocky Mountains but not always at the highest points. It is called the Divide because creeks and streams on the west side (known as the Western Slope) flow toward the Pacific Ocean, while those on the Eastern Slope of the Rockies drain toward the Atlantic.

"Dry fly": an emblem of fruitless hopes. It consists of feathers, thread, and sometimes chenille wrapped around a hook in a pattern which the fisherperson is convinced resembles an actual insect. The dry version is intended to float on the surface of the water and attract trout. The wet version is intended to sink beneath the water and fool the fish into thinking it is an emerging insect. Samples of both versions may be seen festooning willows, aspen, pine, dead logs, rough rocks, and articles of clothing. Some also show up attached to such protruding appendages as noses, ears and fingers.

"Elk": local jokers have a story about a tourist who asked, "what time of year to the deer turn to elk," hah, hah, hah. Elk are taller and heavier than deer and have longer antlers and can run faster, which is good to remember if you are tempted to send Junior out onto the meadow to pose with one of them. Local lore also believes that "the Indians" (whoever they were) called the elk "wapiti," a word no one could pronounce until a ranger with nothing else to do came up with the rhyme "hippity hoppity it's a wapiti."

"Flat hat": generally called a military campaign hat, the NPS flat hat has four symmetrical dents in the crown and a brim that is absolutely flat. Some rangers store their hat in a wooden press so it will stay flat. If you see a picture of Smokey the Bear, Smokey is wearing a flat hat. But that is very odd, considering that Smokey the Bear is a symbol of the U.S. Forest Service and U.S. Forest Service rangers don't wear flat hats. (Smokey is also shown with a shovel as if he's on his way to fight a forest fire. Without shirt, shoes, gloves, or a hard hat. He's only wearing his pants and a NPS uniform flat hat he probably stole somewhere. Dumb, Smokey.)

"Front Range": I don't know about other states the Rockies run through, but in Colorado the long line of high mountains dividing the state into two halves is itself divided up into "ranges." To the north we have the Mummy Range, so named because the collection of peaks resembles either a reclining mummy or a severely constipated boa constrictor, and the Never Summer Range in which there actually is summer every year. There's the Front Range (for which there is no correlative Side Range or Back Range), and the Arapaho Range named for the Indian tribe from whom it was stolen (sometimes referred to as The Indian Peaks, but God help any Indian who would try to claim any of it).

"Gate, The": as in "who is manning the gate" or "I'm only going up to the gate and back" or "they will give you a map at the gate." The term refers to one of the automobile entrances to the national park, where there are no actual "gates" (unless "gate" is another local idiom and means "orange traffic cone").

Glade: A couple of miles up the road from my childhood home is a place called Aspenglade Campground. Had someone not named it Aspenglade, I would not have heard the word until college when I took voice lessons and practiced Handel's "Where e'er you walk cool gales shall fan the glade" over and over until my roommate began tying venetian blind cords into hangman's nooses. I was never sure whether a "glade" was an open spot in the woods, or a collection of trees. It's a lovely sounding word, a romantic word, an altogether pleasant word. But locals never use it. They probably don't know what it means, either.

"Kinnikinnick": In the Rockies, kinnikinnick is an ankle-high plant whose glossy leaves resemble mistletoe. Non-natives sometimes call it "bearberry" but I've never actually spoken to a bear who has eaten the little red berries. According to legend, Native Americans smoked kinnikinnick or mixed it with tobacco. However, it was never made clear to us whether they smoked the dried leaves, the dried bark, the roots or the crushed and dried berries. Trying to answer this question, high school boys have inhaled most of the local kinnikinnick patches.

"Lichen, Krummholz and Skree": crusty moss on rocks; stunted and twisted trees at altitude; and loose sliding stones where you want to walk. (My sister, who is a RMNP Volunteer, has other words for krummholz and skree, but we can't print them.) I've also been told, by unreliable sources, that "Lichen, Krummholz and Skree" is the name of a pop music group. Either that or it's the title of a story about three squirrels.

"Lodge": (1) a large private home made of logs chinked with ten dollar bills and credit card receipts; (2) a tiny summer shack with grandiose name like Nest of the Eagle Lodge or a silly name such as Wee Neva Inn, Dew Drop Inn or Lily's Li'l Lodge; (3) a poshy establishment with a few rental rooms inside and a dozen or more cabins outside, plus a livery stable upwind of the dining room and a volleyball court no one has ever used.

"Moonshine": illegal alcohol. According to folk legend, it was distilled by the light of the moon in order to avoid the authorities.

Also known as "shine," "hooch," "popskull," "varnish remover," "who-hit-John," and even "beer."

"Moraine": few terms confuse visitors as much as does the term "moraine." Locals use the term sparingly, because they don't always understand it either. Some say it means a ridge of rocks that looks as if it was dredged up and stacked by huge machines—it was actually done by a prehistoric glacial flow—while others say it refers to an expansive treeless clearing. Locals sometimes take visitors to Moraine Park and point at the distant ridge, the flat meadow and the campground and say "that's the moraine." Residents along Fall River Road have built their home on one of three distinct moraines and none of them knows it.

"Mountain sickness": also known as "altitude sickness." Do you feel clammy, feverish? Dizzy and diuretic? Have a hangover-size headache? Nausea, aching joints, death wish? Have you been bitten by a wood tick lately? Have you sipped water from one of our trout streams? If not, you probably don't have tick fever or giardia. You probably have mountain sickness. Go home.

"National Forest": a usually vast area set aside and under the protection of the U.S. Department of Agriculture and managed "for the greatest good of the greatest number in the long run." Land within National Forests is used for logging, mining, grazing and recreation. (And by teenagers for necking.)

"National Park": a usually vast area set aside and under the protection of the U.S. Department of Interior and managed so as to preserve and protect it in its natural state for the benefit and enjoyment of future generations. The principal ideal is expressed in the slogan "take nothing except pictures, leave nothing except footprints." (Which, by the way, will get you arrested in The Louvre.)

"**Park**": a flat open space in the mountains, often named for a pioneer and ranging in size. Parks range in size, not the pioneers. Pioneers came in standard sizes. Some parks are a few acres (Allenspark, Hermit Park) while some include hundreds of square miles (South Park, North Park). Locals joke about tourists who arrive in Estes Park Village and ask where to find the roller coaster and Ferris wheel, or the caged animals. No one in human memory has ever laughed at that joke.

"**The Park**": Rocky Mountain National Park, the only important industry of Estes Park and the main reason for the village's existence. Villagers speak lovingly of trails and peaks and lakes in "The Park" but roughly seventy percent of residents have never ventured off the pavement.

"**Pass**": (1)a small card, slip of paper, or phone app allowing you to bring your car into the national park. But you already knew that. (2)In local parlance, a "pass" is a route over the mountains. There are more of these mountain passes than you might assume. It is ironic that many of them are practically inaccessible. Foreigners to Estes Park might be confused by the fact that one famous pass, El Paso del Norte in New Mexico, lies south of the village, while historic South Pass crosses the Wyoming Rockies to the north.

"**Pika**": a chubby little alpine rodent. If you wander into their territory you'll think you're surrounded by puppies playing with squeaky toys. Can you tell a hamster from a gerbil? No? Then you probably can't tell a pika from a hamster either.

"Piton": a device formerly used in rock climbing. A strip of metal about as thick as a butter knife and as long as your hand, pointed on one end and having a large hole in the other end. Early rock climbers would secure themselves to a cliff face by "whanging" or hammering pitons into little cracks in the rock where (they hoped) the soft metal would become permanently stuck. With their climbing rope threaded through a metal ring attached to the pitons, climbers knew they were safe from everything except gravity.

"Ranger": there are two kinds, and woe be to he or she who confuses them. In the USFS (which see below) a ranger is an important chieftain in charge of a very large district of the National Forest. In the NPS a ranger might or might not be a temporary summer employee, i.e. a school teacher wearing a uniform and badge. A National Forest symbol shows Smokey the Bear wearing a flat ranger hat, which National Forest rangers don't wear. But National Park rangers do. Park rangers are known locally as "flat hats" and sometimes "tree cops." National Forest rangers have the authority to cancel your permit for grazing, mining, logging or commercial recreation and thus are known locally as "sir," or "ma'am."

"Rappel": in French, the word means "coming back to oneself." In rock climbing, it means that you may not be coming back to anybody. You rappel by taking a rope between 120 and 260 feet long, doubling it through the eye of a piton or looping it around something that you hope is immovable, securing it around your body with a carabiner and leaping off a cliff. The size of this rope, approximately the same diameter as your middle finger, does not inspire confidence. Oh, and nowadays it is made of nylon; if you rappel too rapidly on a nylon rope, it gets hot enough to melt the material and fuse it to the carabiner, a phenomenon which gave rise to the phrase "don't leave me hanging."

"Rut": the history of this word goes back through Old French, Middle English, and Long-Gone Latin where it meant *"roar"* and referred to the annual onset of sexual activity among mammalian males. During the rutting season male lions begin to roar, male ungulates begin to slam their heads into one another, and elk spend hours making a weird, almost painful howling noise known as "bugling." In some college towns you'll find human males who do much the same thing, except that they call it Spring Break.

"Sam Brown": in addition to the iconic flat hat, Park rangers used to wear iconic Sam Brown belts (presumably invented by the iconic Sam Brown), a wide leather belt which had a narrower leather belt that went over the shoulder. Some say the function of the shoulder strap was to support a heavy pistol and holster. Some say it was left over from WWI, when the shoulder strap was used to drag iconic wounded soldiers out of harm's way. Some say the function of the shoulder strap is simply to make the uniform look cool. Or iconic, whichever comes first.

"Sign": (1) in a word, "poop." When a hunter/gatherer is asked whether he came back with venison, he often replies "no, but I saw lots of sign." Unfortunately, "sign" is not a good substitute for meat, nor do many hunters wish to stuff it and hang it on the wall.

(2) a symbolic, ideographic, alphabetic or pictographic conveyance of information, like a yellow diamond-shaped sign showing a wavy pointed arrow, which warns drivers that the road

is about to go straight up and has many symmetrical curves. In the Rocky Mountains you will frequently see signs saying "Deer Crossing." When the authorities were informed that deer cannot read, many of the signs were replaced with ideographic symbols showing an antlered deer leaping OVER the road. Which is fine for the male deer, but what does a doe do when confronted with the asphalt challenge? Also ideographic is a picture-sign that is supposed to represent range cattle, warning motorists to beware of range cattle who may be grazing on the tarmac or mating on the macadam. Keen-eyed observer motorists will notice that the bovine silhouette on these "range cattle crossing" signs is actually a dairy cow.

"Ski" (n.): In the 1920s, when the McIntyre stories take place, a typical "ski" was a wide board curved up at one end. One measured oneself for a ski by extending one's arm upward as far as it would go and having someone else measure the distance from the palm of the hand to the floor. Or, as in my case, one simply borrowed one's father's skis, which were 7'6" in length. For a binding there was a strip of ribbed rubber mat stapled to the ski somewhere near the center of gravity. Beneath this mat there was a slot through the board. A leather strap went through the slot and was wrapped and buckled around the boot. Ski poles were armpit-length, made of bamboo with a leather wrist loop on one end and a "basket" or woven disk on the other end.

"Ski" (v.): It's the 1920s in RMNP, so don't think you're going to find any ski lifts, ski lodges, ski clothes, *apres* ski parties, or ski instructors. Here is your procedure for going skiing. First, don your woolen long underwear. Pull on a pair of light socks, then a pair of heavier socks, and then a pair of wool boot socks. Now don your corduroy or denim trousers and a turtle neck sweater.

If you have ski pants, or some kind of pants that will shed snow, put them on next. Now you're ready for your heavy ski sweater and large leather boots, followed by your parka, knitted cap and earmuffs (with goggles), a pair of thin gloves, and a pair of heavy leather mittens. You're now ready to strap seven-foot-long ski boards to your boots and begin shuffling uphill. When the slope becomes so steep that you are sliding backward, begin using your "herringbone" technique of walking with your seven-foot skis spread into a wide "V" shape. If you begin to slide again, you'll need to get both skis together and at right angles to the slope and do a little side-step up the mountain. In about a half hour, with legs trembling, you'll probably decide to "make your run" by pointing the ski tips downhill, pushing off with your poles, and praying to the gravity gods for mercy.

Repeat this procedure until you feel you have had enough winter recreation to last you a while. Back at the office on Monday morning your bragging rights include two frostbitten fingers, two legs that will not bend without excruciating pain, a chest that feels as if a camel had stood on it, and a face sunburned red except for the part protected by goggles so that you resemble a parboiled raccoon.

"Skree": a steep slope of unstable small rocks. See "talus."

"The S.O.": Supervisor's Office, or the central administration building from whence flows a relentless stream of orders, regulations, recriminations, requests and regrets. For some reason, employees seem to like pronouncing "S.O." with a suggestive pause after it as if a letter were missing.

"The S.O.P.": a manual of Standard Operating Procedures, kept in the S.O for reference. Updated on a weekly basis until no office shelf is sturdy enough to hold it, the S. O. S.O.P. dictates How To Do Everything, from what to tell park visitors in the event of nuclear holocaust (pray) to how to install restroom toilet paper (roll from the top, not the bottom). Temps in search of answers to questions ("I saw a bear climb into a visitor's car, what do I do?") have been found years afterward as desiccated corpses hunched over the S.O.P. Equally useful is The Compendium, revised almost annually, which tells everyone how to do everything and what not to do. It has been said that the flat hat rangers won't even visit the restroom without taking The Compendium with them.

"Soogan": mostly associated with 1800s cattle drives, a "soogan" is a cowboy sleeping bag. To make one, you first help yourself to your father's 8x10 tarp, the one he covers the bed of his pickup with. Then steal a quilt, preferably an old one. Lay the quilt on the tarp. Fold the tarp over the quilt and sew up the long side and one end. There you go. A soogan. There's a down side to it: it's heavy. On trail drives, they were carried in a wagon. But two cowboys had to share one. And trail drive cowboys seldom bathed. Or brushed their teeth. And ate a powerful amount of beans.

"Sub-alpine": When the first Europeans to visit the Rocky Mountains saw stunted high altitude trees, it reminded them of a pod of submarines with only periscopes visible, hence "sub" alpine. That isn't true. Actually, the existence of the term "sub alpine" shows what happens when scientists are allowed to wander unsupervised. They seem driven by a need to name everything. First they decide that "alpine" will mean a place with no trees. Next they notice that there's a zone slightly lower in elevation where there ARE trees, but the trees are wind-twisted and stunted and so are the bushes. And the same flowers grow there. So they call it "sub" alpine. Kind of like calling a Chihuahua a sub-canine.

"Summer hire": with more than a million visitors traipsing through the National Park each year, the Park depends heavily on summer employees to keep everything (particularly restrooms) clean and functioning. People of all ages and education levels are hired to maintain hiking trails, clean toilets, paint signs, clean toilets, direct traffic, clean toilets, answer questions, clean toilets and pick up trash. Sometimes the rangers help them answer questions and clean toilets.

"The Canyon": there are two major highways between Estes Park and "The Valley" (which see below). One highway follows the Thompson River and is always called "The Canyon" as in "I'm going down The Canyon to The Valley to load my car with stuff at Sam's Club if you need anything." The other route, Highway 36, doesn't have a name. It also doesn't have much of a canyon. Sometimes local people can't recall the highway number and so tell people "I'm going down... uh... to Lyons."

"Talus": a steep slope of unstable large rocks. See "skree".

"Tarn": (1)a mild swear word uttered by a person who has problems with preaspirated glottal stops and cannot pronounce "darn" correctly; (2)a hydraulic anomaly usually associated with tundra and occurring due to accumulation of atmospheric moisture in depressions caused by glacial excavation or terminal moraine occurrence. In other words, itty-bitty ponds way up in the high mountains. They get water from melted snow and rain.

Tarns are shallow and inviting, but don't jump into one. The water is cold enough to freeze the patellae off a brass tourist.

"Telephone exchange": Not where you young whippersnappers (see def.) go to swap smartphones. There are persons still living who remember how telephones had wires. The wire from the phone was attached to the wall wire, which went out of the building and was attached to a wire strung on tall poles (known as "telephone poles" because calling them "wire poles" sounded silly), which led to a building known as the telephone exchange. An "operator" there, usually female, sitting at a switchboard, got a signal that you had picked up your end of the wire and she would ask "Number, please?" Then she'd connect your wire to that number's wire. If you wanted a number other than a local number, she would write down how many minutes you talked. The long distance charge would appear on your monthly statement for you to explain to your parents. My own father went to his grave still wondering whom I had talked to in Parsons, Kansas for forty-five minutes.

"Tie beam": Inside a log cabin you might notice a heavy timber that stretches from the top of one wall to the top of the opposite wall. Back in the 1920s the vast majority of men (and many of the women) wore neckties even when hiking or picnicking, and the cabin tie beam provided a convenient place to hang these ties when they were not being worn. (If you don't believe that one, maybe you'll believe that the tie beam ties the two walls together so they don't sag outward.)

"Timberline": 10,500 feet above sea level. Or thereabouts. Early settlers discovered that at that altitude the trees would not grow large enough to be cut down for lumber. And "timberline" sounded more euphonic than "lumberline." Some modern fussy little know-it-all decided that it should be called "tree line" instead, which confuses things because stunted, runty little trees can be found higher than 11,000 feet in some locations. But that fact, like having a word like "timberline," has little or no significance.

"Tundra": in Russian, the term "tundra" means "if you plan to sleep on the ground bring plenty of goatskins." It is an area above timberline, usually flat except for the place you chose to pitch your tent. It is devoid of trees, bushes, tall grass and any kind of public restroom. Mosses, lichens and flowers grow there although (by definition) the subsoil is permanently frozen. As you will also be if you try to sleep there on the ground without a goatskin. In fact the only creatures who sleep there are mountain goats and bighorn sheep, who bring their own sheepskins and goatskins.

"Up top" or "Up on top": locals who say they drove "up top" or took guests "up on top" are referring to the highest section of Trail Ridge Road where they can scratch their names into the snowbanks in August at two miles above sea level. They can also enjoy driving a two-lane highway that (a)has almost no guardrails and (b)drops off more than a thousand feet from the edge of the pavement to the bottom of Forest Canyon. Restrooms are available Up Top. Sometimes for a reasonable gratuity a local high school student will agree to accompany you in order to pry your fingers from your steering wheel and drive you back down to your lodgings.

"The Valley": one Estes Parkian might say "I'm going down to The Valley" and another will ask "which one?" and the reply will be "Longmont." This may confuse those who don't know that "The Valley" refers to Loveland or Fort Collins, or in some cases any town or city north of Denver. Cheyenne is not "The Valley" nor is Colorado Springs. One also drives "up" to Fort Collins and "over" to Greeley, both of which are approximately two thousand feet lower in elevation than Estes. You also go "over" to Grand Lake, which is on "the other side," and you go "down" to Allenspark, which is higher than Estes Park (unless you're looking at a road map you've tacked to the wall, in which case, being south, it appears to be below Estes). I hope this clarifies the matter.

"Whippersnapper": I'm kidding. I don't have a clue why a pretentious neophyte should be called a whippersnapper. But I made you look.

"Wrangler": *n.* One who wrestles with livestock. In Anglo-Saxon "wrangle" meant to come to grips with, to argue, to debate, to twist the argument. It came from an even older term meaning "to twist." Livestock employees sometimes argue with cattle or horses. Sometimes they try to control an animal by "twisting" the tail or an ear. But it doesn't always work; just ask Pat "Lefty" Brown or "Toothless Tim" McCoy or any hostler who rides with an ice pack clamped over his spleen. By the way, people who sit on the fence and offer advice to the livestock wranglers are known as "harangulers."

About the Author

During his formative years young Jim Work was frequently found staying after school, sitting in the school library. Unlike the other kids who were there in detention, he was not there because of misbehavior. He was simply waiting for a ride home. Since Estes Park had no school bus, some days he had to wait until his father got off work. Home was three miles away, a mile from the entrance to Rocky Mountain National Park.

Having eventually read most of the library's books, he began passing time by scribbling stories and poems of his own. His English teacher, Mary Thomas, took notice. She encouraged him. She and another teacher, Rena Roberts, went so far as to organize a writer's club for Jimmy Work and other youngsters. One thrilling day Mrs. Thomas took him to meet Edna Davis Romig at Ms. Romig's house, where the poet gave the kid a signed copy of her book *The Torch Undimmed*. And with that, as they say in shooting craps, the die was cast.

In college, our author tried to escape the writing life by majoring in practical subjects, beginning with physics. He tried an agriculture major, then journalism. He considered forestry, but after he failed basic chemistry (for the third time) his academic advisor urged him to find a major that would not require either science or discipline. In short, English. The English department did not offer a creative writing concentration, so he studied American literature and took all the writing courses he could find. When the time came to begin graduate studies he did the most logical thing he could think of, which was to switch to English literature because it came before American. After finishing his PhD in Victorian poetry, he once again changed his "major." Leaving the Victorian poets of England behind, he set out to learn about the literature of the American West.

More than a dozen colleges were offering courses in Western American literature, but there was a need for an extensive and comprehensive textbook. Therefore Professor Work spent nearly six years compiling and editing a 600-page anthology, *Prose and Poetry of the American West* for the University of Nebraska Press. He served as president of the Western Literature Association and contributed dozens of literary articles to various journals. He did another about-face, however, when he wondered whether he could write a novel. Twenty books later, he's still trying.